TWISTED PATH

Path Series

by:
Neri Lopez

Twisted Path
The Path Series: Book 5
Neri Lopez

Siren Book & Craft LLC

Other books by this author:

Path Series
Book 1: Red Path
Book 2: Unconquered Path
Book 3: Wagering Path
Book 4: Unexpected Path
Book 4.5: Double Trouble Path – Wedding Novella

Disclaimer

This work includes themes of sexual assault and rape that some readers may find disturbing or triggering. Viewer discretion is advised.

If you or someone you know experienced sexual assault, please know you are not alone and that resources exist to help you during this difficult time. If you are or have been a victim of sexual assault, you can contact your local police department or call the number below.

National Sexual Assault Hotline: 800-656-4673
Or chat online at: http://www.rainn.org

RAINN (Rape, Abuse & Incest National Network) is the nation's largest anti-sexual violence organization. RAINN created and operated the National Sexual Assault Hotline in partnership with over 1,000 sexual assault service providers across the country.

For victims of a roofie assault, please contact: 844-960-2939
http://www.theedgetreatment.com
Help is available 24/7 on the Suicide and Crisis Lifeline. You can call or text in English or Spanish.

The number is: 988 or reach out to them online at http://988lifeline.org

Rock 'n' Roll Resort & Casino
Family Floor
Resort
Casino
Front View

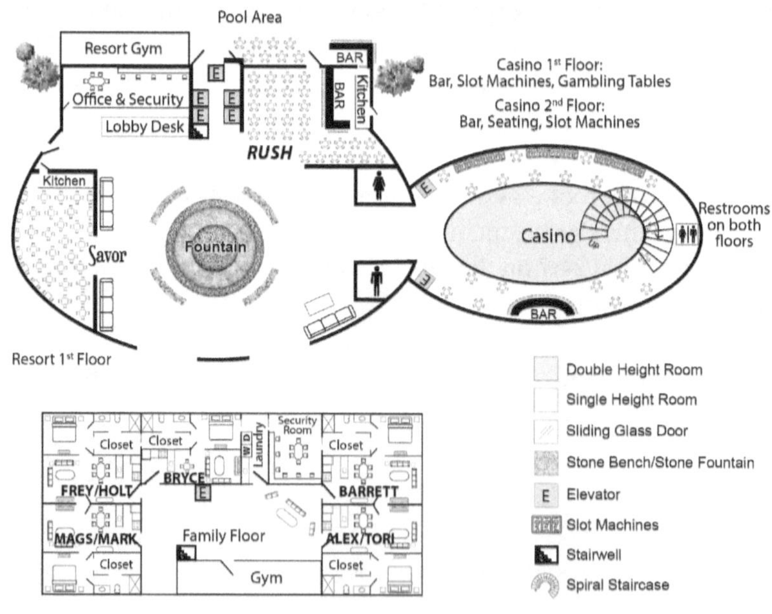
Pool Area
Resort Gym
BAR
Kitchen
Office & Security
Casino 1st Floor:
Bar, Slot Machines, Gambling Tables
Lobby Desk
Casino 2nd Floor:
Bar, Seating, Slot Machines
RUSH
BAR
Kitchen
Restrooms
on both
floors
Savor
Fountain
Casino
BAR
Resort 1st Floor
Double Height Room
Single Height Room
Sliding Glass Door
Stone Bench/Stone Fountain
E Elevator
Slot Machines
Stairwell
Spiral Staircase
Closet
Closet
Security
Room
W D
Laundry
Closet
FREY/HOLT
BRYCE
BARRETT
MAGS/MARK
Family Floor
ALEX/TORI
Closet
Gym
Closet

Path Series Family Trees

d.-deceased ❧ div.-divorced ❧ a.-adopted ❧ shaded box is a spouse

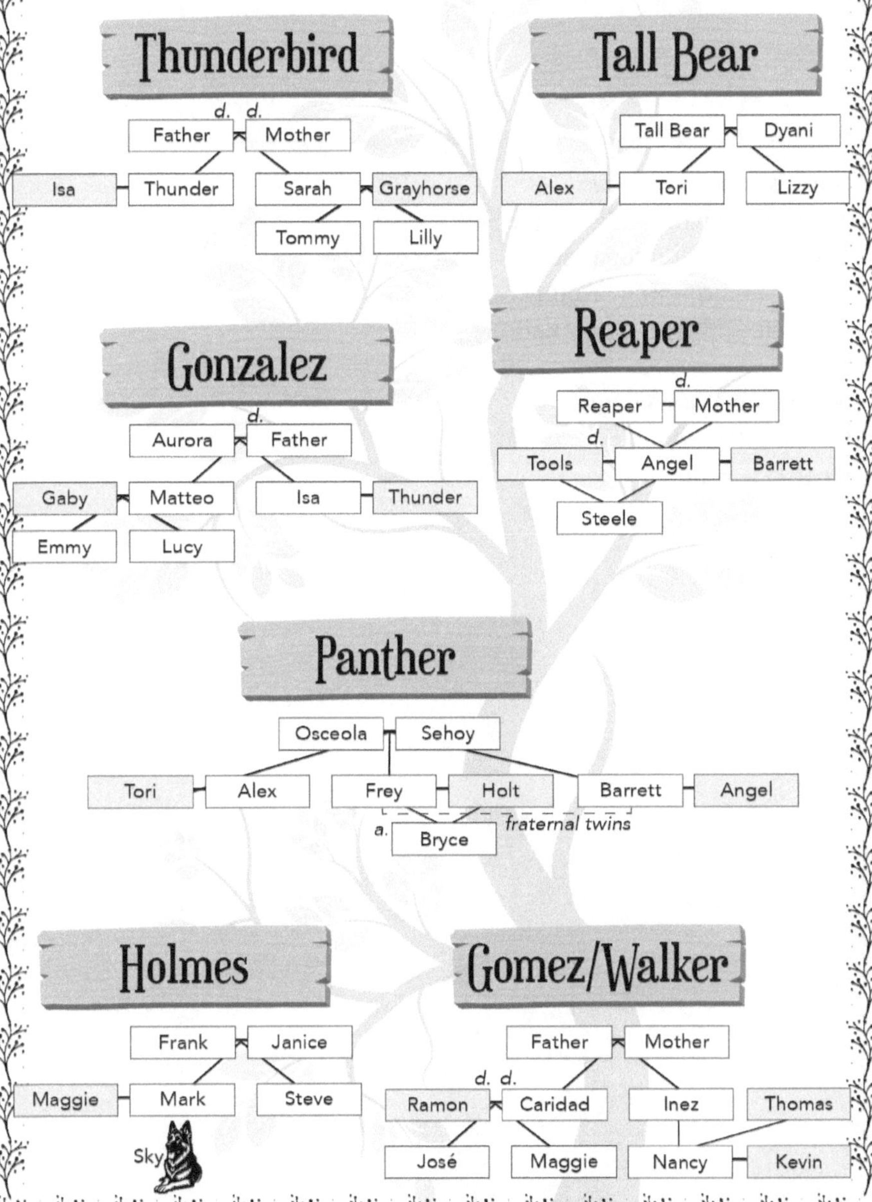

Translations

Spanish Translations
¿Agua, por favor? – Water, please?
Comprende – Understand
Correcamino – Road runner
Machete – Broad, heavy knife

Seminole Translations
Chakpootsi – Son
Chatski – Mom

Contents

Chapter 1

Am I a Terrible Person?

Angel

Though Angel felt guilty about leaving Barrett in pain and bleeding on the floor, she had to get her son away from Numbers. Guilt-ridden and shivering, she left, a sense of doom heavy in the air. Barrett's hushed conversation with the mysterious helper carried thru the doorway. Angel was relieved to know help was on the way for him. But it also meant she had to leave quickly, before George arrived and asked too many questions and delayed her from reaching Steele.

Just as Angel was about to open the apartment door, it swung open, revealing a police officer. *Shit, she hadn't been quick enough.*

"Ma'am, where's Barrett?" the officer burst into Barrett's apartment.

A wave of terror washed over Angel, her heart pounding, her breath coming faster as the officer pushed his way into the room.

Angel pressed her back against the wall and pointed toward Barrett's bedroom. "He's in there." With a surge of adrenaline, Angel turned and ran out toward the elevator. She needed to get to Steele quickly before Numbers did anything stupid.

Angel could hear the officer shouting at her, but his voice was growing faint, and she didn't stop. Her focus was on saving her thirteen-year-old son, even though he didn't realize he needed saving. The last time she saw Steele, he was on the back of Numbers' motorcycle. Numbers was now VP in Lucifer's Renegades Motorcycle Club, and her father's best friend. Her father was Reaper, the president of the MC, who was serving time for the attempted kidnapping of Tori Panther.

Steele idolized his grandfather and wanted to grow up to be just like him. In his mind, his father Tools and his grandfather were important members of the MC, and he was a legacy, the next future president. But Angel would rather die than have her son become a prospect. When the police arrested Reaper, she had hoped Steele would understand the consequences, but he ended up believing his grandfather's lies. According to Reaper, it was all a setup, and he maintained his innocence in the kidnapping attempt. Unfortunately for Angel, Steele believed him.

With Reaper absent, Numbers befriended Steele, poisoning his mind with malicious lies. Angel was fighting a losing battle, but she wasn't giving up yet. Steele was her son, and she would do whatever it took to get him away from the MC.

Stepping outside the hotel, she saw the chaotic scene around her. Police officers fanned out across the parking lot, apprehending members of the LRs and their rivals, Los Lobos, who had taken part in the shootout. Angel darted and ducked between cars in the parking lot, evading the police, to reach her own vehicle. Once inside her car, her shaking hands gripped the steering wheel. After nervously glancing around, checking for pursuing police officers, she backed out. To avoid attracting attention, she drove carefully through the parking lot. After leaving the lot, she gunned the engine and drove directly to the clubhouse.

Her phone rang inside her car—it was Numbers.

Angel pushed the answer button on her screen. "Where the hell is my son?" She wasn't in the mood for pleasantries.

"Well, hello to you too. Where are you?" Numbers sounded calm.

"I had to run an errand." Angel bit her lip and hoped Numbers hadn't seen her.

"Don't fuckin' lie to me!" Numbers screamed. "I know you went to that fucking resort because I saw you. What I want to know is, what the fuck were you doing there?"

"None of your business. Is Steele with you?" She knew Numbers had Steele but had to play dumb. Now that she was halfway to the clubhouse, all she could think about was holding her son close and getting him away from the murderous LRs.

"Yes, he's in his room."

"What room?" Angel wasn't sure if Steele meant a room in the clubhouse or his bedroom at home.

"His bedroom." Numbers sighed. "I'm waiting for you in your house."

Great, would this night never end? A heavy sigh escaped her lips as she acknowledged the need to remove Numbers from her home. Angel pulled a U-turn and headed home, her eyes glistening with unshed tears. Her mind raced, trying to come up with an excuse for her unexpected presence at the resort, a cold sweat breaking out on her brow. If Numbers saw her there or found out she had warned the happy couples, she might not survive the beating.

"You don't have to stay," Angel prayed Numbers would leave. "I'll be home in about twenty minutes." She hesitated to leave her son by himself, yet she dreaded confronting Numbers.

"I don't mind. Besides, I wanted to see you. We need to talk."

Fuck! Her body tensed. She knew Numbers talked with his fists if he didn't like her answers. He was already mad at her for not representing her father and getting him out of jail. However, Angel believed in the law and Reaper had to face the consequences of his actions. Tori seemed like a nice person, and she didn't deserve what Winston or Reaper had done to her. Unfortunately, Numbers didn't care. He just wanted his president and best friend out of the slammer. As far as Numbers was concerned, it was her fault her father was still in jail.

"I gotta go. I'll be home soon." No sooner had Angel spoken, she heard a click in her ear.

That asshole hung up on her. A heavy weight settled in her chest as the reality of the long night ahead sank in. Tears spilled with urgency for the next five minutes before she gathered herself together and thought through her story. It had to sound convincing if she wanted to survive that night.

Chapter 2

Nice Guys Finish Last

Barrett

The failed attempt to help Angel left a knot of anxiety twisting in the pit of his stomach. She was the first woman to abandon him when he needed someone the most. And he'd needed her. *What if he bled out? How could he keep her safe? And why the fuck did he still want to help her and keep her safe after she bailed on him?*

"Shit, Barrett." Deputy George rushed to his side and pulled Barrett's hand away from the wound.

Thank fuck Deputy George came so quickly. "Hey, man." Barrett knew he sounded groggy. He had to stay awake. Angel was still out there, unprotected. *What if those assholes hurt her kid? Or used him as leverage to hurt her? He had to get up and help her.*

Deputy George gently pulled him away from the door. *Fuck, that hurt!*

"It looks like the bullet went all the way through. Hang on. I'm gonna get a couple of towels and apply pressure until the paramedics get here."

He was acting like a pussy. Since he didn't have a bullet travelling through his body, he needed to suck it up and go after her. As soon as George ran into the bathroom, Barrett bent his legs and pushed up with every bit of his waning strength. His ankle screamed in pain, but he continued to slide up the door until he got to his feet. Taking a few deep breaths, he contemplated taking a step.

"What the fuck are you doing?" George said as he strolled up to Barrett.

"I need to go help, Angel." Sweat beaded Barrett's forehead as he murmured quietly. As he moved forward, a sharp surge of pain shot up his leg from his injured ankle, causing his body to crumple. "Fuck!"

George caught him, lowered him to the ground, placed a towel on the entrance wound, and another on the exit wound.

"You need to stay the fuck down. The paramedics will be here any minute. What the hell happened out there? One minute you were standing next to me and the next you're on the ground."

"I was trying to get Angel away from the wall. I think someone directed the bullet that hit me towards her." Barrett moaned. "Fuck, that hurts. Do you have to push so hard?"

"Shut up, you big baby. If you hadn't been playing the hero, you wouldn't be sitting on your ass now. And where is your fair maiden?"

"She fucking left me, man." Barrett's head hung. "What kind of woman leaves her hero bleeding on the floor?"

"The kind that doesn't want your help," George smirked at him. "So, why the fuck do you want to go after her?"

"I wish I knew," Barrett sighed.

"Hello!" Barrett heard someone's voice coming from the living room.

"In here!" George shouted and stood.

"Finally." Barrett groaned and closed his eyes. "Hey!" Barrett hollered when George slapped his face. "What the fuck, man?" Barrett glared at him.

"Stay awake," George glared back.

"Sir, we'll take it from here." The paramedic sat down, pulled out the equipment from his bag, and worked on Barrett.

Barrett recounted the events to the paramedic, who agreed with George that the bullet had passed through Barrett's body. The paramedic started an IV to provide Barrett with fluids.

"Sir, we need to take you to the hospital." Another paramedic wheeled a gurney into the bedroom.

"Absolutely not." Barrett shook his head. "George, tell them no. I don't want my family to see me. I need Alex and Frey to go on their much-deserved honeymoon. If they see me, they'll postpone their honeymoon and I'm fine, dammit." Barrett attempted to take out the IV while the paramedics helped him up and onto the gurney. "And I must find Angel. She's in trouble."

"Barrett, stop!" George grabbed his wrist. "If you pull out that IV, I will knock you out. Look, I promise we'll get you in the ambulance without your family seeing you and I'll help you find Angel. But right now, you need to go to the hospital so they can patch you up."

"How the hell are you going to get me out of here without my family seeing me if I'm on a fucking gurney?" Barrett leaned back and relaxed, shutting his eyes. The throbbing in his head was relentless, a steady pulse that made it impossible to focus on anything else but the need for sleep.

"I'll create a distraction. Don't worry. I'll make sure Frey and Alex don't see anything. But I gotta tell your mom and dad, or your mom will kick my ass." George walked out with them.

"Really? You're afraid of my barely five-foot mom?" Barrett grinned. "Pussy."

"Have you seen what that woman looks like when she's mad or worse, disappointed in someone?" George shook his head. "Hell no, I do not want the wrath of Sehoy."

"Of course I've seen her wrath. She's my mom, you idiot." Barrett sighed. The pain medication was not kicking in fast enough.

"Barrett? George? What is going on?"

Barrett heard his mother's voice and strained to hear their conversation. Grinning as he thought, "George was so busted!"

"Mrs. Panther, Barrett is being taken to the hospital. He doesn't want Frey or Alex to know. I'm going to follow the ambulance. I'll give you an update as soon as the doctor checks him out."

Despite having his eyes closed, Barrett could sense he was in the lobby from the soft music playing and the familiar voices of people nearby. The wave of heat from the outdoor temperature hit him seconds later, urging him to open his eyes and take in the chaotic scene outside.

"I'm going with him. What hospital are we going to so I can text Osceola?" Sehoy ran behind the gurney and jumped into the ambulance.

"Broward General, ma'am," one paramedic said before he shut the door and sat down next to her.

"*Chatski*, I'm okay." Barrett mumbled to his mom. Sehoy looked up from texting with tears in her eyes. "The bullet went all the way through. They just gotta sew me up."

"Shh, *chakpootsi*. Keep your strength." Sehoy reached her hand out and grabbed Barrett's.

Barrett felt like the journey to the hospital was endless, even though he knew it normally took thirty minutes with traffic. He believed the flashing lights and sirens cleared the way like Moses parting the Red Sea. With a sudden screech, the ambulance came to a stop and the back door was flung open. A nurse standing by the ambulance hurriedly took him to the ER. He remembered counting backward from one hundred and reaching ninety-five before the room faded.

Chapter 3

Storytime

Angel

Angel pulled into her driveway and spotted Numbers' motorcycle. Why couldn't anything go her way today? Pulling herself together, she stepped out of her car and made her way to her front door. Angel took two deep breaths and prepared herself for the verbal sparring she knew she was going to get from Numbers.

Despite being old enough to be her father, Numbers started behaving like a jealous husband. She was worried because the thought of having another husband who was a member of the LRs was the last thing she wanted. Hell, she didn't want another husband, period—especially not Numbers. She had her hands full with Steele. He ignored her, ditched school all the time, and never did his homework. Lately, all he talked about was joining the Lucifer's Renegades MC and becoming president like his grandpa.

Steele was unaware that Tools had put in a lot of blood, sweat, and tears to make the club legal by setting up the garage. When Tools first joined the club, he was involved in plenty of illegal activities but as soon as Angel got pregnant, they got married and he prioritized his family above all else. Angel begged him to leave the club, but Tools exact words were, *"No one leaves the club. But I can make things better by helping them go in a different direction."*

Angel felt a wave of relief when Reaper approved his plan to build the garage. Things were going well until El Loco murdered Tools. Although Tools was not involved in the shooting that resulted in the death of El Loco's family, he was an innocent bystander who got caught up in the violence.

The bullet not only took Tools' life but also shattered her family. Angel sought comfort from Steele, only to find Steele seeking solace from Reaper and Numbers. With Reaper in custody, Numbers seamlessly transitioned into being Steele's mentor at the club. Only now it seemed Numbers was acting like his father instead of a mentor.

Angel needed to get this over with and send Numbers home. She inserted her key in the lock, but it turned easily. It was unlocked. Numbers must not have worried about intruders. Asshole. He should always lock her door, especially with Steele in the house. Hell, she wished he would've locked Steele in and left.

Strolling into her house, she found Numbers sprawled out on her couch. His biker boots resting on her coffee table and a beer in his hand. Steele sat next to him as they watched a show about officers and laughed at them.

"I'm home, Numbers." Angel stood next to the couch. "You can go now."

"Son," Numbers patted Steele's knee. "Go on to your room. I need to talk to your momma."

Angel hated when Numbers called him son. He was NOT Steele's father and never would be!

"Okay." Steele gave Numbers a hug and glared at his mom on his way out.

Why the hell was her son glaring at her? She's not the one that rode in and began shooting innocent people. Angel waited until she heard Steele's door slam shut.

"What did you tell my son about today?" Angel pointed her finger in Steele's direction. "Why did he look at me like that? You need to stop spewing your venom at my son. And stop calling him son!"

"Are you done?" Numbers got off the couch and stood in front of her with his arms crossed, and an eyebrow raised.

"No, I'm not done. Get the hell out." Angel turned around but before she stepped away, Numbers grabbed her arm and spun her toward him, trapping her against his chest.

"You have a nasty mouth on you tonight, especially after what you did." Numbers glared at her. Both his hands gripped her biceps. She was sure he was going to leave bruises.

"I didn't do anything." Angel bluffed.

"Did you fuckin' run to those assholes and blab about our hit?" Numbers growled.

"Take your hands off me." Angel pulled back, but he shook her so hard her teeth rattled.

"I will take my hands off you when I'm fuckin' good and ready."

Angel had enough of his manhandling and wanted to distract him from his question, so she kicked his shin, hard.

"What the fuck, bitch!" Numbers released her and slapped her face so hard she dropped to her knees.

Angel stared at Numbers in horror. Kicking him had not been a good idea. Out of the corner of her eye, she saw movement and glanced in that direction, only to see Steele standing in the hallway with a smirk on his face. *Why was he smirking? Why was he not coming over to help her or asking Numbers to stop?* There was only one reason. Reaper and Numbers had gotten to him and brainwashed him into believing that women were their servants and just because she was his mom, she had no power. She needed to get Steele away from them—now. Tools would roll over in his grave if he saw his son behaving like that.

"Look at me when I'm talking to you." Numbers turned to see what she had been looking at.

"Steele, go to your room." Angel's voice trembled as she said. "I'll be there in a minute." She did not want to give Steele the impression that this was how women ought to be treated.

"Son." Numbers pointed at Angel, still on the floor. "Your mother needs to learn her place."

What the hell was Numbers trying to teach her son? Warning Tori about the hit had been a dangerous move, and now she was paying for it. Angel stayed on her knees, looking at the ground, hoping if she stayed still, he would leave her there. Unfortunately, he didn't. He grabbed her by the back of the hair and pulled until she stood in front of him, head tilted back so he could stare into her eyes. Numbers' red angry face showed no leniency. She'd never seen him like this before.

"Why did you make me hit you!" Spittle flew out of Numbers' mouth onto her face.

Fear crept up Angel's spine as she watched his face distort into the face of a monster instead of her father's best friend. There was a time when he treated her like family. *What the hell was she thinking? Why hadn't she run sooner and taken Steele? Did she really think he would never hit her again after that first time?* Angel felt stupid, terrified, and trapped. She wasn't family now. Now, she was the enemy, and she needed to choose her words carefully if she wanted to get out of this alive.

"I'm sorry." Angel cast her eyes to the floor. It was best if she showed weakness, so he wouldn't continue to hurt her. "I'm just tired. It's been a long night, and I just want to go to sleep."

"I can stay with you." Numbers released her hair and cupped her ass, pressing her into his body. "I know what you can do for me to get into my good graces again."

Angel felt queasy from the mingling odors of cigarette smoke and bad breath exiting his mouth when he spoke. "I think it's best you go home. I don't want Steele to see a man sleeping with me in my bed who isn't my husband."

"Sugar, I don't think he'd mind if that man was me." Numbers moved forward to kiss her. "Besides, I can remedy that real quick."

Angel turned her head, and his kiss landed on her cheek. *Was Numbers serious? Did he want to marry her? Was that his end game?* There was no way in hell she would be his wife. She'd die before that happened.

"Please, not tonight. My head is pounding, and I just want to take some medicine and go to bed." Angel prayed he believed her and left her alone.

"Some other night then." Numbers held Angel's chin, so she couldn't turn her head this time.

Angel held her breath and endured the kiss, pulling back after a couple of seconds. Growing up with her abusive father, Angel learned how to mask her feelings. Whenever Reaper thought she was going to put up a fight, he would hit her harder. Reaper called it "beating the uppity out of her." Angel just called it abuse. But no one would listen or help her. Reaper loved to boast about how he'd beat the uppity out of her mom.

Tools had stopped Reaper's abuse when he married Angel. He told Reaper Angel was his wife, and he would reprimand her however he saw fit. Reaper didn't know that Tools had never laid a hand on her. Tools didn't believe in hitting women, much less his wife and the mother of his child.

Glaring at her with intense eyes, Numbers stood watchful, prepared to pounce on her at the first sign of deceit. Now was a good time to school her facial features and pretend to like Numbers' kiss. The quicker he believed her, the quicker he would leave her house. She ran her hand over his cheek and smiled.

"Goodnight, Numbers."

"Goodnight, sugar." Numbers kissed her again. "Next time, I won't stop until I bury myself deep inside you."

Angel's body trembled slightly. Despite what Numbers may have thought; she shivered not with excitement but with apprehension. Angel walked behind Numbers to the door and locked it as soon as he exited. Sliding down to the ground, she leaned back against it for support. Her heart sank as a feeling of despair swept through her. *How was she going to get away from Numbers?* Contemplating a fresh start in a different town with Steele brought tears to her eyes, knowing it meant leaving behind her memories of her life with Tools. This was where things got tricky. She turned her head towards Steele, only to find that he was no longer there. The urgency to escape gripped her heart as she realized they had to run. It was her only option to evade the looming threat of Numbers.

Chapter 4

Find Her...Please!

Barrett

Barrett opened his eyes in the hospital bed, greeted by the sight of Sehoy, Osceola, and George. Dull, persistent throbs pulsed in his shoulder and ankle. Constant reminders of his injuries.

"How long was I out?" *Was that his gravelly voice?*

"Between surgery and recovery, about five hours." Sehoy squeezed his hand. "They took a CT scan of your shoulder. You were fortunate that the bullet went straight through, causing no additional harm."

"Yay," Barrett mumbled. "What about my ankle?"

"The x-ray showed it's only sprained," Osceola grabbed his other hand.

"You're going to live!" George slapped Barrett's thigh, causing him to jump.

"George," Sehoy reprimanded him.

"Fucker," Barrett croaked.

"Barrett! Language," Sehoy glared at him.

"Sorry, *chatski*." Barrett pointed to the glass on the nightstand. "Water, please?"

"Of course." Sehoy hurried to do his bidding.

Barrett smirked at George, who rolled his eyes at him. After a drink of the cool water, he handed the glass back to his mom and stared at George. "Have you found Angel?"

"No. I've been here waiting for you to stop being lazy sleeping the day away." George grinned at him.

"F...," – Barrett attempted to insult George, but his mother's expression stopped him– "fine. Can you try to locate her now that I'm awake? I'm worried about her."

"Who is Angel?" Sehoy shifted her gaze between the men. Osceola shrugged and George quirked his eyebrow.

Fine, no help from George. No worries. He could handle his parents.

"The girl who tried to stop the wedding." Barrett sighed.

"Why do you want to help her?" Sehoy squinted at him with her inquisitive, motherly gaze. "She ruined the wedding."

"No, that's not true." Barrett shook his head. "She came to warn us. The LRs would've attacked whether or not she had interrupted."

"She left you bleeding on the floor." Sehoy squeezed his hand.

"That's because fear for herself and her son gripped her," Barrett looked pleadingly at George. "A little help here."

"What do you want me to say?" George shrugged. "They're right. She left you."

"Because she had to. Is no one listening to me?" Barrett's agitation set off a cacophony of beeping monitors, each sound a sharp reminder of his boiling anger. "She had to go to her son. She's in trouble."

"Okay, calm down, son." Osceola laid a hand on his shoulder and looked at George. "I promise to help George try to find her and make sure she is okay."

"What's going on in here?" the nurse entered the room and checked Barrett's vitals.

"Nothing." Barrett laid his head back and took a deep breath. "I'm fine."

"You don't look fine." The nurse turned off the beeping. "Do I need to ask these people to leave? You need your rest."

"No, it's fine. I'll be fine." Barrett mumbled. "But thank you."

"Okay, but another outburst like that, and I'll give him enough morphine to knock him out so he can rest." The nurse stared at everyone in the room. "Understood."

"Yes, ma'am," Barrett nodded.

"You're a cop." the nurse pointed at George. "You know better."

"I do." George crossed his arms and looked her in the eyes. "It won't happen again."

"We're sorry." Sehoy wrung her hands while she stared at the ground.

What the fuck? Barrett had never seen his mom appear so docile. She must really want to stay in the room to continue her interrogation.

"I'm watching you guys." The nurse pointed from her eyes to all of them. "He needs to stay calm. Don't make me come back in here."

"We won't." Sehoy walked her to the door. "Thank you for letting us stay."

The nurse shook her head and left.

"Well, that was close." George walked to the side of the bed. "I'll start looking for Angel. Do you know her last name?"

"No." Barrett shook his head. "I just know her name is Angel. She has a son, and she's Reaper's daughter."

"Fuck, if she's Reaper's daughter and he finds out she tried to warn us, she's in deep shit." George rubbed his face.

"Language!" Sehoy glared at George.

"George," –Osceola put his arm around his wife and kissed her cheek before releasing her– "why don't we leave them alone and come back with some answers for Barrett?"

Barrett could read between the lines. He knew his father was trying to keep him calm. "George, text me with anything you find out. Don't sugarcoat it, I'm fine." Barrett glared at him.

"I'll let you know what I find." George slapped his good leg and left with Osceola.

"Tell me about this Angel." Sehoy sat on the edge of the bed next to him.

So much for peace and quiet. Barrett knew his mother wouldn't give up, so he told her everything about Angel and the events following the shooting. Although his mom was a good listener, he preferred discussing relationship problems with Frey and Holt. It was difficult to share certain details about a girl with his mom when Barrett typically had casual, short-term relationships. Sehoy wanted her kids to find the right person, settle down, and give her lots of grandbabies. It's a good thing two out of three kids were married. Barrett figured Alex and Frey bought him some time. Unfortunately, after this conversation about Angel, he placed himself directly in Sehoy's happily ever after path.

Chapter 5

We Need To Go!

Angel

After Numbers left, Angel rushed to her room and retrieved her suitcase from the closet. Placing the suitcase on her bed, she carelessly threw clothes inside. She needed to leave town quickly before Numbers realized she had warned everyone at the wedding and returned to finish the beating he started. Picking up another suitcase, she hurried into Steele's room.

"Steele." Angel dropped the suitcase on the floor beside his bed. "I'm glad you're still awake. I need you to pack."

"Why?"

"Be...because we're going on a trip." Angel opened a drawer, grabbed his clothes, and threw them onto his bed. Some made it into the suitcase, but others she would grab as soon as she emptied his other drawers.

"Mom, stop." Steele bolted out of bed, grabbed his clothes out of the suitcase, and shoved them back in his drawer. "I'm not going anywhere."

"Yes, you are." Angel grabbed the clothes again. "We need to leave, NOW."

"Why?" He wrenched his clothes out of her arms, flung them into the drawer, slammed it shut, and stood in front of it. "What's going on?"

"I..I think we need a vacation, that's all." Angel turned toward his closet. *Why was he arguing with her?* Before Tools died, there was a time when she'd simply tell him to do something, and he would obey instantly. She'd let her grief and work overwhelm her so much that she'd stopped noticing how much of an influence Reaper and Numbers had over her son. She needed to change that starting today.

"Where are we going?" Steele followed her into the closet. "Did you call the school? Is Numbers coming with us?"

Angel froze. "Why would Numbers come with us?" *What had Numbers said to Steele over these past two days that made him turn against her?*

"Because he's your boyfriend, and he wants to marry you."

"What?" Angel spun around so fast, her vision blurred. She caught herself on the doorframe to avoid falling. "Numbers is a friend, my father's best friend, to be exact. What made you think he's my boyfriend?"

"He told me and so did grandpop." Steele shrugged.

"When did you speak to your grandfather?" *What the hell was happening?* How many times had Reaper talked to Steele without her knowing? After Reaper's arrest, she foolishly thought she had created distance between Steele and the LRs. *How had she not seen this coming?*

"A couple of days ago, when we planned the hit."

Angel's mind was spiraling. "You were a part of that?" Since when did her son talk about hits and take part in MC business? "I told you not to go there and listen in on MC meetings. I thought you were going to Ned's house after school to do your homework." Ned was Steele's closest friend at school. They'd been best buds since kindergarten.

"It was fine. Numbers invited me." Steele huffed. "Where have you been? I haven't gone to Ned's house to do homework in over a year."

"What?" Angel was astonished. "Where have you been going every day after school until I get home?"

"To the clubhouse." Steele shrugged.

"How are you getting there?" Angel knew the answer before she asked her stupid question.

"Numbers picks me up on his bike," Steele answered nonchalantly, "and drops me off before you get home."

Of course he does. After Tools death, she broke down and stopped taking cases. But when the bills piled up and Reaper offered her money, she snapped out of it and took on more cases. Angel was a highly successful and well-paid defense attorney.

Now, she realized the impact of her not being home when Steele got home from school. Angel needed to get them out of there, a sense of dread urging her on. Numbers was driving a wedge between them. She recoiled at the idea of marrying Numbers. The mere thought of a date with him caused her to shudder.

"Okay, well." Angel cleared her throat. This was not the time to talk about Steele's after school extracurriculars. They could discuss that on their way out of town. "Let's go to that theme park place for a few days." Angel intended to run away and never return, a secret she kept from Steele. If he knew her plan, he would never go with her. "I'll call the school right now, you pack."

"Yeah, okay."

Though surprised by his calmness before she left, Angel ignored it to finish packing and call the school. Pulling her phone out of her back pocket, she dialed the school on her way to her room. The receptionist told her phone calls weren't necessary. They had an online form that needed to be submitted within forty-eight hours of their return to school. Perfect, she'd worry about that later. Running into her room, she hung up, grabbed some cash out of her safe, finished packing, and went to get Steele.

"We need to go." Angel burst into his room and saw Steele's zipped up suitcase next to the bed. *Why was he pacing and murmuring into his* phone? "Steele?" Angel called out.

Steele stopped in his tracks. Glaring at her, he said, "I gotta go," before he hung up the phone.

"Who were you talking to?"

"I'm not going anywhere until Numbers gets here." Steele confronted her with his arms crossed.

"Is that who you were talking to? Why did you call him?" Angel couldn't believe Steele called Numbers. Since when had Numbers become his confidant. She thought she'd been a great mom all along, unaware of the danger Numbers posed. He infiltrated their lives as subtly and dangerously as a viper. Injecting poison into her son's thoughts and actions.

"None of your business." Steele glared at her and sat on the edge of the bed.

When had her sweet little boy become so defiant? Angel stepped forward, dropping to her knees before him. She had to make him understand the severity of that phone call. They had to leave before Numbers got there.

"Steele, I love you. I'm sorry I haven't been around as much lately, but you are my everything." Angel clasped his hands in hers. "I will always keep you safe and hanging out with the MC is not what your father and I wanted for you."

Steele shook her hands off and stood abruptly, stepping around her. "You're never home. And when you are, you're working on your computer." Steele whirled around. "And how can you say that about dad? He built a garage for the MC. He loved it there. They were his brothers, just like they will be mine one day."

"No, Steele." Angel stood and reached for him. "Please, let's get out of town for a few days and talk about your future. Yes, your dad loved his brothers, but he also wanted them to go legit. That's not what's happening. Don't you see that?"

Angel couldn't believe she was having a stare down with her son. Her baby boy, who always looked at her like she hung the moon, now looked at her as if she were a monster, ripping her away from his future brothers.

Ding Dong

"There he is." Steele ran out of his bedroom, before Angel could stop him.

Chapter 6

Steele, What Have You Done?

Angel

With a heavy heart, Angel shuffled to his bedroom door and pressed her forehead against the wall. She needed a minute before she faced Numbers. "Oh, baby boy. What have you done?" The weight of impending doom settled on her shoulders. All she could think about was protecting Steele and herself. Her throat constricted, a cold sweat prickling her skin as she forced a smile, schooling her expression, and walked toward the front door.

"You're taking Steele out of town without my permission?" Numbers stormed toward her.

Not even a miracle would have stopped the slap to her face. Angel fell back into the wall. Anger boiling within her. *Who the hell did he think he was?* She would not act like the battered wife when they weren't even married. "You are not his father." Angel glared at him.

"I will be soon enough." Numbers grabbed her arm and pulled her up to his chest. "Grab your shit. You are both coming with me."

"I'm not going anywhere with you." Angel tried pulling out of his grip, but it was no use. "Steele, call the police." She said over her shoulder.

"Steele, go get your shit and grab your mom's. I need to have a word with her."

As Steele's footsteps faded, Angel turned her head and yelled. "Call the po... ahh!"

A searing pain shot through her stomach, freezing her with terror as she gasped and doubled over.

"Why do you make me hurt you?" Numbers grabbed her arms and shook her so hard her head bounced around.

Having trouble catching her breath, Angel cried, "Why can't you just leave us alone?" Tears streamed down her face. Then the world tilted, a suffocating weight crushing her windpipe as icy fingers tightened around her throat and shoved her against the wall.

"Because he is the future of the LRs. He needs to take his rightful place until your fucking father gets out of prison." Numbers angrily shoved his finger in her face. "So shut the fuck up and do as you're told." Numbers squeezed harder before releasing her throat.

Angel thought she was going to die by strangulation until he released her. Gasping for breath, she continued fighting him.

"Never." Angel choked out. "He will be president, over my dead body."

"That can be arranged," Numbers murmured. A sly smile playing on his lips as he held her gaze and shoved her aside.

An icy shiver raced down her spine at the tone of his voice. He was serious. She was nothing. It was Steele he was after. If she became a problem, he would kill her. She wondered if her father had approved of that plan.

"My father will never let you kill me." Angel squinted at him. "He still loves me in his own warped way."

"He doesn't need to know," Number growled before he pushed Angel toward Steele's room. "Help Steele get all your shit and let's go."

"Where exactly are we going?" Angel stumbled, her heart pounding in her chest, but caught herself before she fell.

"To the clubhouse. You are going to be my new roommate until we're married." Numbers sneered at her.

"What? No. I'll stay with Steele. I'm his mother and he's underage. He shouldn't be alone in the clubhouse. Besides, I...I don't want to get married again." Angel attempted to remain calm while she was trembling with fear on the inside. If she stayed with Numbers, he would require sexual acts, and she wasn't ready to pretend to enjoy them. And she would have to pretend to avoid a beating.

"This isn't up for debate. You will stay with me, and we will get married as soon as possible. But if you don't want to get married, that's fine. You can be my ole lady. I really don't give a shit, as long as I get to fuck you every night."

Steele stood at the end of the hallway carrying their luggage. "I got all our bags. We're ready."

"No, Numbers, please don't do this?" Angel stood next to Steele and placed her arm around him. "We'll stay in town, I promise. Let us stay here."

"Bitch, I can't trust you. Let's go."

Angel felt Steele flinch when Numbers called her a bitch. There was hope for him.

"Why don't I make us some breakfast and we can talk this out?" She had to convince Numbers to let her stay in her own house. On her way to the kitchen,

Numbers shoved her into the wall, again. He just loved that fucking wall. Her head bounced off and her nose gushed blood.

Numbers pressed his body against her back and growled in her ear. "You will fucking listen to me when I tell you to do something. Now, get your shit and keep your mouth shut unless you want your son to watch me beat the shit out of you. Do you understand me?"

Hot tears mingled with the blood trickling down Angel's nose, each drop a bitter reminder of her vulnerability. "Y...yes." Angel nodded.

Numbers pushed her again before releasing her. "Let's go."

After wiping her nose with the back of her hand, Angel picked up her keys and purse. She watched Steele stride past. The heavy suitcases bumped against his legs, his gaze fixed straight ahead, ignoring her completely. Maybe she had lost him. *How could he just stand there and watch Numbers push her around?* Once again, like so many times before, she closed her eyes and wished Tools was there to protect her. As she walked outside, she noticed Numbers had arrived in one of the club's cars instead of his motorcycle—he'd come prepared.

The ride to the clubhouse was uncomfortably silent. Once there, Steele grabbed his bag and Numbers held onto Angel and her suitcase, dragging both inside. Several brothers were at the bar drinking while others were fucking girls. Angel immediately turned to Steele.

"Steele, close your eyes and come with me." Angel tried to hold his hand, but he pulled away.

"I've already seen all this, mom. Stop treating me like a baby."

"You're still my baby and you're not eighteen yet."

"He's fine." Numbers nodded to some brothers and dragged Angel to the stairs that led to the bedrooms. "Shit, I had just turned thirteen when I fucked my first girl, and he's almost fifteen. He's long overdue."

"No," Angel glared at Numbers and shoved him. "He is not old enough to be here. Tools wouldn't do this."

Numbers dropped her suitcase and pulled her up to his face. Once they were nose to nose, he let her have it.

"I don't give a shit what Tools would have done. He's dead. You're mine now and you will do as you're told. I will not fuckin' warn you again. Do you hear me? Now shut the fuck up and go up the fuckin' stairs." Numbers growled and pushed her up the stairs.

"Mouthy one, huh, Numbers," one brother said while others laughed.

"She'll learn her place soon enough." Numbers followed her and pointed to a door. "Steele, that was your dad's room when he lived here. It's yours now."

"Wow, really?" Steele burst into the room, looking around in awe.

Angel wasn't sure what he was looking for because all of Tools' belongings had either been thrown out or were at their house. The room contained one bed, one dresser, and a desk surrounded by bare walls. Angel saw Steele run his hand over the dresser and desk, probably imagining his father sitting there. She didn't want to ruin it for him, but she had been in this room with Tools many times, and he never had a desk. Numbers must have scrounged it up for Steele so he could do his schoolwork on it. After looking around, Steele plopped onto the bed.

"Let's unpack." Angel stepped forward, but Numbers stopped her.

"Where do you think you're going?" Numbers blocked her path into the room. "He can unpack himself. You are needed elsewhere."

Angel was not looking forward to being in Numbers' room. She knew they were going there and had tried to delay the inevitable, but her plan failed.

"Steele, when you're done, head downstairs." Numbers spoke while staring at Angel. "I'll be down in a few minutes. What I have to do won't take long." Numbers sneered at her.

Angel shuddered. Could he be any more blatant and disgusting?

Numbers grabbed her arm and dragged her into his room, slamming the door.

"Take your fucking clothes off and get on the bed."

Angel hesitated. She thought she would at least have a breather. "I need to unpack."

"No, you fuckin' don't, because I'm keeping you naked and chained to my bed until you learn to behave and listen to me."

"What? No!" Angel backed away from him. "What if Steele needs to talk to me?"

"He won't." Numbers continued to approach her. "I'll take care of Steele. Now, do as I said, or I'll fuckin' cut your clothes off." Numbers showed her the knife strapped to his belt.

Angel tried to control her trembling, but it was difficult with him staring at her. She attempted to run out the door, but he caught her and spun her around. Angel took off her shirt, threw it at his face and tried to escape, but Numbers was now blocking the door. Every time she tried to outsmart him earned her a slap or punch to the face. At this rate, she would be black and blue.

"Behave! Dammit!" Numbers snarled. "Do you want me to get your son to help me handcuff you naked?"

"You wouldn't dare!" Angel spit in his face.

"Try me," Numbers bellowed. The knife, now in his hand, raised between them. "Take the rest of your clothes off, now!"

Angel undressed and covered her nudity with her hands, but Numbers wasn't having any of her modesty. He quickly shoved her so hard she fell onto the bed. Not giving her a chance to get up, he sat on her chest and pulled her head up by her hair, breathing his stale breath into her face, he muttered. "Be nice to me, bitch, or I'll share you with all my brothers."

The evil shining in Numbers eyes stopped her cold. She could feel him hardening between her breasts when he mentioned sharing her. Fighting him wasn't getting her anywhere, now that he had total control over her body. Angel slowed her breathing while he finished handcuffing her arms to the railing on the headboard. *How the hell was she going to get out of this one?* She had to calm down and think of a plan.

Wiping his forehead, he stared at her. "I'm gonna go talk to Steele and teach him all about what it means to live in the clubhouse. He's gonna learn to drink and fuck tonight whether you like it or not."

Numbers didn't bother covering her with a blanket, he left her buck ass naked on his bed for any brother to see if they came into his room. *How could he do this to her? Did her father know what Numbers was up to? Had they been planning this all along?* Her despair over Steele downstairs overwhelmed her, and she cried herself to sleep.

Chapter 7

I'm Fine, Gotta Find Angel?

Barrett

It had been two fucking days since the shooting, and he still didn't know where Angel was. The hospital had kept him until they were sure he didn't have an infection from the bullet. The doctor also wanted to wait for the results of his CT scan and x-ray. Since he wasn't in danger of losing his life, those results had taken two days. As soon as the nurse arrived with his release papers and a crutch to help with his bad ankle, he signed himself out, called a local car service, and went home. He hated lying around doing nothing when he had to find Angel.

"*Chakpootsi*," Sehoy ran up to him in the lobby. "What are you doing here? Shouldn't you be in the hospital?"

Barrett hobbled into his mom's arms. "No, *chatski*. I'm okay. They said I could go. It's just a mild sprain, so they wrapped it up for me. I gotta do some RICE method they wrote in my release papers." Barrett lifted his free hand to show her. He hated the fucking crutch. They would've given him two crutches, but with his bad shoulder, they only gave him one.

"What about your shoulder?" Sehoy glanced over the paperwork.

"They said rest, ice, and pain meds." Barrett took the papers back when she finished.

"How did you get here?" Sehoy stepped back and stared.

"I called a car service."

"We would've come to get you."

"I know, *chatski*." Barrett leaned down and kissed his mom's cheek. "I just wanted to get out of there."

"You should rest. Go upstairs and I'll bring you some soup."

"I don't have a cold, *chatski*." Barrett chuckled. "But I would love a sandwich."

"Okay." Sehoy pointed to the elevators. "Go up and I'll bring you a sandwich."

"I love you, *chatski*." Barrett hugged his mom one handed before making his way to the elevator. He was hungry and a sandwich would hit the spot. He hated hospital food and was glad to be eating food from their restaurant. Once in his room, he laid on the couch and used several throw pillows to prop up his foot. He'd take ibuprofen when his mom brought his lunch. He refused to take his prescription pain meds. Besides, he needed a clear head for the conversation he was about to have with George.

"Hey, man, how are you? When are they releasing you?" George answered his cell on the first ring.

"I'm good and I'm home."

"No shit, that's great news. How are you feeling?"

"I'd be better if you told me you found Angel." Barrett closed his eyes.

"I have an address. I went by and knocked, but no one answered."

"Can I ask for a wellness check and go with you to check again?" Barrett held his breath, praying George could do this for him. Luckily, he didn't have to hold it for long.

"I'm not supposed to take a civilian with me, but for you–yes, you can come."

"Thanks, man. Can we go now?"

"You are not going anywhere, *chakpootsi*." Sehoy strolled in carrying a bag and a drink.

"Is that your mom? Tell her I said hello."

"George says hi." Barrett gave Sehoy the message and sat up. "*Chatski*, I'm fine and I really need to find Angel. I'm afraid something bad happened to her."

"Give me the phone." Sehoy put his food on his cocktail table and stuck her hand out.

Barrett handed it to her and pulled his sandwich out. He needed to eat quick.

"George, how are you?"

Barrett could only hear her side, since it wasn't on speakerphone.

"Is this dangerous?"

"You promise me. Because with his bad foot, I don't think he could run fast."

"*Chatski*, really?" Barrett stared at his mom. *What the hell?* He wasn't a pussy. He could run if he needed to.

"Okay, I'll tell him."

"Tell me what?" Barrett spoke with a mouthful of food.

"Don't talk with your mouth full." Sehoy reprimanded him. "George said he'll be here in about an hour."

"Perfect. Tell him to text me and I'll come down."

"Did you hear that, George? Yeah, he'll come down. Okay. See you later."

Sehoy hung up and handed Barrett his phone. Barrett put it in his back pocket.

"Thanks again, *chatski*."

"Yeah, yeah, yeah, now it's thanks again, but when George gets here, it's stay out of it. I see how it is." Sehoy went into the kitchen and screamed from the opening. "Where's your ibuprofen? I think you should take some with your food."

"In the cabinet to the right of the sink, best mom ever." Barrett always called her that when he was trying to sweet talk her, and she knew it.

"Here, you smooth talker, you." Sehoy held her hand out to him and placed the pills in his palm.

Barrett chuckled and took them after the last bite of his sandwich.

Chapter 8

Where the Hell is She?

George

George knew he couldn't let Barrett go with him for the wellness check. Officers were never supposed to take the civilians with them. But how the hell was he going to keep Barrett away? George told Sean O'Reilly his partner, hoping they could convince Barrett to stay in the car. It was a stretch, but he was willing to try. Sean agreed to meet them at the address.

As soon as he reached the resort, he texted Barrett and waited by the front door. It didn't take long to see Barrett limping toward him on one crutch.

"Hey, how are you feeling?" George asked when Barrett flung the door open and got in.

"Just peachy." Barrett buckled in and held the crutch between them. "Let's go."

"It's good to see you using a crutch." Barrett held up his hand to say goodbye to Sehoy before he pulled out.

"I'm only using it because she's watching. I'm fine."

"Who pee'd in your Wheaties?" George wasn't used to Barrett being in a pissy mood. He was usually the upbeat one ready for a good time. This grouchy behavior was unusual for him.

"Can we just go to Angel's house?"

"About that," George glanced at Barrett. "You can't come in with me."

"Why the hell not?" Barrett turned and glared.

"Because a wellness check is police business and you're not an officer of the law."

"I'm your friend. What the fuck, man?"

"Just stay in the damn car. Once she opens the door, I'll ask her if you can come in, okay?" George sighed. "Sean's gonna meet us there."

"Is he my babysitter?" Barrett huffed.

"Does he need to be?" George retorted.

"No. I'll stay in the car. It's fine," Barrett sighed. "Whatever."

"Hey, I'm sure she's fine." George remained calm even though inside he was hoping the LRs hadn't gotten a hold of her. After what they did to Maggie and Lola, he would hate for Angel to be their next target. Then again, she was Reaper's daughter, so how bad could it be?

George pulled into the driveway. Only Sean's patrol car sat outside. But he saw a garage, so maybe she parked her car inside. Most deputies were weary of wellness checks if the person had been missing for more than a couple days because they might find them deceased.

"Okay. Just stay put." George unbuckled and turned to Barrett before he got out. "I'll wave you over as soon as she opens the door."

"Fine." Barrett crossed his arms and stared at the front door.

George met up with Sean in the driveway and pointed toward Barrett in the car. Sean held up his hand, but Barrett just glared at them like an angry bear. George chuckled and walked with Sean to the front door. Sean knocked, but no one answered.

George banged on the door. "Angel, this is Deputy George Smith and Deputy Sean O'Reilly. Can you please open the door? We need to speak to you." George waited a couple of seconds and repeated his words and actions.

George leaned in, placing his ear against the door, trying to hear for any sounds. He grabbed the doorknob and turned it. Surprisingly, the door opened; it wasn't locked. He immediately pulled out his gun, nodding to Sean, who got his as well. George saw Barrett get out of the car, limping toward them. Idiot. He was going to get himself killed if someone was armed in the house.

"Dammit, Barrett." George whispered when he reached them. "I told you to stay in the car."

"I'm your backup, just in case."

"I have backup," George gestured to Sean before putting on gloves. He wasn't sure what he was going to find, but if it was a crime scene, he didn't want to leave his prints.

"Yeah, and I must say I'm pretty good." Sean smiled.

George turned and saw Barrett cock his gun. "Where the hell did that come from?"

"My back," Barrett smirked. "You didn't think I'd accompany you unarmed, did you?"

"One can dream," George whispered. "Okay, do as I say and stay behind me. And for the love of God, don't touch anything."

"You got it."

"Sean, go around back in case we have a rabbit." George slowly opened the door.

"What the fuck is a rabbit?" Barrett stood behind George.

"A person who runs from us." George entered slowly and looked around, both clearing every room in Angel's house.

"Well, she's not here." George holstered his weapon and walked to the sliding glass door in the back and waved to Sean to come in the front.

"Is that blood on the wall?" Barrett stormed toward the wall near the kitchen.

"It sure is, and it doesn't look fresh," George sighed. "Sean, call it in while I talk to Barrett."

"Fuck!" Barrett rubbed his face, staring at the blood splatter. When George saw Barrett reach his hand toward the wall, he grabbed it.

"Don't touch it!" George screamed.

*** Barrett ***

Barrett knew she had left him bleeding the day of the wedding, but she was worried about her son. If the MC had his son, he would've left in a hurry too. "Where the hell is she, George?" Barrett asked George. "The first time I saw her was when she came in like a bat out of hell to stop the wedding, then left me to die."

"Dramatic much." George smirked at him and pulled him into the kitchen.

Barrett ignored George's sarcasm, his arms flailing as he said, "That was two fucking days ago, George! They could be hurting her. You saw what they do to women."

"Believe me, I know." George crossed his arms and braced his feet, blocking the doorway. "Sean called it in. They'll be sending a detective and forensics. Let's stay here until they arrive.

"Can I walk around and see if anything else looks wrong or bloody?"

"No." George shook his head. "Sit your ass down."

"I gotta find her." Barrett rubbed his face. "What if they have her? What if they're torturing her, as we speak?"

"Look, I get that you're worried. But her son isn't here either." George shrugged. "Maybe they went to the mall or to get a bite to eat."

"It just doesn't feel right."

"What are you, a psychic, now?"

"Fucker." Barrett was about two seconds away from punching that smirk off George's face. But what good would that do? Hitting an officer, even if he was his friend, could land him in jail. He wouldn't put it past George, making him sit in jail to cool off, and that was not an option when Angel was God knows where. "No, I'm not. But it doesn't take a mind reader to know school is out, no one's home, and there's dried blood on the fucking wall!" Barrett's voice pitched at the end of his rant.

"Forensics is here. Sit tight." Sean said from behind George.

Well, no shit Sherlock, Barrett could hear the fucking sirens blazing.

"Deputy Smith, can you tell me what happened?" Barrett saw a man in a suit approach George.

"Sean and I were conducting a wellness check when we noticed the unlocked door. We came in and saw the blood." George pointed to the wall. "Then we checked the house and found it empty."

"Where's Forensics?" The man in the suit asked Sean.

"They just pulled up." Sean answered.

"Who's this?" the detective pointed to Barrett, who leaned against the kitchen counter with his ankles crossed. Barrett was seething inside because George was keeping him in the kitchen.

"This is Barrett Panther." George motioned toward him with his hand. "He called in the wellness check."

"Hello, Mr. Panther. I'm Detective Appleton. Why did you call in a wellness check?" the detective pulled out his pad and turned to Barrett.

"Because I think she's in danger. I wanted someone to check on her because I didn't have her address." Barrett said through gritted teeth.

"How do you know her? Why do you think she is in danger?"

"George, do we really have to do this now?" Barrett stepped away from the counter, attempting to leave the room. "Can we please go find Angel?"

"Mr. Panther, I just need to ask you a few more questions." The detective stepped in front of Barrett. "Then you will be free to go."

"Fine." Barrett threw his arms up and winced. "Ask your fucking questions."

"Who is Angel to you?" the detective waited with his pen poised on the pad.

"Look, all I know is she showed up at our resort and casino attempting to stop my brother and sister's wedding on New Year's Eve. She said Lucifer's Renegades were coming to take revenge...."

The detective interjected, "I heard about that."

"I think everyone has heard about that by now." Barrett wiped his forehead. His shoulder was throbbing. It must be time to take another ibuprofen pill. Unfortunately, he didn't have any on him.

George grabbed Barrett's bicep. "I think you need to sit down, Barrett."

"I'm fine. I just want to get this over with."

"Please continue," the detective nodded.

"Anyway, she tried to warn us, but the shooting began. When I moved her out of the way, I got shot in the shoulder and tripped trying to protect her. I followed her to the lobby, and that's when she saw her son riding bitch on the back of an LRs member's bike. I stopped her and pulled her to safety, but she left my ass when I nearly passed out." Barrett turned around and braced his hands on the counter. "We need to find her. She could be in grave danger."

"Why would her son be on the back of a biker's bike?" the detective looked confused.

"Because she's Reaper's daughter, the president of Lucifer's Renegades!" Barrett slammed his hand on the counter and spun around to face the detective. "Can I go now?"

"Of course, but let me have your number, so I can call you if I have further questions."

"I have his number." Barrett was grateful for George stepping in because he was losing his cool. "I'll text it to you."

"Great." The detective closed his notebook. "I'm gonna have a look around."

"Finally," Barrett muttered.

George glared at him and whispered. "Shut the fuck up and sit your ass down before you fall down."

"I'm not a pussy. I'm fine." Barrett said, before he leaned on his bad ankle and winced.

George got a chair from the dining room and put it behind Barrett. "Sit your ass down."

"Fine. Mom." Barrett sat and sulked.

"If she's missing...," George placed his hand on Barrett's good shoulder. "...we will find her."

"Can we go to the LRs clubhouse?" Barrett looked up at George.

"Uh, that's not a good idea unless you want to get shot." George leaned on the counter.

"Don't you guys have anyone on the inside?" Barrett looked up at him. "Undercover or something?"

"I'll talk to my sergeant and see what I can find out. But in the meantime," George pointed his finger at Barrett, "You need to stay put and not go over there."

Barrett looked down, not making eye contact with George.

"Are you listening to me?" George kicked Barrett's good foot. "Fucking promise me, you won't go over there. I don't want to find you in a bloody heap in their clubhouse. Let's be smart about this."

"Fine. I promise I won't go over there."

"I'll talk to some people and make a plan, okay?"

Barrett agreed to stay put–for now. "Yeah."

They waited in silence until the detective and the forensics team finished cataloging their findings.

"Gentlemen." The detective came back into the kitchen. "Mr. Panther, thank you for staying. We've collected all the samples we could find. We'll go talk to the neighbors to see if they heard anything. George, Sean," the detective shook their hands, "I'll write up my report and we can discuss the case tomorrow. Mr. Panther, call me if you hear anything." The detective gave him his business card and left.

Barrett stood. "George, you will keep me updated, right?"

"Yep, I promise." George clapped him on the back. "Come on. I'll take you back to the resort."

"Thanks." Barrett shook Sean's hand. "Good to see you too, Sean."

"Likewise," Sean sighed. "Just wish it was under different circumstances."

"Me too."

Barrett followed George to his police car for the drive home.

"Thanks for everything, George." Barrett grabbed his crutch and opened the car door.

"What are friends for?" George smiled.

Barrett scooted to get out, but George grabbed his arm and Barrett faced him.

"Listen, man. I'll call you with any updates."

Barrett nodded and got out.

*** George ***

George drove to the police station. He had an idea rattling around in his head, but he wanted to run it by his sergeant before he got Barrett's hopes up. George knew he needed to come up with a plan quick because Barrett was acting crazy over this girl. The last thing he needed was for Barrett to act like a lone wolf and get himself killed.

If this idea worked, they might know where Angel was and how to get to her by tomorrow night. Fingers crossed that his sergeant, captain, and whoever else had to approve it, were on board.

Chapter 9

Hell on Earth

Angel

Angel didn't think life could get any worse, but she was wrong. For the past couple of nights, Numbers left her naked and handcuffed to the bed. He only let her get up to eat and pee while he taunted and humiliated her. Going to the bathroom was the worst because he made her go naked and didn't care if any of the brothers were out in the hall. Several times they stared at her, and she was sure they were going to touch her, but Numbers would tell them to leave her alone. It surprised her because she thought Numbers would have enjoyed seeing her further humiliated like he'd threatened when he made her strip.

Lucky for her, Steele was never in the hallway. Numbers kept him busy with all the sluts that hung around the clubhouse. She prayed Steele was wearing a condom, because she was sure these whores were full of diseases.

Numbers hadn't forced her to fuck him yet. He was focusing on Steele's lascivious education for now from the little bit of information he gave her every night before he dropped into bed drunk. Angel wasn't complaining, she'd rather he passed out than notice her.

On the morning of her third day in hell at the clubhouse with Numbers snoring next to her, she needed to use the restroom but crossed her legs attempting to hold it. She didn't want to wake him. Unfortunately, if he didn't wake up within the next hour, she would wet the bed. *How did she get here? Why was Steele acting like such a badass biker? Where had her little boy gone?*

"What are you thinking about so hard over there?" Numbers grumbled.

"Nothing." The last thing Angel wanted was to make Numbers privy to her thoughts. "I have to use the restroom."

"Fuck." Numbers uncuffed her and pulled her to the door. "Let's go."

"When are you going to let me put my clothes on?" Angel mumbled.

"When I'm fuckin' good and ready. Besides, I like to see you naked and tempting my brothers. This way, if you misbehave, they will be happy to fuck you into submission."

"If any of them were friends with Tools, they wouldn't...ahhh!" Angel never saw the punch coming. When was she going to learn to keep her mouth shut and stop mentioning Tools to Numbers? Her face was going to have permanent indents from his punches soon.

"I told you never to talk about Tools again." Numbers pulled her down the hallway and shut them in the bathroom. "Now, pee."

Angel didn't know how she was going to get away from him, but one day, she would run away. Thinking of her escape put a smile on her face.

"What the fuck are you smiling about?"

"Can you please at least turn around and give me some privacy?"

"Why? I've already seen everything you've got and tonight I'm gonna test drive it." Numbers licked his lips. "But first we have an important meeting."

"About what?" Angel wiped and stood.

"None of your fuckin' business." Numbers grabbed her arm after she washed her hands and pulled her back into their room. "If you please me tonight, then I'll uncuff you and let you put some clothes on."

"Can I see Steele?"

"Maybe. Let's see how you behave tonight."

Tonight's ordeal disgusted Angel, but she realized unless she pretended to obey his rules, she would remain trapped in his room. Once she could wander the clubhouse freely, she could plan her escape. Not knowing what was happening outside that bedroom was killing her. *Was Steele going to school? Had they started giving him drugs to go along with the alcohol?* She had to do everything in her power to please Numbers so she could help her son. She didn't care about herself anymore. Saving Steele and getting him as far away from here as possible was her main priority.

Chapter 10

Shitty Night

Barrett

They were still short staffed at the casino since Holt and Frey were on their honeymoon for another week. Being short staffed in security made for endless nights, especially since he was still using one crutch for his bad ankle. Maybe it was time to call Mark and ask him if he could work a few hours at night until Holt came back. Anastasia and Abigail covered Frey's table, but he missed seeing his sister's face.

"Hi Barrett." a buxom blonde stopped him on his rounds. "What happened? Can I help you with anything?"

Barrett couldn't remember her name, only that he had fucked her before. "Uh, hey. I'm good. How are you?" He tried to make small talk, so he didn't come off as being a prick since he didn't remember her name. In his ear, he could hear kissy noises from the other security officers who could hear his conversation. *Fuckers.*

"I'm great now that you're back." The blonde twirled her hair and stroked his shoulder. "I've missed you. Do you think we can get together when you get off work?"

"Um, not tonight. This crutch really wears me out."

"I'm sure she'd like to wear you out," Travis mumbled in his ear. *Fucker.*

"I can help you relax with a full body massage." The blonde winked at him.

"Oh, Barrett," Travis said in a girly voice in his ear. "I can massage that big cock of yours."

Barrett chuckled. "Well, at least you agree it's big." All the security officers joked with each other every night when they weren't taking care of business. It's what made the night shift fun.

"What's big?" the blonde mushed her breasts against Barrett's arm with a puzzled look on her face.

"Nothing, sorry." Barrett pointed to his earpiece. "Talking to other security officers and they're telling me something big is happening and they need my help. I gotta go. It was nice to see you."

"Something big is happening in your pants." Travis laughed.

Barrett stepped away from the blonde and whispered. "You are such a dick."

"I'm the dick? Do you even remember her name, fuck boy?" Travis mumbled.

"Not at the moment, but it'll come to me," Barrett smirked.

"Oh, she would've come for you if you'd given her half a chance."

"Travis, you're a sick fuck." Barrett strolled around the casino checking for issues.

"That's why you love me. Hey, why don't you take a break and I'll walk around the main floor."

"You just want to leave the monitors so you can check out the hot blonde that was flirting with me." Barrett left the main floor, heading to the security office's main monitoring station behind the lobby desk.

"I do not want your sloppy seconds."

Barrett opened the door and glared at Travis. "Since when has that stopped you?"

"Valid point." Travis stood and nodded. "You look a little pale. You should take off and get some sleep. It's Wednesday, and it's quiet. I can call someone in if I need to."

"Thanks, man," Barrett slapped his back. "I think I will."

"Good. See you tomorrow."

"*Chakpootsi*, are you okay?" Sehoy came into the room. "I just saw Travis, and he told me you were going up to your room for the night."

"Yeah, I'm more tired than I thought I would be."

"Go rest. I'll have your father make a few rounds before we leave."

"Thank you, *chatski*." Barrett kissed his mom's cheek. "Have you seen George today?"

"No, was he supposed to come by?" Sehoy frowned.

"No, I just thought maybe he'd found Angel."

"I'm sure he's trying. Why don't you get some sleep so when he finds her, you can go see her."

Barrett hugged Sehoy. "Okay, see you tomorrow."

"Goodnight, *chakpootsi*."

"Barrett!"

Barrett spun around and saw Maggie approaching him in a full out run with her fists clenched, leaving Mark behind.

"I didn't get the chance to tell them how you were," Sehoy whispered.

"Great." Barrett smirked, "Hey Maggie. How are you?"

"How am I?" Maggie smacked his good shoulder. "What the hell happened to you?"

"I need to check on something. See you all later." Sehoy walked away.

"Thanks." Barrett mumbled and glared after his mother. The least she could do was help him out with Maggie instead of leaving him flapping out in the wind.

"Well, are you going to tell me what happened? It's been two days since the wedding, and I didn't know what happened to you? Last time I saw you, you were bleeding. Where's the blonde bitch, anyway?"

"Killer, we talked about this." Mark wrapped his arm around her shoulder pulling her toward him. "Calm down and let Barrett tell us what happened to him."

"Hey, Mark." Barrett put out his hand for a handshake. "Good to see you guys are okay."

"We're fine. You wanna tell us about the shoulder and the crutch?" Mark gave him a raised eyebrow.

"One of the LRs bullets got me. I think they were trying to hit Angel, but I took the direct hit when I pushed her away. It went all the way through my shoulder, but it hurt like a bitch. To make matters worse, on my way down, I tripped over a chair and sprained my ankle. That still hurts and I can't put weight on it, hence the crutch."

"Why didn't you tell us?" Maggie crossed her arms and glared at Barrett.

"You were a little busy wanting to kill Angel and looking for your brother." Barrett grinned. "Besides, as you can see, I'm fine."

"Where is the bitch?"

"Can we not call her that, Maggie?" Barrett sighed. "She put her life on the line to warn us at the wedding. Besides, I think she's in big trouble."

"What do you mean?" Mark immediately went on alert. "Where is she? Are they planning something else?"

"Fuck if I know." Barrett leaned against the lobby desk. His ankle was throbbing, and he really needed sleep. "She's not at her house and we found dried blood. George is looking for her. I just want to make sure she's okay. But I'm so fucking tired and not much help. Shit, I couldn't even finish out my shift in the casino cause my ankle is throbbing."

"I have an idea," Mark snapped his fingers. "Maggie, help Barrett upstairs. I'll work your shift in the casino."

"Is that okay with you, Maggie?" Barrett hoped she said yes, because Travis could really use the help.

"Yeah, that's fine." Maggie gave Mark a peck on the lips and turned to Barrett. "Let's get you to bed."

"Not with you in it, Jessica Rabbit," Mark growled.

Barrett remembered a time when Maggie wasn't feeling well, and Mark caught them in a compromising situation. It was all innocent, and it took Barrett a lot of explaining to calm Mark down. Now, he just liked to mess with him. "Why not? The best nurses sleep next to their patients in case they need anything."

"Not Nurse Nightingale." Mark pointed at Maggie. "She will leave your bedroom door open and lay on the couch in case you need anything. Right?"

"Yes, Surfer Smurf. I promise not to snuggle with Barrett." Maggie winked at Barrett.

"Margarita Gomez, do not test me." Mark growled, but Maggie walked over to him, whispered something in his ear and gave him what looked to be a sinfully delicious kiss.

Barrett chuckled. She loved to bust Mark's balls. And deep down, Barrett thought Mark loved it too.

When the kiss ended, Mark smacked her ass and headed to the casino.

"Come on, you pain in the ass, let's go." Barrett hobbled on the crutch to the elevator with Maggie in tow.

Chapter 11

I Will Survive This for Steele

Angel

Numbers had stormed out earlier today, mumbling something about a club meeting. Angel prayed for an extra-long meeting that would keep him out all night because the nights were the worst. She remembered from when she visited Tools as a teen at the clubhouse how the brothers would drink and get high before they went to bed either alone or with a sweet butt. That's what they called the girls that hung around the club and made themselves available for sex with any of the brothers—they weren't picky. All a sweet butt ever wanted was to snag a brother and become his ole lady (his girlfriend or wife). Ole ladies had some say in things and never got passed around. Some things never change.

As she laid in bed, pain shooting down her arms from being cuffed for so long, she could hear several brothers in the hallway and hoped they didn't confuse this room for theirs. She wasn't sure what they would do. Would they turn around and leave or hurt her?

During the day, they might think twice about violating Tools' widow, but at night, it was game on. They threw out their inhibitions and morals. Every night she would doze in and out of sleep, but jar awake every time she heard footsteps or voices in the hallway stomping past the door. Her body would tighten in fear of being caught naked and helpless. Numbers never left a light on when he left the room, so it was pitch dark when she finally heard the door open.

From the rhythm of his walk, and the quick slamming of the door, she knew it was Numbers. As expected, he locked the door. He wasn't stumbling around, so he must be sober...*shit*. Angel heard a zipper being lowered. He always slept naked beside her, but hadn't touched her these past couple of nights. Maybe he'd remembered she was more like a daughter than a wife. No, that couldn't be it because what normal father would sleep naked next to his daughter? She didn't know what he was waiting for, but was glad for the reprieve.

Angel slowed her breath and pretended to be asleep. She prayed for another night of being left alone. Then his pants hit the floor, and he slid onto the bed. Although she was not willing to have sex with Numbers, she hoped that if it happened, it would be quick and without pain. She'd find no pleasure in it. Her body was just a vessel until she could leave this horrible nightmare. Angel felt something goopy being spread on the inside and the outside of her pussy. This was it, the moment she had been dreading. He was going to rape her.

"I know you're not sleeping, so stop pretending." Numbers rammed his cock into her.

Angel screamed out in agony. She hadn't been with anyone since Tools died and the excruciating pain of being ripped open was worse than she thought. It didn't matter if he was big or small. It had been years since she had been intimate with a man, and the lubricant he used wasn't effective.

"Scream louder bitch, it turns me on." Numbers grunted as he continued to force himself on her.

Between the weight of his body and the handcuffs, she couldn't move. Tears streamed down her face from the pain. She tried to shut out the horrible things he was doing to her with his penis, hands, and mouth. Her mind tried to wander outside of her body, but then he would bite her and bring her back to her horrible reality. She bit her lip and refused to scream out since it turned him on. She wouldn't give him the satisfaction. *Fuck him.* She would endure this assault so she could see her son again and plan her revenge. He could take her body, but he would never take her soul or her mind.

In the morning, he fucked her again. When he finished, he got up and uncuffed her.

"Go take a fucking shower." Numbers threw a long t-shirt at her. "Then I'll let you see Steele."

"Okay." Angel scurried away, down the hall into the bathroom, locking the door behind her. Her performance must have pleased him because this was the first time in three days that he hadn't followed her into the bathroom. Turning on the water as hot as it would go, she scrubbed her body until it was a deep shade of pink. Leaning on the tile, she cried for the naïve girl that thought everything would be okay without Tools. The woman who thought she could fight off the boogie man who turned out to be her father's best friend, and the little girl that broke tonight because her daddy didn't protect her.

Numbers was pounding on the door. "Why are you taking so long?"

"Sorry." Angel pulled herself together. "I'm almost done!" It was now all about Steele and her survival. He would not break her. She would get away with Steele and create a new life for them somewhere far away from here where Numbers couldn't find her. She didn't know where that would be, but anywhere was better than here. After drying off, Angel put on the t-shirt and opened the door.

"I'm sorry. The hot water just felt so good."

"Come on." Numbers put his arm around her shoulders. Angel tried not to flinch. "Steele is waiting for you."

Angel was excited to see Steele. She wasn't sure which Steele she was going to get. The little boy that loved her beyond words or the rude teenager that wanted to be a club member more than her son.

Numbers knocked on Steele's door.

Steele swung the door open, standing before them in only his underwear. "Mom?"

Angel looked behind him and saw one of the club's sweet butts getting out of bed naked. She hoped he wore a condom. Seeing her fourteen-year-old acting like a man broke her heart. He should not be doing this at his age. He should be playing outside with friends, gaming, skating, playing sports, anything but sleeping with a girl in a dirty clubhouse room. Then again, hadn't she done that with his father at fifteen? Now she knew how her mother had felt when she found out she was sneaking around with Tools at the clubhouse. Her life had come full circle. The only difference was their age and their love.

There was no way Steele was in love with that woman or vice versa unless she knew they wanted to make him president one day. Now more than ever, Angel was determined to get them both out of there as soon as possible.

Chapter 12

Awkward Much

Steele

The last person Steele expected to see on the other side of his door was his mom. A flush of heat crept up his cheeks as her eyes passed him, taking in the state of his room and the girl behind him. Cherry had spent the night and taught him what it was to be a man. He did things last night he had only heard about from the LR brothers and seen in the porn magazines Numbers gave him.

"Uh," Angel cleared her throat. "Good morning. Can we talk?"

Steele stared down at the floor, not sure what to say with a naked woman in his room. He was afraid to see the disappointment in his mother's face.

"Cherry." Numbers pushed his mom out of the way and stepped into the room. "Get your shit and leave Steele with his mom."

"Sure." Cherry snatched her dress off the floor and bolted naked out the door, shoving his mom in her haste.

"Angel, come in." Numbers snapped his fingers in her face, jolting her out of her trance. "I'll give you both twenty minutes, then I'll take him to school."

Angel walked in and turned to Numbers. "You're letting him go to school?"

"For now." Numbers pointed in her face. "Don't let me regret this." Numbers slammed the door on the way out.

"Mom." Steele sat on his bed. "What do you..."

Angel interrupted him. "I'm not gonna yell at you for losing your virginity or possibly getting drunk or high last night. I know you were forced into it. This fucking clubhouse has a way of doing that."

"I wasn't forced." Steele bolted off the bed and faced her. He had to make her understand. He went willingly with Cherry. It was a rite of passage. With his father gone, he'd had a lot of questions that were embarrassing to ask his mom. At least with Cherry, she took over and taught him what he needed to do. Now he understood what all the hoopla was about. It had felt damn good. The only awkward part was facing his mom this morning, with Cherry naked behind him.

"Okay. Let's sit and talk." Angel looked around the room and sat in the desk chair. "I'm so happy to see you."

Steele sat at the edge of the bed facing his mom. "I'm glad you're okay. It looks like you have more bruises. When are you gonna learn to do what Numbers says. Stop making him hit you." If she could just behave like the sweet butts, Numbers wouldn't beat on her.

"Wow, is that what you think?" Angel raised her eyebrows. "That I'm asking for it. How would you have liked it if every time I asked you to do something and you said no, I smacked you around?"

"You're right, I wouldn't have liked it, but all you gotta do is stay quiet. It's not the same thing."

Angel nodded and whispered, "I...I don't know what to say. I can't believe you are okay with someone hitting me for any reason. Where's the son I raised to be a good man? Your father never hit me. He loved me and I loved him. I do not love Numbers and don't want to marry him."

Steele pointed a finger at her. "Watch what you say. If Numbers hears you say that he'll really hurt you."

Angel's eyes widened. "How could I marry someone who hits me if I don't behave or say the right things? How can you be okay with that as my son?"

"I think you should leave. I gotta shower and get dressed for school." Steele stood and walked to the door. He didn't have any answers for her. He felt conflicted and confused. Numbers treated him with respect, giving him anything he desired, whereas his mom gave him rules and punishment. Numbers made him into a man, and his mom wanted to hold him back like her little baby. But he wasn't a baby anymore, and he was tired of being treated like one. *So, what if he got drunk, had sex, or even got high? He could handle it. He was a man now.*

"Will you come see me when you get home?" Angel followed him.

"If you behave and Numbers allows it, sure." Steele opened the door and saw Numbers leaning against the far wall of the hallway. "Numbers is waiting for you."

As Angel walked by him, Steele mumbled, "Don't do anything crazy and make it harder for me in here."

Angel mis-stepped and tripped, but Steele caught her and shoved her out the door toward Numbers.

Steele closed the door behind her and leaned back against it with his eyes closed. It was best that he not see her. The hurt in her eyes was more than he could bear. He loved his mom, but this was their new reality and the sooner she accepted their future, the better it would be for both of them.

Dropping his head, he saw he was still in his underwear. *Fuck!* He needed to take a shower, go to school, and act the part of a normal teenager. Living here was about survival and if he could get a break for eight hours every day away from the drinking and drugs, he would take it.

When he gathered his stuff to go shower, his mom was gone. She must be back in Numbers' room. He knew he had broken her heart by the way she looked at him with horror and sorrow reflecting in her eyes. His words had been harsh. He hated everything he said to her, but he truly didn't know how to act or what to do. Going along with Numbers seemed like the best plan for now.

He didn't know what was happening to her in Numbers room, although going by the way she was dressed, it probably had to do with sex. *Fuck!* He couldn't think about that. He had to pretend everything was okay until he could get her out of there. His father had lived here and loved his brothers, he would too. Unfortunately, he would have to do it without his mom. He would get her to safety, then never see her again. Numbers was already inviting him to the club meetings, and he wasn't even a prospect yet. He couldn't wait to get his kutte with the 'prospect' rocker label on the bottom.

Chapter 13

Friend or Foe?

Angel

Numbers escorted her to their room. Seeing her teenage boy after losing his virginity as he stood in front of her, mostly naked, was one of the most awkward experiences of her life. She had hoped his first time would be a beautiful experience like it was with her and Tools. Not with a sweet butt that was twice his age. But that hadn't been the worst part of her morning. The worst had been his attitude toward her. He spoke venomously to her. She wasn't sure how she was going to get him to leave with her, but she had to try.

"I have shit to do today." Numbers faced her. "You are free to walk around the clubhouse, but you are not to leave. I've left strict instructions with my brothers and if anyone sees you leaving, they will follow you and call me. Trust me, you won't like the consequences."

"I won't go anywhere." Angel gulped and cast her eyes down. "Thank you for not cuffing me again."

Numbers lifted her chin with his finger and stared into her eyes. "Don't fuck with me."

"I won't." Angel shook her head. "I'm gonna head downstairs to get something to eat."

"Let's go." Numbers grabbed her hand. As soon as they entered the main living space, Numbers kissed her in front of the brothers, who were lounging around.

She realized he was staking his claim and deliberately keeping others away from her. However, if she disobeyed him, he only needed to give the command, and they would attack her with the ferociousness of rabid dogs, their snarls echoing through the air. Overwhelmed by the urge to wipe her mouth and avoid gagging, she returned his kiss and smiled until he left.

"So, you're Steele's mom?" Angel turned to face Cherry.

"I am. You're Cherry."

"Your son is awesome. He's a quick learner." Cherry smirked and several brothers laughed.

"I'd rather not talk about my son's sex education, if you don't mind." Angel walked around her into the kitchen in search of a refrigerator and something to eat. She wasn't sure what she would find, but was hungry and needed sustenance. She had to be strong and healthy for when she escaped. On her way, she saw the tarp that covered the missing wall from the fire Los Lobos set.

"If you're looking for food, it's slim pickin's," Sandy, Brick's old lady, said from the small table. "How are you, Angel?"

Sandy had always been nice to her before she hooked up with Brick. She didn't know what she saw in him. But Angel figured after years of being passed around, it was better to sleep with one man than the entire club.

"Hey Sandy." Angel opened the fridge and saw a new container of yogurt behind a row of beers. That would have to do. When she went on this food finding mission, she didn't know if all she would see would be beer and leftovers. Leftovers at a clubhouse scared her because she didn't know who cooked it. At least the yogurt was sealed and hadn't expired. Angel grabbed a spoon and sat across from Sandy. "I wish I was at my house. Will you help me go home?"

Angel knew asking Sandy was a long shot, but she hoped because of their friendship, Sandy would help her. She'd known Sandy since she was married to Tools. Brick used to help Tools in the garage. On the day of the shooting, Brick offered to run out and pick up a part for the car Tools was working on. Tools had been standing outside shooting the shit with some of his other brothers waiting for Brick when El Loco did his drive by shooting, killing Tools, Gears, and Ink.

Numbers had been heading toward the brothers when the bullets started flying. A bullet struck his leg, and he arrived too late to help his brothers. By the time he reached them, they were lying dead on the floor. He was the only survivor.

"No can do." Sandy shook her head. "I won't go against Numbers. Besides, Brick would kill me."

Angel sighed. "Yeah, I figured," Angel sighed, crushing her hopes that Sandy would help because of their past with her three words, 'no can do'. Word travelled fast from brother to ole lady. Angel knew Sandy had the lowdown on her situation and none of them were going to go against Numbers or Reaper, but she had to try.

"But we can still be friends. Lord knows you need one. Just don't ask me to go against our president."

"Sandy, Numbers is not your president." As far as she knew, the members hadn't voted on a president. They were still hoping that Reaper would get out on a technicality. Reaper was standing by his statement that he didn't know Winston was going to kidnap Tori. He'd thought they were just robbing the American Indian Cultural Center.

"That's because you won't help get Reaper out." Sandy glared at her. "So, Numbers is taking over until Reaper comes home."

"Shouldn't that be the job of the VP?" *What the hell was going on?* The club wasn't following protocol. If the president wasn't around, the VP, in this case Butch, would take over.

"Not when Reaper himself put Numbers in charge." Sandy looked at her like she was an idiot.

"I didn't know that. I mean, I saw him giving directions, but I wasn't sure he was in charge." If Numbers was acting president, he had all the brothers behind him. Finding an ally here was going to be next to impossible. *Fuck!*

"Any suggestions about food?" Angel lifted the empty yogurt container. "This didn't cut it."

"I can ask a prospect to go get us something." Sandy shrugged. "What do you want? I'm not picky and I'm hungry, too."

"How about a breakfast croissant from any fast-food restaurant and coffee?"

"I'll tell them to get the food, coffee we have lots of. I'll go make a pot." Sandy stood.

"I'll go with you so I can see where the coffee stuff is."

Angel followed Sandy to the main living area where the prospects were hanging out, waiting for assignments other than to clean up after the party last night.

"Red," Sandy called out to a thin, red-haired man slouched on the couch. "I need you to go get us some food."

"Sure thing, Sandy." Red stood. "What can I get ya'?"

"Get us," Sandy pointed to Angel and herself, "some breakfast croissant sandwiches from the fast-food king place."

"I ain't getting her food." Red shook his head and pointed at Angel.

"Yeah, you fuckin' will," Brick came from around the corner and put his arm around Sandy. "If my ole lady tells you to do somethin' you do it. Besides, Angel is Numbers ole lady now." Brick winked at her.

The corner of Angel's lip twitched as she attempted a grin. Not agreeing with Brick would get her locked back up in Numbers' room. *And when the hell did she become Numbers ole lady?*

"Oh shit." Red's face turned a deep pink. "I didn't know. Sorry, Brick. I'll go right now."

"While you're at it, get about 20 of those sandwiches for the rest of us." Brick whipped out several twenties from his pocket and handed them to Red. "I want my change when you return."

"Of course." Red nodded and bolted out the door.

"Ladies, I got shit to do. Good to see you back, Angel." Brick gave her a hug, which surprised the shit out of Angel since in her mind she was a prisoner here. "See you later, babe," Brick kissed Sandy, slapped her ass, and left.

Angel turned away to give them some privacy. Now that they knew she was Numbers ole lady, perhaps she could deceive some of the prospects or hang arounds to help her escape. It would be tricky because to become a full patched member of their MC, hang arounds and prospects would do anything. But, if they figured out she lied to them, they'd betray her in a heartbeat.

"Let's get that coffee going." Sandy tapped her shoulder. "You look like you could use a cup."

"I could use an entire carafe." Angel rolled her eyes and followed Sandy.

Chapter 14

Her Fate was Sealed

Numbers

"How are you doing, boss?" Numbers asked Reaper as soon as he entered their meeting room at the jail. They kept Numbers name in the roster as one of Reaper's lawyers so they could meet face-to-face instead of over the phone where conversations were recorded. They would soon catch on, but for now, they took advantage of what they could get.

"How the fuck do you think I'm doing?" Reaper sat, braced his elbows on the table, and leaned into Numbers' face. "You all fucked up a hit and now half of my brothers are sitting here with me. Don't get me wrong, it's nice to have family around to fight off the assholes in Los Lobos, but I'd rather be out there." Reaper pointed behind him.

"I get it. I want you guys out too." Numbers crossed his arms and placed them on the table. "Our lawyers are working on it."

"What's going on with Angel? Why was she at the wedding when the hit went down? And why the fuck did you take my grandson on that hit?" Reaper snarled at Numbers.

"Angel is out of control. She went there to warn everyone about our hit. I'm not sure how she found out, but I will get to the bottom of it. I know she wants nothing to do with us and is trying to keep Steele away from us, but I'm working on it."

"I told you," –Reaper pointed his finger in Numbers face– "to force her to marry you."

Numbers nodded. He remembered that conversation. "That's what I'm working on. I already took her and Steele to the clubhouse. She's in my room and I put Steele in Tools' old room." Numbers wasn't about to marry anyone, but he did want to fuck her and play with her.

"Is she behaving?" Reaper smirked. "You know she has a mouth on her. Probably why she's such a damn good attorney."

"She's fighting me every step of the way. But she'll learn her place soon."

"Just beat that uppity shit out of her. That's what I did when she was a child, and she always came around." Reaper ran his hands over his head.

"Been doing that. She's better today."

"Watch her. She can be conniving." Reaper sat back.

"It's under control." Numbers mumbled.

"What about Tori and Maggie?"

"As far as I know, Tori is on her honeymoon and Maggie has been holed up at the resort." Numbers braced his elbows on the table, fisted his hands and leaned his chin on them.

"I want them both dead," Reaper's nostrils flared like an angry bull. "Do you hear me?"

"Loud and clear. I'll work on that, too."

Reaper stood. "As far as my daughter, kill her if you can't control her. Steele is the future of the LRs. She doesn't matter."

Numbers' smile spread. He couldn't believe his luck. He knew Reaper wasn't too close to Angel, but to give him full reign on how to treat his daughter, was unexpected. She better start behaving or she was going to see his dark side.

Chapter 15

Waiting Sucked

Barrett

Barrett woke up with stiff muscles. He was used to exercising every morning, but because of his injuries, he'd stopped. What the hell, maybe he could lift some light weights without damaging his stitches. Getting out of bed, he tried to stand on both feet and immediately lifted his bad ankle. No running for him. Well, that sucked. Barrett limped into the bathroom and decided on a bath instead of a shower. He was the only one with a nice jacuzzi tub in his bathroom. Something everybody teased him for having. Barrett didn't give two shits about what they thought. When his sore muscles hurt, his tub filled with Epsom salt made him feel better.

He waited until the water was deep enough, then settled back, resting his head and letting the warm, salty water work its magic. He needed to be in fighting form for when they found Angel. His imagination ran wild with crazy scenarios of what could happen to her. After what the LRs did to Maggie and her brother's girlfriend, Lola, he wouldn't put anything past them. They were evil men who preyed on women.

When the water cooled, he got out of his tub, got dressed, and grabbed his phone to call George for an update.

"Hey, how's my gimpy friend doing?" George answered on the first ring.

"Ha, ha." Barrett used one crutch to relieve some of the weight on his foot as he walked into his kitchen to make some coffee. That always helped him wake up. "Have you found Angel yet?"

"No good morning. How are you?"

"Good morning. How are you? Have you found Angel yet?" Barrett poured ground coffee into a filter. Today was a full pot day instead of just a cup.

"Well, since you asked so nicely." Barrett could hear the sarcasm in George's voice. "We still haven't found her, but we think she's with her son at the LRs clubhouse. We haven't seen her go in or out, but we have seen her son. An MC brother takes him to school every morning and picks him up to take him back to the clubhouse."

"Fuck!" Barrett slammed his hand on the counter. "We have to go in there and get her out."

"We can't do that. Unless we have a search warrant, we can't enter their property."

"Well, I'm not a cop. I can get in."

"Are you fucking stupid? Did that gunshot rattle your brain? If you go in there, you're a dead man. The LRs won't even give you a chance to open your mouth before they put a bullet in your head. Or they could use you as leverage to get to Tori and Maggie. Don't you fucking dare go over there? We have a plan in place. It just might take a few days."

"She doesn't fucking have a few days!" Barrett ran his hand over his hair, pulling it with frustration.

"She's a lawyer and she's smart. She'll play it safe to keep her son safe."

"How do you fucking know that? You don't even know her." Barrett watched the coffee pouring into the pot.

"I'm a cop. I've seen what people are capable of when they are put in shitty situations. A mom will always protect her child."

"Yeah, but who's gonna protect her?" Barrett sighed.

"It's just a couple more days, then we'll have enough intel to get her and her son out. Just bear with us."

"Okay, but can you please keep me updated? I'm going out of my mind wondering how she is." Barrett leaned against his counter, waiting for the pot to fill with coffee. The aroma of his favorite blend helped to wake him up.

"I'll tell you as much as I can."

"Can I go with you when you guys bust them? I can help her." Barrett shut his eyes and held his breath, waiting for George to say no.

"We'll see."

Barrett let out his breath. At least George didn't say no. There was hope he could be there. "Okay, thanks."

"Listen, I gotta get up and go to work. I'll call you if I hear anything."

"Thanks, George." Barrett hung up and poured a cup of coffee as soon as the last drop landed in the pot.

He missed not having Frey, Holt and Alex to talk to. He could call, but didn't want to interrupt their couples' honeymoon. They'd be back soon enough. He hoped they were all relaxing and enjoying Hawaii. Hell, he wished he was with Angel in Hawaii. How had she come to mean so much to him in just a few hours? Was it his protective side that wanted to keep her safe, or was he attracted to her? Only time would tell, but for now, he wouldn't know anything until he found her.

Barrett grabbed the bag of frozen peas from the freezer and his cup of coffee and limped into his living room while trying not to spill his coffee. He sat on the couch, rested his foot on the coffee table, and dropped the bag of peas on his ankle. It looked better today, less swollen. He watched movies to pass the time. Eventually, the peas thawed out, and he got up for an icepack, refreezing the peas. He would never eat those peas, so refreezing them was perfectly fine. He then sat his ass back down, hoping that if he relaxed and babied his ankle during the day, he could work his full shift tonight.

Chapter 16

Finding a Friend

Angel

Angel stayed with Sandy during the day, helping her with anything she needed. She hoped befriending Sandy or anyone else there could help her in the long run. She knew some of the older brothers from Tools' time, but the shooting killed his closest friends, besides Brick.

The brothers accepted her because of Numbers and Reaper but remained distant because of her previous hate filled outbursts toward the club when she would get Steele after spending time with Reaper. Her refusal to help Reaper get out of jail was just the icing on the cake. Angel knew it was an uphill battle, but she had to try. It was the only way to get out of there. She had to earn their trust quickly.

With that in mind, she catered to them all day long. If they wanted a beer, she got it for them. If they wanted food, she either ordered it or made it. If they were bored, she sent the club sweet butts to please them. Hell, she even helped the prospects clean the clubhouse.

It had been a good day with Numbers gone and the brothers accepting her. But the day turned dark as soon as Numbers came in with Steele. The mood shifted and any brother who was sitting near her got up and walked away, leaving her alone at the bar. She could feel the change in the air. It was like a storm cloud entered the room, sucking out all the sunshine and happiness from within.

Angel spun around in her chair and ran over to Steele. "How was your day?" Angel hugged him, but he never lifted his arms to hug her back, so she stepped back. He always hugged her back. His attitude change was breaking her heart a little piece at a time.

"Go with your mother, Steele." Numbers slapped his back. "I have a club meeting to attend to."

"Can't I go with you?" Steele took off his backpack and shoved it at Angel.

Angel grabbed it before it fell to the floor.

"Not for this meeting. Go do your homework." Numbers turned and faced his brothers. "Call a meeting now! I'll be in the meeting room."

"But I want to come with you?" Steele screamed when Numbers turned to walk away.

Numbers froze and pivoted to face Steele. Angel saw Numbers face fill with rage, his eyes squinting as he glared at Steele. It's the way he always looked right before he hit her. *Oh Shit!* Angel dropped the backpack and tried to step in front of Steele to take the hit but wasn't quick enough. Numbers swung back and backhanded Steele in the face.

"Don't' you ever talk back to me." Numbers pushed Angel away and got in Steele's face. Leaning down, he snarled at him. "If you ever do that again, I will teach you a lesson you won't soon forget." Then he pointed his finger in Steele's face. "Got that."

Steele's body was trembling. "Yes, sir." Steele nodded.

"Now, go do as you're told." Numbers pushed him away and stormed out of the room.

Angel watched in horror as her son took several deep breaths and closed his eyes. Looking around, all the brothers scurried around doing Numbers bidding. *What could be so important that Numbers was calling an emergency meeting?* When she looked back to where Steele had been standing, he and his backpack were gone. Angel whirled around, searching for her son. She found him climbing the stairs to his room and hurried to catch up.

"Steele, wait." Angel reached him and put her foot in the doorway, stopping him from slamming the door in her face.

"I have nothing to say. I don't need help with my homework."

"Okay. But can I sit with you for a while?" Angel rested her hands on the door, pushing it open. "Are you okay?" His cheek was already turning pink from the hit.

"Fine." Steele released the door and let her in.

Angel sat on the edge of the bed, hoping she sat in a clean spot. She wasn't sure what was on those sheets from the previous night, and she'd spent so much time buttering up the brothers downstairs today, she didn't have time to wash his sheets like she'd wanted to.

Steele walked to his desk, sat down, took out his homework from his backpack, and got to work. He was ignoring her, but Angel wasn't giving up.

"How was your day?"

"It was fine."

He was shutting her out. Maybe food or water would help. "Can I get you a snack, water, or an icepack for your cheek?"

"I said I was fine. Can you please leave me alone?" Steele snapped at her.

"I can help you with your math. If you want?" Angel had always been the go-to parent for math.

Steele stood so abruptly, his chair tipped back as he spun around to face her. "I said I'm fine. Can you go, please? Stay away from me."

Angel stood and tried one more time. She approached him and placed her hand on his cheek. "I know it's crazy here, but I have a plan. Please don't shut me out. You're all I have left." She thought she had gotten through to him, but he slapped her wrist, pushing her hand away from his face.

"Just go," Steele snarled and pointed to his door.

Angel held her wrist. Shocked, her son had done that. Right then and there, she made a vow to never spend another night there. She planned to escape with her son the following day. Having already lost her husband to the club, now more than ever, she was determined to save her son.

Slowly, she walked backward to the door, staring at her son. "I'll come back later and check on you." Her voice trembled.

"Don't." Steele followed her and shoved her out the door. This time, he slammed the door in her face.

Angel jumped and walked back to Numbers' room. She didn't want anyone to see her so distraught. She didn't know how long Numbers would be at his meeting, but she hoped he'd be gone all night. With nothing else to do, she put on pajamas, got into bed, and planned her escape.

Chapter 17

Kill Orders Given

Numbers

"Now that everyone's here, I have news from Reaper." Numbers slammed the gavel down to start the meeting.

"How is Reaper?" Brick asked.

"He's pissed as shit that our hit didn't kill Tori and Maggie. Not to mention he's still in fucking jail." Numbers pounded on the table. "How do you think he's doing?"

"Sorry, boss." Brick looked down.

"It's fine Brick, I'm just pissed."

"So, what does Reaper want to do?" Butch asked.

"He wants us to come up with another plan to kill Maggie and Tori. We can't fail this time. Do you all hear me?" Numbers looked around the room. "We need to be all in, kill or be killed. Tori can't survive because his hearing is coming up."

"Can we use Angel again to get info?" Brick looked around.

"No, she won't help us. I'm pretty sure she was the one who warned them we were coming." Numbers scowled.

"So, what are we going to do with her?" Butch questioned.

"I'm working on it. But I got Reaper's approval to kill her if she doesn't fall in line." Numbers looked at everyone around the table. Some knew Angel since she was a little girl, like him. But business was business, and no one could come between what they had to do to get their president out of jail. "Everyone on board with that."

All the brothers nodded, although some hesitated. "She's my ole lady now. What I say goes. Do not forget that? "Numbers glared at all of them. "Whatever order I give, you will follow. Understood?"

"Yes, brother." They all responded. Some were louder than others. Numbers made note of the ones that hesitated. He would have to watch them and make sure they didn't befriend Angel. He wouldn't put it past her to go to them for help.

Chapter 18

Another Agonizing Night

Angel

A ngel had her plan in place in her mind. She would clean the bathroom and make a show of cleaning Numbers and Steele's rooms. Taking a trash bag, she would fill it with a mix of her and Steele's clothing. She had to be careful not to arouse Numbers' suspicions.

Her biggest challenge would be keeping the brothers occupied long enough to sneak out. While she considered alcohol and drugs, she realized that neither would be quick enough to get into their systems in time for her to get Steele from school and run. She needed something that was fast-acting to give her most of the day before they realized she was gone, and Steele wasn't in school.

Girls, that's what she needed. The brothers loved to fuck. With everyone busy, she'd sneak out the kitchen back door, using the trash bags as her excuse. She would run to the closest convenient store, which was less than a mile away, and call a car service to drive her to Steele's school.

Calling the school on her way there would speed up the checkout process. She needed Steele to be ready and waiting for her in the front office when she got there. She would ask the driver to wait for her and then drive them to her house. Despite the danger of going home, she needed to get her car, money, and Tools' gun for their escape.

Angel and Tools had a vacation fund where they put away extra money so they could visit different places throughout the US and teach Steele about American History. Some places were famous battlefields and others were places to hike or camp.

When Tools died, she pulled out all that money and stashed it in her closet. Seeing the growing bank statement account was a constant reminder of the life they would never have. Instead, she kept enough in her account to pay her bills, but tossed the extra cash in her safe every week. Only when Reaper was imprisoned did she understand how free she truly was—until now.

She had thousands of dollars in her closet so she could drive far away and trade in her car for a cheaper model. Now, she had cash and didn't need to make yet another stop at the bank before leaving town. She didn't think Numbers would chase her forever, but she wasn't taking any chances. Tools' gun would be her protection in case Numbers found them and threatened their lives.

Once she went over her plan in her head several times, she relaxed and fell asleep.

***

Angel jolted awake when someone pulled her pants off. Blinking, she saw it was Numbers.

"I've told you to sleep naked." Numbers continued to pull off her clothes.

"Uh, sorry," Angel murmured, trying to stay calm. If she could get through tonight, she would never have to see this monster again.

"For your punishment, get on your fucking knees and suck me off." Numbers pulled her out of bed and pushed her to the floor.

She could do this. She just had to pretend to enjoy it. He never lasted long. The faster she went, the quicker he would climax. Thinking of it as a horrible job, she cleared her mind and swore to herself that this would be the last time she did this. Numbers was already naked and pulling her face toward his cock. She didn't open her mouth quick enough and received a slap to the face.

"Open your fucking mouth and give me the best head of my life, now!" Numbers grabbed the back of her hair and shoved her face in his crotch.

Angel opened her mouth and attempted to give him the best performance of her life, because her life truly depended on it. He roughly fucked her mouth. Tears streamed down her face as pain shot up her jaw. She wanted to bite his cock off, but how could she leave with her son if he called out for his brothers while his cock bled? The pain of him shoving his cock down her throat was becoming unbearable. She couldn't breathe and was gagging.

Numbers pulled her off and bent down to snarl in her face. "If you fucking throw up on me, bitch. I will make you eat your throw up and do this again until you can take my full cock all the way down your throat. Do you understand?"

"Y..Yes." Angel swallowed and nodded. She had to do this. Taking several calming breaths, she opened her mouth and Numbers rammed into her again. Placing her hands on his thighs, her nails digging into his skin, she tried to hold on. Luckily, that bit of pain turned him on, and he gushed his come into her mouth. Some coming out the sides.

"Swallow, bitch!"

Angel looked down, wiped her mouth, and swallowed his disgusting come, glad it was over. But it wasn't.

"Get on the fucking bed, doggie style."

Angel got on her hands and knees. *How could he fuck her after that?* Didn't he need a few minutes? She soon realized he had no intention of fucking her, as she felt a sudden sting on her ass. He was going to spank her into full submission. *Asshole!*

He continued to strike her until her ass was throbbing from the pain. Angel kept quiet, trying not to cry out. She could do this.

"You're enjoying this, huh?" Numbers rubbed her ass. "How about this?"

Angel felt the sting right after she heard the crack of a whip and couldn't stop from crying out.

"That's more like it. You were good today, so I'll only give you a couple lashes, but if you disobey me during your stay, I will rip your ass to shreds." Numbers gave her another lashing before he bent down and whispered in her ear. "Do you understand me?"

"Y...Yes." Angel's voice trembled. "I...I understand."

No sooner had the words left her lips, Numbers rammed into her causing her body to jerk forward. The asshole got off on her pain. When had he turned into such a monster? She remembered camping with Uncle Numbers when she was small. But now that she thought about it, her mom always avoided him and flinched every time he touched her. *Had he hurt her? Did Reaper know? Had Reaper passed her mom around the club?*

Numbers pulled her head back by her hair before screaming his orgasm. Angel was so glad to be on the pill, although he must have worn a condom because she couldn't feel his come dripping out. The last thing she needed was to be pregnant with this monster's child or worse, end up with some disease. It was bad enough she had to put her mouth on his cock. She loved children, but it would be hard to carry his seed.

Dropping down to the bed, Numbers pushed her over. "Get some rest. I might need you later."

Angel saw him rip off the condom and hurl it across the room—so gross. She was positive he would expect her to clean it up in the morning. Curling up in a fetal position on the edge of the bed as far away from him as possible, she held her fist in her mouth to stop her cries of pain. Her butt was throbbing, and she could feel something rolling down her left butt cheek to her side. Was she bleeding from the whip? She was too afraid to look. Tomorrow, she would leave this hellhole or she would die trying.

Chapter 19

Undercover Helpers

José aka El Loco

The past few days had been a rollercoaster ride. His club, Los Lobos de Muerte MC, had agreed to help the police. Los Lobos didn't want to be a one-percenter club anymore. They had dealt with too much loss. They wanted to make honest money and help their community instead of hurting it. The members who still wanted to sell drugs left the club a few weeks before the wedding shootout, when they were told the club was going legit–no more drugs or illegal gun running. What José and their president Machete didn't tell them was that they were also helping the police in arresting the LRs.

Some Los Lobos members went to the LRs and were now prospects, while others were happy to help their local law enforcement agency. Police arrested several people during the wedding shootout, and anyone with information about the shootout, Angel, or Steele, could receive a reduced sentence for cooperating.

Correcamino, the Los Lobos road captain, volunteered to go undercover and become a prospect for the LRs. He was insistent on wanting to help, so Machete gave the all clear. The LRs knew he was a Los Lobos deserter, so they kept a close eye on him. Machete and José would meet with Correcamino in different locations at night to keep his cover a secret. If the LRs found out Correcamino was working with the cops or Los Lobos, his fate would be worse than death.

Machete and José found out that Angel and her son Steele were being held at the clubhouse. Correcamino had seen the boy, but he hadn't been able to confirm the mother's presence until last night. José knew Deputy George would want an update since he'd called him half a dozen times over the last couple of days. A phone call was in order. After all, Deputy George and Mark had kept Maggie safe before, during, and after the shootout.

"José, what's happened?" Deputy George answered.

"My inside guy just told me that girl you've been looking for, Angel, and her son are staying at the clubhouse."

"Fuck! I was afraid of that." George sighed. "Can your guy keep them safe?"

"No, he's just a prospect and they're already wary of him because he was one of us. I think they just love to fuck with him, which is why they made him their prospect so soon." José sat down with a beer. "Shit, to be honest, I'm shocked they haven't shot him yet or tortured him for information."

"They must be gearing up for something else."

"Yeah, that's what I was thinking, too." José took a drink.

"We gotta stop them."

"I agree." José nodded. "My guy found out they have a huge shipment coming in on Saturday. We can get as many as we can then."

"Drugs?" George asked.

"No, humans."

"Fuck! They are worthless pieces of shit."

"That they are, my friend, that they are." José watched Lola curl up under the covers. She still wasn't accepting his comfort. He didn't want to fuck her, he just wanted to hold her. Yet another reason the LRs had to pay. His ole lady was still suffering from their torture.

"Okay, let's meet tonight and put a plan in place. I want those fuckers in jail."

"Agreed." José finished his beer. "I'll talk to Machete and call you back with the details."

Chapter 20

Gotta Get Steele

Angel

After a grueling night of pain and humiliation, Angel was ready to put her plan in action and get the hell out of there.

"You're not going into work today, right?" Numbers cautioned.

"No, I took a leave of absence because I wasn't sure what you wanted me to do." Angel had a bitter taste in her mouth after that lie. But it wasn't a total lie. She took a leave of absence, just not for him.

"Good, then you can work on your dad's case. I'll have his lawyer contact you later today."

"Fine." Angel got out of bed, her muscles stiff and in pain from everything Numbers had done to her. She could feel the dried blood cracking on her butt as she grabbed some clothes. "I'm gonna shower and clean the bathroom while I'm in there."

"That's good. It needs a good scrubbing." Numbers stopped Angel from leaving to kiss her. "You did good last night. I'll let you heal today and grab some new toys for tonight."

Oh, hell no! Angel let him kiss her so she could start implementing her plan. He didn't know it yet, but it would be the last time he did anything to her.

Angel hobbled slowly to the bathroom, giving him the impression that she was in pain from the whipping. Which she was, but if she played it up, he might stick with his plan to leave her alone during the day. It worked because she heard him chuckle behind her. *Asshole! Fucker! Son of a Bitch!*

In the bathroom, she checked her backside in the mirror. She'd been right. There were scabs of dried blood from where the whip had cut into her skin. Thank goodness the cuts weren't too deep or she wouldn't be able to walk, let alone leave today.

After her shower, she cleaned the bathroom as best she could. She knew that nobody had cleaned it in years, and that no amount of scrubbing would remove all the mildew from the grout, but it looked a little better. She grabbed a couple trash bags and proceeded to clean Numbers' and Steele's rooms, all the while tossing some of hers and Steele's clothes in the bags.

When the bags were half full, so she could carry them easily, Angel checked the time and knew she had to hurry. If Numbers wanted her to talk to Reaper's lawyer, she had to be gone, well before the lawyer called to talk to her. When she walked through the main room, Sandy was on the couch sitting on Brick's lap. Angel was relieved to see they were fully clothed and only kissing.

"Hey Sandy, Brick." Angel stopped in front of them. "I cleaned the bathroom upstairs along with Numbers' and Steele's rooms." Angel lifted the trash bags. "I'm gonna clean the kitchen next and take out the trash."

"Well, you've been a busy little bee this morning." Sandy smiled.

"I want to pull my weight around here if we're going to be living here."

"Sounds good. We could use a little sprucing up." Brick agreed. "Hey." Brick jolted when Sandy pinched his waist.

"Are you insinuating that the girls and I do nothing around here?" Sandy smacked Brick in the chest and tried to get off his lap, but Brick held her tight.

"No, babe. I know you do a lot around here. It's just nice for you to have more help, that's all." Brick nuzzled her neck; calming Sandy, before they went back to kissing.

Angel cleared her throat to get their attention. "It's awfully quiet." Angel looked around and only saw a couple brothers shooting pool besides Brick and Sandy. "Where are all the girls?"

Butch, who was shooting pool, turned to her and answered. "Taking a nap in there." He pointed to the bedroom downstairs by the kitchen.

"Gotcha." Angel nodded and went into the bedroom. It was time to get the girls up to take care of Butch and Smiley.

"Hey, ladies." Angel stepped in and closed the door. The girls were half naked, only wearing their undies lying on the bed. Great, there were two of them. One for Butch and one for Smiley. "Butch and Smiley were asking about you. Why don't you go out there and show them a good time? They would love to see you."

"You think?" the bleach blonde asked.

"Oh, I think." Angel winked at her.

"Come on, Lisa, let's show them what a good morning looks like."

Angel stepped out of the way as the girls left the room and made a beeline for Butch and Smiley. The men put down their pool cues and grabbed them, lifting them onto the table to ravish them.

"Well, that was easy," Angel mumbled before hightailing it out of there and continuing with her plan. With the two love birds busy on the couch and the other men fucking the sweet butts, she easily slipped out the back door. Looking both ways, she didn't see anyone around, so she made a mad dash run to the bushes. Crouching down, she looked back. Once she realized no one was following her, she ran to the closest gas station a couple of blocks away, and texted a car service. They were three minutes away, so Angel hid behind some hedges. It was the longest three minutes of her life.

As soon as she saw the car approaching, she ran out and got in.

"I need to get my son from school. Can you please wait for me when we get there?"

"Sure." The driver answered. "But you'll have to re-text the app and select me."

"Oh, okay." Angel didn't want her final destination to show up on anything. "I'm in kind of a hurry. Can I pay you cash?"

"It'll cost you an extra hundred bucks."

Angel knew that was way too much money, but if he waited at the school and then drove her home, she was willing to pay anything.

"That's fine. I appreciate you helping me out."

When they reached the school, he parked and held his hand out. Angel knew she shouldn't pay anyone before receiving their services.

"I'll pay you after you drop me off at home."

"Fine." The driver huffed.

Angel got out and walked up to the ladies sitting at the front office desk.

"Good morning. How can we help you?" one of them asked.

"Hi, I'm here to check out Steele Barnes. He has a doctor's appointment."

"We'll send a note to his class. Please take a seat. He'll be here shortly."

"Thank you." Angel watched the lady write a note and ask a student to deliver it. She had forgotten to call Steele's school when she got in the car. Her adrenaline was so far off the charts she wasn't thinking straight. This kink in her plan was taking longer that she hoped. "Can you call into the classroom? I totally forgot about this appointment and we're running late."

"I'm sorry, Mrs. Barnes, but we can't call into a classroom during instruction time. He'll be here shortly."

"Of course, thank you." Angel sat mad at herself for not calling ahead like she'd planned. She looked outside to make sure her driver was still there. He was staring at her when he pointed at his watch. Shit, he was going to charge her more money. It's a good thing she had it at home.

"Mom, what are you doing here?" Angel spun around when she heard Steele's voice.

"I...uh...forgot you had a doctor's appointment. We need to go, or we'll be late." Angel motioned for him to walk ahead of her, but turned back to thank the ladies.

"What doctor's appointment? I know nothing about any doctor's appointment. Why aren't we using one of the club's cars?" Steele looked confused.

"I had forgotten and there wasn't a car available. Get in. We need to get going."

Angel and Steele got in and the driver pulled away.

"Which doctor am I going to see?" Steele frowned.

"Uh, the dentist." Angel didn't want to get into it in front of the driver. The less he knew, the better. God forbid Numbers found out who her driver was. She didn't want someone's life on her hands.

"But I just went a couple months ago?"

"I know, but they called because they thought they saw something in the x-ray and want to double check." Angel was spewing anything that came to mind.

"Yeah, I hate the dentist too, kid." The driver interjected.

"If we're going to the dentist, why are we heading home?" Steele looked outside and then glanced at Angel. "What's going on?"

"I asked the driver to take us home so I could get my car. These rides get pricey." Angel squirmed and hurried out as soon as the car stopped.

"Hey," the driver yelled out his window.

Angel turned back and walked to the driver. She still had the money she'd hidden from Numbers before he dragged her to the clubhouse. "I'm sorry. Here's a hundred and fifty for all your help."

"Thanks, ma'am. Call me anytime." The driver pocketed the money and drove off.

Angel followed Steele into the house.

"I just have to get a couple of things, go get in the car."

Chapter 21

So Close to Freedom, But Not Quite

Angel

Angel ran upstairs and opened her safe in the closet. She shoved some money into her bra, the rest into the trash bag, and she slid her passport into her back pocket. Wanting to keep Tools' gun hidden from Steele, but needing it for protection, she tucked it into the back waistband of her jeans. The trash bag she took from the clubhouse contained enough clothing for a week. It would have to be enough, because she didn't have time to get more clothes. Pausing at her dresser, she stared at the photo of herself with Tools and Steele.

She remembered they were gonna to take a family photo that day. The boys were sitting waiting for her to set the timer on the camera and run to get in place. But when she sat between them, Tools and Steele tickled her right as the camera went off. It captured the perfect moment when they were all laughing and looking at each other.

Running her fingers down the photo, she stared at it, missing the happy times with Tools. She wanted to keep the photo to remember those good times, so she quickly pulled the photo out of the frame, folded it, and tucked into the other side of her bra.

Then she picked up the trash bag and ran out of her bedroom.

"In a hurry?" Numbers stood in front of the door, blocking her exit.

"Uh...Numbers what are you doing here?" Angel came to a halt. Gripping the trash bag in front of her.

"Steele, said you checked him out and are taking him to the dentist." Numbers approached her slowly. Angel took a step back for every step he took forward.

"Yes, I am."

"Why didn't you tell me he had an appointment?"

"Uh...because I forgot. How did you know I checked him out, and that I was here?" Angel's pulse was racing. He knew she was lying. He was going to make her pay.

"I had you followed. Imagine my surprise when one of my prospects told me where you were." Steele had her backed up to the couch. "I have a question for you?"

"O...okay."

"Why are you carrying the trash from the clubhouse? Our trashcans aren't good enough?" Numbers pushed her.

She toppled back onto the couch. When she dropped the trash bag, it burst open because she hadn't closed it. Her money spilled out onto the floor. She rolled over onto all fours on the other side of the couch and shoved the money back in.

"Is that a gun on your back?"

Before Angel could reach out and grab the gun, Numbers jumped over the couch, pulled her gun out of her pants, and kicked her in the stomach. Angel curled up in pain with her head tucked down, attempting to avoid any other hits.

"What else are you hiding from me?" Numbers searched her pockets and found her passport. "Where the fuck are you going?" Numbers pushed her onto her back and sat on her.

Angel fought him, but it was a losing battle. His hands were everywhere. She heard footsteps and turned toward the front door. Steele walked in and stared at them. Angel stilled, giving Numbers the advantage to continue searching her.

He ran his hands under her shirt and found her money in a bra cup. "That's a lot of cash to be going to the dentist?" He pulled it out and pocketed her money. "What else we got here?" He pulled out the photo of Tools and her during a happier time. "Yeah, you won't need this anymore." He tore it down the middle.

"No, stop." Angel tried to pull the two halves from his hands. She could still glue them back together. But Numbers laughed at her attempt and tore the rest into pieces, throwing them at her face like confetti before standing and laughing at her as she grabbed all the pieces.

"Mom? Numbers?" Steele said from the front hallway. "What's going on?"

"Your fucking mother lied to me. You don't have a doctor's appointment. She was trying to take you away." Numbers kicked her leg. "Get up. We're going back to the clubhouse to teach her a lesson."

"No, Numbers, I'm sorry, please just let us go," Angel pleaded.

"Shut your fuckin' mouth." Numbers backhanded her. "And get in the fuckin' car! Steele, grab the trash bag. It's got your clothes and apparently your college fund." Numbers snickered. "The club thanks you for your donation."

Angel's body jolted from his anger. *Fuck! How was she supposed to leave now when he had taken everything she came to get?* Glancing at Steele, she saw him walk over to the pieces of photo that Numbers had ripped apart. Numbers was so focused on her, he didn't notice Steele collecting all the pieces and putting them in his pocket before he grabbed the trash bag.

The ride to the clubhouse was eerily silent. Once they entered, Numbers called all the brothers into the main room and pushed Angel's chest so hard she fell backwards on the floor. Angel attempted to get up, but he kicked her hand, and she fell back.

"Stay down!" Numbers screamed at her. "That's where liars and filth belong. I trusted you to behave. I told you if you didn't, I would beat the shit out of you." Numbers was circling around Angel. "Well, guess what?"

Angel tried to scoot around, facing him. Her body was trembling in fear. She had never seen Numbers so angry. His face was full on red and she could see the veins popping across his forehead.

Numbers pointed at her, "I'm gonna teach you a lesson you won't soon forget, and my brothers and your son are going to help me."

Numbers turned, facing all his brothers. "Today, this bitch needs to learn her place. She's lied to me, to us, her son, and her father. She refuses to help get Reaper out of jail. Oh, and as a final nail in the coffin, she warned everyone about our hit at the wedding, which got more of our brothers arrested and killed. Today, she pays!"

"No, Numbers, please?" Angel raised her hand and pleaded. She knew Numbers spoke the truth, but deep down she hoped some brothers wouldn't take his side.

Numbers didn't wait long before he kicked, punched, and slapped her. Angel tried her best to cover her vital organs, but it was difficult with so many brothers joining in. She saw Brick approach her. He was a big boy. His kick or punch would hurt like a bitch.

"Brick, please?" Angel was crying and shaking with fear.

"I've been nice to you, and you lied to me and my ole lady this morning." Brick pointed at himself. "To our faces!"

"I'm so sorry," Angel whispered before he kicked her ribs so hard she swore she felt the crack. *Oh shit, that hurt.*

"Steele, your turn." Numbers turned to Steele and pushed him forward.

"What?" Steele shook his head. "But...she's...my mom."

Even though most of Angel's face was swollen, she saw Steele trembling. He didn't want to have any part in this.

"Do you want to be a member of this club?" Numbers grabbed his arm and pushed him toward Angel. Steele stumbled, but straightened before he landed on her.

Steele nodded.

"Then give her the beating she deserves for deceiving us. Your grandfather would want you to do this. She's a lying bitch, not your mom."

"Are you sure my grandfather would approve of this?" Steele looked between Angel and Numbers.

"Yes." Numbers nodded. "He said we could kill her if she worked against us."

"B...But she's my mom?" Steele wrung his hands while he rocked back and forth.

"Are you going against your acting president's orders?" Numbers growled.

Angel used all her strength to sit and face Steele. She could see the internal struggle Steele was facing. Hit his mom and please the club or don't hit his mom and pay the price.

Steele glanced down at his mom. Angel gave a slight nod. He had to hit her. His life depended on it. She would gladly give her life for him. *Soon Tools, she thought, I'll be with you soon.*

Steele swallowed and kicked her thigh. It was a light tap. Angel knew it wasn't enough.

Numbers reached down and pulled Angel up by her hair, then whispered in her ear. "I'm gonna make a man out of him and you're not gonna be here to watch it. We could've built something, but you had to go against me and my club." Angel closed her good eye. "Open your fucking eyes. I want you to see your son when he hits you. I want him to be the last thing you see before you die."

Numbers pushed her away. Angel stumbled, trying to hold on to any brother near her, but they all shoved her toward the center of their circle.

"Steele, now!" Numbers screamed like a madman.

With tears running down his face, Steele slapped Angel. Her head jolted to the side, but Numbers gripped her hair and turned her to face him. Angel was in so much pain her entire body was throbbing. The only thing holding her up was Numbers crushing grip on her hair. "Give him a kutte. Steele put it on." Numbers mumbled in her ear, "he's one of us now." Numbers looked around the room, making eye contact with his brothers. "From now on, he will be known as Junior. One day he will be our president, but for now, he is a president in the making." Numbers glared at her before he turned to face Steele.

"Finish it! Junior!" Numbers hollered in Steele's face.

Steele punched her and it was lights out. Angel felt her body crumpling to the floor and everything faded to black.

Steele punched her and it was lights out. Angel felt her body crumpling to the floor and everything faded to black.

Chapter 22

Mom!

Steele aka Junior

Steele couldn't believe what he had done. His mom lay unmoving on the floor. *Had he killed her?* He never wanted to hit her; she was his mom; he loved her. But when Numbers pressured him and she nodded, he followed orders. If he hadn't done it, he would be lying on the floor next to her. He couldn't believe she had nodded, giving him permission to hurt her. *What the hell?*

All the brothers patted his back, congratulating him on becoming one of them. They were celebrating while his mom lay dead on the floor. That was so fucked up. He smiled and nodded, but his heart was splintering inside. Losing his father had been hard, but being a part of his mother's death was soul shattering.

"Alright, alright," Numbers held up his hands. "We can celebrate later. For now, we need to get rid of this lying bitch." Numbers bent down to grab her legs. "Brick, grab her arms. Let's carry her to the car and put her in the trunk. Red, you and the prospects grab some shovels and follow us. Steele, you're coming with me."

Steele followed Numbers. He was numbly following orders as he got in the back seat. It all felt so surreal. Like an out-of-body experience or a horrible nightmare, he would wake up and find that she was okay. But it wasn't a dream—he'd killed his mother. How had it come to this? If she'd only behaved, she would still be alive.

That was a selfish thought. Steele was old enough to know that Numbers wasn't treating his mom right, he just chose to ignore it for his own self-preservation. He was a horrible son. He was supposed to be the man of the house; he should have protected her. His father would be so disappointed and disgusted with him right now if he were alive. Hell, he was probably rolling over in his grave. Speaking of graves, his mom wouldn't be able to be with her true love even in death. Steele had sealed her fate. *He was an asshole.* Brick drove them to a secluded area near the Everglades.

"Pull over there." Numbers pointed to a dirt road that led off the main road. "We don't have to bury her too deep. She can be gator meat."

Steele's stomach revolted, and he almost threw up. He had been a shitty son recently. His mom deserved better. Numbers had told Steele that he loved her. But how could Numbers do what he did to her if he loved her? Then again, he professed to love his mom and had dealt her the final blow. When they came to a stop, Steele got out and threw up.

"You'll get used to it, kid." Brick patted his back and handed him a waded-up t-shirt.

Steele didn't want to get used to it. He wished he'd listened to his mom and stayed away from his grandfather. If he had done that, she would still be alive. They would be home eating dinner, playing a board game, or even helping him with math. Anything was better than this. He couldn't believe he would wake up tomorrow and never see his mother again.

"Brick, pick her up and follow me." Numbers waved to the prospects and everyone followed him.

They walked a few feet when Numbers pointed to the ground. "Start digging, prospects. It doesn't have to be too deep. She's gonna be gator bait."

Steele covered his mouth, his body convulsing as if he was going to throw up again. After a few minutes, Numbers stopped the prospects.

"That's enough. Brick, drop her in."

Brick let her body drop into the shallow grave.

Steele saw her finger twitch. Maybe she wasn't dead. He had to find out, but he couldn't do it if everyone was standing around.

"Numbers, Can I have a minute with her?"

"Why?"

"She was my mom. I know she was a lying bitch, but I feel like I need to say my peace." Steele moved toward her. "You can go. I'll finish burying her and leave with the prospects."

"Go ahead, but we'll wait in the car until you're done." Numbers turned and walked away.

"You guys can go to the car." Steele pointed at the prospects. "You started it, and I'll finish it."

"Fine, but don't bury her too deep. Numbers said she's gator bait." They all smacked each other, laughing all the way to the car.

Steele waited until they left and knelt down. "Mom?"

Angel's one eye squinted open and her mouth whispered, "Steele".

"Mom, I'm so sorry. Please hang on. I'm gonna call the police and get them over here." Steele looked around and pulled his phone out of his back pocket.

"911, how can I help you?"

"This is Steele Barnes. The LRs beat and left my mom at this location. Please hurry, she's barely alive."

"Are they still there? Please stay on the line." The operator said.

"Do you have this location?"

"Yes, but we need more information."

Steele interrupted her. "I can't stay on the line. They're here and I need to leave with them. Please help my mom." Steele hung up and erased the call from his cell.

"Mom, someone's coming. Please stay awake."

"Steele, be careful," Angel murmured. "You did nothing wrong. I love you."

"I love you too, mom."

With tears in his eyes, he partially buried his mom, leaving her face out of the dirt so she could breathe. He hoped the police got here before the gators. He shivered at the thought. Steele wiped his face with the back of his hand and grabbed all the shovels. He'd taken long enough. He didn't want them to find him and see that his mom wasn't totally covered in dirt.

"It's done." Steele said as he walked by Numbers. "I'll put the shovels in the back of Red's car."

"No, put them in the back of this car and get in." Numbers motioned with his thumb. "We have some celebrating to do."

Steele nodded and put the shovels in the trunk. There would be no celebrating for him tonight. Only praying and hoping that his mom made it to the hospital alive. He hoped he saved her.

Chapter 23

Let's Go!

Barrett

Barrett was working his regular shift when he got a call from Deputy George.

"Get your ass downstairs. I'm outside."

"I am downstairs. I'm in the casino working. Give me a minute."

Barrett clicked his headset. "Hey, something's going on. Can one of you cover the floor? Deputy George needs me, and I don't know how long I'll be gone."

"Fucking Slacker," Travis grumbled. "I was comfy in the security office, but I'll cover your ass on the floor tonight."

"Gee thanks. Have a good night." Barrett clicked off his earpiece and headed to the lobby. Still on the phone with George, he said. "What's going on? Are those your lights on?"

"Yep, lights and sirens, hurry."

Barrett hung up and limped to George's patrol car. His ankle was healing, but he still couldn't put his full weight on it or stand for long periods of time. Opening the door, he got in. "What the hell's going on?"

"Dispatch just got a call from a boy named Steele Barnes asking us to help his mother, who was beaten and dumped near the Everglades. I have the location. I'm assuming it's Angel."

"Motherfucker!" Barrett slammed his hand on the dashboard. "Is he okay? Is she alive?"

"Not sure because I stopped here to come get you." George drove like a Nascar driver to the scene.

Barrett bolted out of the car, ignoring the pain shooting up his ankle as soon as the car stopped. Someone had already put up a police tape.

"Sir, you can't come in here." An officer put his hand up to stop Barrett.

"He's with me. Let him through." George went first. When they got to Angel, she was sitting up, taking sips of water with dirt pooled in her lap. The paramedics were checking her out.

"Angel." Barrett ran to her. "What the hell happened?"

"Barrett?" Angel looked up, but black and blue bruises swelled one eye shut.

"Yeah, it's me." Barrett and the paramedics helped her stand.

"Aahhh!" Angel screamed out in pain.

"Sir, help me get her on the gurney." The paramedic said to Barrett.

Barrett nodded and picked her up, laying her on the gurney. "Where are you taking her?"

"To Sunrise General." The paramedic answered while he wheeled her into the ambulance.

"Come on." George grabbed Barrett's arm. "I'll take you there."

"Angel!" Barrett screamed. "I'll meet you there."

Barrett was grateful to be riding along with George. Because of his lights and sirens, they reached the hospital immediately after the ambulance. Someone escorted Barrett and George to the waiting room while they wheeled Angel into the ER.

"Fuck." Barrett rubbed his hands over his face. "They really messed her up. Was it the LRs?"

"During his call to dispatch, Steele mentioned the LRs but didn't name anyone. I'm gonna let them know I need to speak to her as soon as possible."

Barrett nodded and took a seat. God, he could really use Holt and Frey right now. He was close to Alex, his older brother, but Holt and Frey were his rock. He needed to hear their voices. Make sure the happy couples were safe. With that in mind, he called them.

"Hey, man. How's it going?" Holt sounded happy.

"How are you guys?" Barrett was relieved to hear the joy in Holt's voice.

"We are all good. We're at the beach. I'll put you on speakerphone so everyone can say hi."

Barrett relaxed. "Hey, guys."

"Hi, baby brother," Frey shouted.

"Hey, Barrett," Tori interjected.

"Hey, Bro," Alex blurted.

"Bare, you have got to come here for your honeymoon," Frey spoke up.

"Uh, he's not even dating anyone, babe." Holt said.

"Stop giving Barrett a hard time." Barrett heard Tori defend him.

"What's going on back home?" Holt got back on the line. "Did they catch the LRs? What about the girl who tried to stop the wedding?"

"Yeah, some of the LRs and Los Lobos were arrested." To avoid ruining their celebration, Barrett kept Andrew's death and his shoulder wound a secret. "The girl, Angel, ran. I'm not sure where she's been, but we just found her beaten and dumped by the Everglades. I'm at the hospital now with George, waiting to get an update."

"Oh shit. Does Maggie know what happened to her? Did José get arrested?"

"José got arrested, but I don't know all the details. As far as Maggie, I'm not sure she cares what happens to Angel." Barrett stood and paced.

"Give Maggie time. I mean Angel came in to warn us, so she can't be that bad. Plus, it sounds like she received one hell of a punishment if the LRs beat her so badly." Holt sighed. "Wish I was there with you, but I am enjoying seeing your sister in her teeny tiny bikini."

Barrett smiled. "You are such a fucker, but thanks for trying to cheer me up."

"Yeah, I gotta go, but keep me posted." Holt screamed, "I'll be right there." Then spoke into the phone, "See ya in a week, bro."

"Yeah, see ya then." Barrett hung up and pocketed his phone just as George walked in with two cups of coffee.

"It's not the best." George handed him a cup. "But it's all I could find."

Barrett took a sip and smirked. "Not great, but it'll do. Thanks. Any news?"

"No, not yet."

Barrett and George sat down for what felt like hours. But when the nurse walked in and Barrett looked at his watch, it had only been thirty minutes.

"Deputy George." The nurse waved him over. "You can see her now."

"What about me?" Barrett walked to the nurse. "Can I see her?"

"I'll ask when I escort Deputy George. Wait here, please."

Barrett went back to his seat and drank his watered-down coffee. Closing his eyes, he leaned his head against the wall thinking about all the things he wanted to ask Angel.

"Sir," the nurse interrupted his thoughts. Barrett opened his eyes and stood. "Yes, ma'am."

"Barrett, is it?" the nurse asked.

"Yes, ma'am. I'm Barrett." Barrett looked up hoping she was coming to get him.

"Come with me. Angel would like to see you." The nurse turned and walked away. Barrett quickly threw out his coffee and followed.

"Hey," Barrett said as soon as he walked in. "What can I do to help you?" Walking to the side of the bed, he gently picked up Angel's bruised hand.

"I wanted to tell you," Angel cleared her throat. "I'm sorry for leaving you to bleed out when you were trying to help me. Deputy George," Angel glanced at him, "told me he reached you in time and that you're going to be okay."

"I'm better than you, unfortunately," Barrett smirked. "I wish you'd stayed with me. You could've avoided all this." Barrett motioned his hand down her body.

"I had to go after my son." Angel's lips partially smiled. "I almost got us out, but Numbers found me."

"Angel, I need to know everyone that did this to you so we can arrest them." George took out his pad.

"It was mostly Numbers. I know other brothers kicked me, but I was curled up, covering my face and body throughout most of the attack. Brick only hit me once, and then he drove the car with me in the trunk. Red and another prospect that I don't know dug the hole," Angel shivered. "And...and..."

"And what Angel?" Barrett sat on the side of the bed, running his thumb over the back of her hand. He didn't know why he was so drawn to her when she had left him. But she looked so helpless laying in the bed. There wasn't a place on her body that wasn't bruised.

"Numbers made Steele hit me." Tears rolled down Angel's cheeks.

Barrett stiffened.

Angel squeezed Barrett's hand, her eyes pleading with him and George. "They made him. If he hadn't done it, they would've hurt him."

"He should've defended his mother." Barrett growled.

"He couldn't," Angel cried out. "There were too many of them. It was his quick thinking when they all thought I was dead that saved me. Please, don't hurt Steele. He tried to help me as best as he could."

"Okay," George rested his hand on Angel's leg. "Calm down. We're not gonna hurt him. But I gotta go so I can get a warrant for Numbers' arrest. Are you going to be okay? We can post an officer outside your door?"

"I'll stay with her until she gets released, then I'll take her home with me." Barrett stood up and shook George's hand. "Thanks, George."

Barrett watched George leave.

"Why are you doing this?" Angel frowned.

"Helping you?" Barrett sat back down and stroked her fingers.

Angel nodded. "You don't know me. Because of me, you got hurt."

"It wasn't your fault I got hurt. You tried to save all of us." Barrett rested his other hand on the bed next to her hip leaning over her. "Listen to me. I don't know why I feel drawn to you, but I do, and I want to help you. As soon as they release you, you will need a safe place. I can keep you safe at our resort. We've kept Maggie safe and away from the LRs there. I can do the same for you. Please."

"What do you want from me?" Angel quirked an eyebrow.

"Nothing."

"Men never want nothing. I'm not gonna sleep with you. Been there, done that and," Angel pointed to her body, "I have the scars and bruises to prove it."

"Did he rape you?"

Angel looked down and pulled her hand out of his. "That's none of your business."

"It's not, but I think you just gave me an answer, anyway." Barrett rubbed the back of his neck. "I promise not to do anything that makes you feel uncomfortable. You can have my bedroom. I'll sleep on the couch in the living room. Will that work for you?"

"Why?"

"Why, what?"

"Again, why are you being so nice to me?" Angel winced when she crossed her arms.

Barrett stood up and paced at the foot of the bed. "The truth is, I don't know. Maybe I want to be your hero and save the damsel in distress."

"I can take care of myself."

"Yeah," Barrett snorted, "I can see that."

"Get out," Angel whispered.

"Look." Barrett placed his hands on his hips and glanced down before looking at her. "I'm not trying to be mean or condescending. I just want to help you and your son. Can you please just accept that? Where else are you gonna go?"

Angel leaned her head back, staring at the ceiling. "I don't know where else to go and I have to get my son."

"So, let me help you?"

"Okay," Angel sighed and glared at him, "but I don't owe you any sexual favors."

"Absolutely not." Barrett nodded.

"And you're gonna sleep on the couch?"

"Yes." Barrett held up his hands in surrender.

"And when they find Steele, he can stay with me in the bedroom?"

"For as long as you both need." Barrett saw her body relax. "You drive a hard bargain."

"I'm an exceptional attorney." Angel grinned.

"I can see that." Barrett nodded. "So what will it be?"

"Okay, I'll go with you. Thank you."

She was a tough nut to crack, but he'd finally gotten her to agree to go with him. Now if they could get her son and arrest the LRs he'd finally be able to sleep at night. Since she'd left him, he hadn't gotten a good night's rest worrying about her and her son.

Chapter 24

Party Time!...NOT

Steele aka Junior

Steele walked into a full-blown party at the clubhouse. He wasn't in the mood for parties. His mother could be dead if the cops didn't get to her in time and, unfortunately, he had no way of knowing. He couldn't ask anyone here to help him or call the local hospital. They were all celebrating her death. It would suck if they found out she made it. He was sure they would send out a lynching mob to finish the job.

"Hey, Junior," Butch slapped his back. "You want a beer?"

He had to pretend to be happy, even though deep down he was dying inside. "Uh, sure. Thanks."

"Well, that's one way to become a brother in the club without the one year waiting period." Red put his arm around him. "I wish I'd thought to beat my mom to death."

Steele flinched, but held his tongue. Now wasn't the time to correct Red. Taking the beer that was offered to him, he walked to the end of the bar where no one was sitting.

"Hey, baby." Cherry came out of nowhere and rubbed her breasts on his arm. "How about we go upstairs for some fun?"

Steele wasn't in the mood, but if he went upstairs with Cherry, he would only have to put on his game face for one person instead of the entire club. She was the lesser of two evils.

"Yeah, let's go." Steele chugged the beer and pulled Cherry with him, ignoring all the cheers and nasty chants as he went up the stairs. He would let Cherry pleasure him and give her what she wanted. He just wanted the night to be over and to be left alone.

*** Numbers ***

"The kid seems fine." Brick stood next to Numbers as they both drank beers and watched Steele take Cherry upstairs to his room.

"Yeah, he does." Numbers clinked his beer bottle. "But let's watch him carefully. Reaper wants him protected. He needs to know his mom was a weakness he didn't need. We gotta convince him, she didn't really love him."

"Sounds good." Brick nodded. "Now that she's gone, what are we gonna do about Tori and Maggie?"

"Tori is on a honeymoon, so we'll wait until they get back and attack the cultural center. They both work there, so it will be a two for one."

Brick laughed, "I like that...two for one special."

"Let's keep Steele busy with Cherry." Numbers finished his beer and snapped his fingers for someone to get him another. "I don't want him feeling sympathy for the bitch."

"What about school?"

"We'll let them know his mom passed, and he needs a few days off to mourn." Numbers drank his new beer. "I'll call them tomorrow and let them know I'm his guardian."

"What if they find out that you're not?"

"I'll figure it out. Worse comes to worse, I'll tell them he's being homeschooled and withdraw him." Numbers ran his hand over his neck. *Fuck! Why did that bitch run away?* He had a plan to keep her as his ole lady until he was the most important adult in Steele's life. Then he'd get rid of her.

"I think that might be best." Brick finished his and waved Sandy over. "When are you gonna tell Reaper?"

"Tomorrow. Let's focus on our shipment on Saturday. I want Junior there. He needs to learn the ropes."

"Hey, baby," Sandy ran her hands over Brick's chest. "You want another beer?"

"Nah," Brick chugged his beer and threw the empty bottle at a prospect sitting on the couch. "I wanna take this party upstairs." Brick threw Sandy over his shoulder and headed to his room.

Numbers laughed and looked around for a sweet butt to fuck.

Chapter 25

Her Hero

Angel

The doctors made her stay overnight because of her concussion, but by morning, she was ready to leave, even if it was with Barrett. She was afraid to stay in the hospital where Numbers could still find out she was alive. Opening her eyes as much as she could, she saw Barrett slouched in the chair next to her bed.

He was still wearing the same clothes from yesterday. Angel couldn't understand why he was helping her after she left him. The only man that had ever helped her was Tools. He looked after her, making every day special. He had been an excellent father and husband. If only they'd had more time together. Barrett reminded her of Tools. He was also a tall, dark-haired, muscular man with broad shoulders that tapered to a narrow waist. Angel heard Barrett clear his throat, darting her eyes up to his.

"How are you this morning?" Barrett grinned.

Angel knew she'd been caught staring at his body. "Why are you helping me?"

"I thought we already went over that." Barrett leaned back, stretching out his legs. Crossing his ankles, he watched her curiously.

"We did, but other than my husband, no one has ever done anything for me."

Barrett sat up. "You're married?"

"I was. He was shot by El Loco."

"Oh, shit." Barrett's eyes widened.

"Yeah, oh shit. Maggie's brother killed my husband." Angel crossed her arms.

"Fuck me!" Barrett shot up and rubbed his hands over his face while he paced the room. "So, are you playing me? Do you want to get access to Maggie to hurt her?" Barrett faced Angel with his hands on his hips.

"No." Angel shook her head. "I know El Loco killed Tools because my father killed their parents."

"Wait." Barrett held up his hand. "What the fuck are you talking about?"

"You didn't know? Ugh," Angel slammed her hands on the bed. "I am so tired of all this MC revenge shit. I just wanted to get away with my son and start over somewhere else, away from everything and everyone here!" Angel bellowed. "When will this all end? The lies. The deceit. The revenge."

"Hey, Angel," Barrett approached the bed and held her hand. "It's gonna be okay. I'll talk to Maggie and make everything right."

"Why does Maggie need to be calmed down? I'm not going to her house, am I? Do you live with Maggie?" Angel removed her hand.

"Not exactly."

"What do you mean, not exactly?"

"Uh, I live at the resort in an apartment on our family floor. Maggie, uh,..." Barrett winced, "lives with Mark on the same floor."

"I can't go home with you. Maggie hates me." Angel was not going to be anywhere near Maggie. Maggie would never understand that she couldn't fully stop the LRs from hurting her when they kidnapped her. She never wanted Maggie to suffer for what El Loco did. Angel was fully aware of how dangerous it was marrying an LR, but she had fallen hopelessly in love with Tools from the first day she saw him. He was an innocent bystander, just like her parents. She could be in the same room with Maggie. Her brother was another story. Him, she never wanted to see.

"Maggie doesn't understand your side." Barrett reached for her hand again. "I'll talk to her. It'll be okay. I promise."

"Good morning." the nurse walked in with papers in her hand. "You'll be happy to know the doctors have released you. Do you have somewhere to go? You're pretty banged up, and I would prefer you not be alone for a few days."

"I'm gonna take care of her." Barrett released her hand and stood. "When can I pull my car around?"

"Go get it now. I'll have her ready. Do you know where to go?"

"Yup." Barrett nodded. "Unfortunately, this isn't my first rodeo." Barrett turned to Angel. "I'll be back."

"That is one hunky man." The nurse sighed after Barrett left.

"Yeah, I guess so." The nurse helped Angel scoot to the side of the bed.

"You guess so. Girl, something must have affected your eyesight more than I thought if you don't find him sexy as hell." The nurse held her arm and led her into the bathroom.

Angel walked in and shut the door so she could relieve herself. A few minutes later, she heard a soft knock on the door.

"Angel, I have some clothes for you." The nurse announced.

Angel opened the door to let the nurse in.

"I'm sorry. I only have scrubs for you to wear." The nurse placed them in her arms. "I'll wait out here in case you need help getting dressed."

"Scrubs are fine. Thank you."

Angel felt like a walking pincushion, but the desire of wanting to leave the hospital outweighed the pain. Dressing as quickly as possible, she left the bathroom.

"I'm ready."

"Okay dear," the nurse smiled at her. "Have a seat in this magnificent chair and I'll wheel you down to Mr. Hot and Sexy."

Angel smiled and sat.

The nurse placed a plastic bag with her shoes inside on her lap. "We could only save your shoes. Because of your bruising, it was easier to cut your clothes off. I'm sorry."

Angel hugged the bag. "It's okay. I'm surprised I had any clothes on."

"Oh, dear." The nurse placed her hand on her knee and squatted down to eye level. She reached into her pocket and handed her a business card. "This is an excellent psychiatrist. She can help you if you want to talk. Please, take care of yourself."

Angel took the card and nodded. "Thank you."

"Of course." The nurse stood. "Now, let's not keep your hunky man waiting."

Angel put the card in the bag with her sneakers. She didn't want to lose it. She wasn't ready to talk to a professional, but she might make that call within a few weeks, depending on how she felt. Right now, she wanted to find Steele and get him out of that damn clubhouse.

Barrett was waiting for her by his truck with the door open. He picked her up out of the wheelchair and placed her in the passenger seat.

"Take care, dear," the nurse waved.

"Thank you," Angel lifted her hand in a wave. "For everything."

"Thank you," Barrett added.

"My pleasure." The nurse grabbed Barrett's arm after he closed the door and said something to him Angel couldn't hear. He nodded and walked around the front of the truck.

"What did she say to you?" Angel asked as soon as he got in the car and buckled in.

Barrett placed his left arm over the steering wheel and gazed at her. "She said you remind her of her daughter." Barrett grinned. "She told me to take care of you or I would have to answer to her. She likes you."

Angel smiled. "I like her too. She was very kind."

Barrett faced the road and put the car in gear. "Yes, she was. By the way, just so you know," Barrett winked at her, "I will take care of you. I promised her and I don't break my promises."

Angel blushed and turned to look out the window. "How can we get my son?"

"Deputy George is working on it."

"What are they going to do?"

"I'm not sure." Barrett shrugged. "I'm not a cop. They don't give me all the details."

"Can you contact him?" Angel placed her hand on his thigh. Barrett looked down. "Sorry." She withdrew her hand quickly. "I'd like to be there when they find him, please."

"Sure." Barrett nodded and drove them home. Angel was quiet on the drive to the resort. When they turned into the employee resort parking lot, he glanced at her and said, "I'll call Deputy George when we get upstairs to get an update. Come on, let's go."

Barrett unbuckled and went around to help Angel. Angel winced, trying to get down.

"Stay there, I got you." Barrett picked her up and shut the door with his shoulder.

"I can walk. Please put me down."

"Okay." Barrett set her down on her feet and wrapped his arm around her waist. "You can walk, but I'm not letting you go in case you fall."

"I'll be fine as long as I can walk slowly." Angel grasped his hand on her waist for support.

"We'll walk as slow as you like." Barrett walked in the side door and saw the look on his mom's face when she saw him. "Heads up...my mom is heading our way. She's gonna ask..."

"*Chakpootsi*, what happened to this poor girl?" Sehoy rushed over, placing her hand gently on Angel's cheek.

"A lot of questions," Barrett finished.

"Wait, are you the girl that interrupted my son and daughter's weddings?" Sehoy took a step back.

"Yes, ma'am. I'm Angel." Angel nodded. "I'm sorry I didn't get to Maggie in time to tell her about the LRs plan. It pained me to ruin the weddings."

"*Chatski*, she was trying to help us." Barrett pleaded. "We need to help her now. The LRs did this to her, and I need to keep her safe."

"This is dangerous *chakpootsi*," Sehoy glared at him. "Do you know what you're doing? We've already had to fix the wedding venue. What if they shoot up our lobby or hurt any of our guests?"

"I understand, but they think she's dead, and the longer I stand in this lobby with her, the more danger she's in." Barrett moved past his mom.

"Fine," Sehoy said behind them. "We'll talk later."

"I don't think your mom likes me." Angel murmured while Barrett rushed her out of the lobby and into the elevator.

"She will when she gets all the details. My mom is the kindest person I know. Well, besides Tori, who married my stick-up-the-ass older brother...now she's a saint." Barrett smirked at her.

Angel smiled. She appreciated Barrett trying to cheer her up. Barrett escorted her to his apartment door, but just as he placed his hand behind her to guide her in, Angel heard a furious woman's voice say, "Oh, hell no!"

Chapter 26

A Woman Scorned

Barrett

Oh Shit! Barrett spun around in time to catch Maggie before she attacked Angel. "Maggie, no...stop." Fuck, where the hell was Mark? "Angel is not the bad guy here."

"She fucking let them beat me, cut me, and ruined my friend's weddings. I'd say she's a horrible person."

"Oh shit, killer, stand down." Mark rushed over, grabbed Maggie from behind, and pulled her away from Angel.

"Surfer Smurf, let me go." Maggie was struggling in his arms.

"Maggie, listen to me." Barrett stood in front of Angel, blocking Maggie from getting to her, but Angel stepped around him.

"I tried to stop them!" Angel screamed before Barrett pulled her behind him again and held her hips, pushing her against his back.

"Ladies, stop." Barrett hollered. "Maggie, look at her."

"I can't, because the bitch is hiding behind you." Maggie grabbed Mark's arms trying to pull them off her.

"Fuck this shit," Angel shoved Barrett's back and peeked around him. "And you miss holier than thou, what about the fact that your fucking brother killed my husband?"

Maggie pointed at her. "Well, your fucking club killed my parents!" Maggie shook with rage.

"It's not my fucking club!" Angel screamed. "I hate that club," Angel pounded on Barrett's back. "I don't want any part of it. I just want my son back. Let me go. I'll take my chances on the street."

"Woman, stop hitting me." Barrett growled before he spun around and grabbed her upper arms. "No, you will not take your chances out there on your own. They think you're dead and we're going to keep it that way." Barrett pulled

Angel in front of him as they both faced Maggie. "Look at her. They beat her to within an inch of her life just like they beat you and they still have her son. Don't you think she's suffered enough? Is still suffering? Can we please settle this fight so we can all work together?" Barrett lowered his arms and glared at Maggie.

Barrett watched Maggie take a deep breath and drop her arms. Mark moved his hands to her shoulders. Maggie stared at Angel. "They have your son, Steele? The one I met at the cultural center?"

Angel nodded.

"Okay, now that we're all calm, let's go in Barrett's room and talk like adults instead of screaming insults at each other like spoiled kids." Mark gestured toward Barrett's room.

Barrett turned and opened the door, letting them all in. They gathered on the couches.

"I'm sorry." Angel looked at Maggie teary eyed. "I tried to stop them the day they had you, but they shoved me out of there and drove me home. Steele was there, and I didn't want him to see them hit me. Not that it matters, he saw all of them hit me before they dumped me in the Everglades."

"How did anyone find you?" Maggie sat on the edge of the couch and reached for Angel's hand.

Barrett took a sigh of relief. These two women had been through so much at the hands of the LRs. Maybe they could help each other heal.

"I guess after my son was forced to hit me, he had a change of heart and called the police." Angel closed her eyes, and a tear rolled down her face. "I can't remember the details, just that I saw him say he loved me and to hold on. Then I felt dirt drop on my body, but not my face. The next time I woke up, I saw the paramedic standing over me."

"Wait, your son hit and buried you?" Maggie gasped.

"Yeah," Angel nodded and looked up, her gaze bouncing between Maggie, Mark, and Barrett. "But he didn't want to. They forced him."

"Oh, shit." Mark grumbled.

"Motherfuckers!" Barrett bolted up and paced like a caged wolf on the prowl. "They will pay for this."

"I'm so sorry," Maggie hugged Angel. "I guess we are both victims of the LRs."

Angel pulled back. "We are not victims, Maggie. We are survivors and we are not gonna let them beat us."

"I like the way you think." Maggie murmured.

"Barrett," Angel laid back and winced when her head hit the pillow on the couch. "Please, call Deputy George."

Barrett pulled out his phone and dialed.

"Hey, Barrett. What's up?"

"I brought Angel to the resort for safekeeping." Barrett sat down next to Angel on the couch.

"Yeah, I heard. I went by to talk to her."

"She's here with me. Can I put you on speakerphone? Mark and Maggie are here too."

"Sure, the more the merrier." George answered.

Barrett pushed the button and set the phone on the cocktail table in front of the couches.

"Hey, George," Mark said.

"Hi, George," Maggie blurted.

"I see the gang's all there." George laughed.

"Can you give us an update?" Barrett grinned.

"It seems they have a shipment coming in on Saturday."

"What kind of shipment?" Barrett held his breath, hoping it was drugs.

"Human trafficking." George sighed.

"Holy Shit." Mark remarked.

"That's only two fucking days." Barrett rubbed his hand over his mouth. "Do you guys have a plan?"

"O, ye of little faith." George chuckled. "Of course, we have a plan."

"Deputy, this is Angel. Do you think they are going to take Steele with them?"

"I think so. My understanding is they need to get him involved in all aspects of the club."

"He's just a little boy. I want to be there." Barrett saw Angel's eyes water.

"Uh, I don't think that's a good idea, Angel." Barrett placed his hand on her knee. She could barely walk and she wanted to be a part of the upcoming take down. That seemed dangerous.

"Barrett's right. You could get hurt. Let us handle it. I promise, we'll bring Steele to you as soon as we have him in custody."

"No." Angel pushed Barrett's hand away and glared at him. "He is my son. He will come to me when he sees me."

"Uh, have you forgotten he hit you and partially buried you alive?" George sounded dumbfounded.

"They forced him. I know he regrets it, please." Angel leaned closer to the phone. "I'll do whatever you say. I'll even stay in the car until it's safe to come out."

Maggie got up and sat on the other side of Angel, rubbing her back. Angel leaned into her, away from Barrett.

"George, I'll stay with her in the car and make sure she stays put," Barrett grunted.

"Yeah, like you ever listen to me," George sounded sarcastic.

"I will this time because the last thing I want is for anything to happen to either of them." Barrett stared at Angel. *How could she not see that he wanted to comfort her and keep her safe? He was so worried about her getting along with Maggie and now she was leaning on her for support. What was he, chopped liver?*

"Let me run it through my sergeant and I'll get back to you guys. I gotta go."

"Okay, thanks George." Everyone else said thank you, and Barrett hung up.

"Come on," Maggie helped Angel stand. "Let's get you to bed. I've been where you are, and I know you need rest. Barrett, we're taking the bedroom."

"Of course." Barrett nodded and leaned back on the couch. His ankle throbbed, and he was worn out. He lifted his foot onto the cocktail table.

"I'm gonna get you some ice for that." Mark got up and pointed at his swollen ankle.

Barrett had been feeling better, but had pushed it too much today. "Thanks. There's a bag of peas in the freezer."

"Got it." Mark came back and placed it on his ankle. "Overdid it today, huh?"

"Yeah," Barrett sighed. "Long day."

"How about I work your shift tonight?"

"Lucky for you, I was off tonight." Barrett said. "But could you work for me Saturday, Sunday, and Monday night? I'd like to stay with Angel for a few days."

"You got it. Anything you need." Mark nodded.

"Okay, she's sleeping." Maggie came out of the bedroom. "I gave her one of your comfy t-shirts." Maggie winked at Barrett and heard Mark growl.

"You're gonna pay for that, smarty pants." Mark walked up to Maggie and smacked her ass.

"Oohh, I can't wait." Maggie shivered and smiled.

"Okay, you two. TMI." Barrett rubbed his forehead. "Take your foreplay back to your room. I'm tired."

"We will." Maggie grabbed Mark's hand and pulled him to the door. "Call if you need anything."

"I will. And Maggie...," –Barrett turned his face toward her– "thank you."

"Anytime. Come on, Surfer Smurf, you owe me a punishment. Toodles." Maggie wiggled her fingers above her head as Mark opened the door.

Barrett smiled. Mark had his hands full with that one. Maggie was a ball of fire, except when the LRs returned her after beating and cutting her. He remembered how much pain she had been in and now Angel was the one feeling that pain. Barrett set the peas aside, got up, and peeked into his bedroom to check on her. She was lying in the fetal position, her hair spread like her namesake on the pillow. The swelling on her face had gone down, but the deep blues and purples were still prominent on her cheeks and around her eyes.

Despite his many past relationships, Angel captivated him like no other woman ever had. He had felt an attraction to her from the moment he saw her at the cultural center. Barrett had hoped to talk to her that day, but she disappeared too fast. He'd given up hope of seeing her again, then she unexpectedly showed up at the ceremony. He was happy to see her, but that quickly changed when the shooting began. Hell, he even took a bullet for her.

Even though she left him, Barrett still vowed to keep her safe. She needed someone in her corner, and he was going to be the man to help her and her son. Barrett quietly shut the door and went back to the couch. Stretching out, he put the peas back on his ankle and decided to take a nap.

Chapter 27

Is She Dead?

Steele aka Junior

It was now morning and Steele hadn't slept a wink. He had to know if his mom had survived. *Did the police find her? Was she okay?* He glanced over at Cherry, who remained passed out next to him. After she pleasured him, she'd taken a shit ton of drugs. Steele slipped out of bed and grabbed his phone off the charger. Before dialing his mom's number, he glanced at Cherry. Yep, she was still snoring away.

Steele hesitated. He didn't know if his mom had her phone with her when they left her, but he hoped she did. He would give anything to hear her voice and tell her he was sorry. How had he gone down such a shitty path? Because he'd chosen to listen to his grandfather and Numbers, his mom could be dead. Or could she be safe? He had to find out.

Steele walked to the corner of the room, far away from Cherry. He dialed the number and held the phone up to his ear. Someone answered, but said nothing. Steele covered his mouth over the phone and said, "Hello? Mom?" But the phone clicked off.

Several seconds later, his bedroom door burst open, and Numbers stood in the doorway holding up his mom's cell phone. *Oh shit.*

"Why the fuck were you calling your mom? Is there something I should know?" Numbers stared him down, looking for any weakness.

Steele knew he had to sound convincing. "I...uh...wanted to hear her voice. I was expecting it to go to voicemail."

"Why? She was a conniving bitch. A traitor to our club." Numbers dropped her phone and smashed it with the heel of his foot, grinding it into the ground.

"Yeah. I know. It was a moment of weakness." Steele pointed to the broken phone. "Obviously, it won't happen again."

"Get cleaned up. We're meeting in the garage in thirty." Numbers turned and walked to the door.

"What about school?"

Numbers stopped and faced him. "I called them. Told them your mom died, and you're grieving. In a few days, I'll call them back and withdraw you from school."

"You're not my legal guardian. I don't think you can do that." The last thing Steele wanted was to be stuck in the clubhouse from morning until night.

"Watch me. I'll figure it out. For now, get cleaned up." Numbers left just as quickly as he entered.

Steele stared down at the broken phone. The connection to his mom shattered into so many damn pieces. Bending down, he put the big pieces together, but it wasn't powering up. He placed the broken phone in the drawer of his desk. Maybe if he glued it.

Dammit! He'd hoped to go through her phone and find someone in her contacts that might know if she was okay. How was he supposed to know now? *Shit, he couldn't even ask for help at school, because he wasn't allowed to go.* Despair washed over him as he realized not only did his mom not have her phone, but he'd just made a grave mistake by calling her number.

He didn't think Numbers believed him. After that call, Numbers would watch him like a hawk. From now on, Steele needed to learn to control his temper and practice his poker face. If his mom was alive, he needed to keep her off Numbers' radar.

"Hey, baby. Come back to bed," Cherry mumbled.

"Sorry, I have a meeting to get ready for. Stay as long as you like." Steele grabbed some clothes and headed to the bathroom for a shower.

*** Numbers ***

Numbers knew he had his work cut out for him. Junior was missing his mom. He hadn't counted on that. For the past few years, Reaper had worked hard on toughening him up. After they arrested Reaper, Numbers promised to continue his teachings. He was going to see Reaper after their club meeting and he refused to tell him he'd failed with Steele and killed Angel. Numbers never failed, well except the wedding fiasco, but to his credit, that wasn't his plan. The wedding shitshow was Reaper's plan.

He'd kept nothing from Reaper, but he wasn't about to tell him Junior tried to call his mom. *Why had he done that if she was dead?* He claimed he wanted to hear her voice, but Numbers wasn't convinced. Junior hadn't looked him in the eyes when he said it. Something was going on, and Numbers was going to get to the bottom of it before he faced Reaper.

"Red!" Numbers stopped in the main room and called his prospect.

"Yeah, boss? What's up?" Red hurried over to him.

Numbers grabbed him by the t-shirt, pulling him up to his face. "I need you to go, alone, to the place we buried Junior's mom and make sure her body's there." Numbers shook him. "Tell no one and call me as soon as you have an answer for me. You got it?"

Red nodded. "Yes, boss. I got it."

Numbers pushed him back and strolled out of the room, bellowing instructions. "Meeting in twenty. Call everyone. Brick!"

"Coming boss." Numbers heard his footsteps behind him. Upon entering the room, Numbers sat at the head of the table. "Close the door for a minute."

Brick shut the door and approached him. "What's going on?"

"I need you to keep an eye on Junior. I think he's up to something. I sent Red to his mom's gravesite to make sure her body is still there."

Brick's eyes widened. "You think she's alive?"

"Maybe, not sure. But I'm not taking any chances. If she's alive, then I want her dead. We need to keep him with one of us before he goes rogue and talks to the police. Got it."

Brick nodded.

"Go ahead." Numbers motioned to the door. "Open the door and let everyone in. We need to plan for the arrival of our shipment tomorrow. It's our largest shipment yet. We can't afford any mistakes. We have a shit ton of money riding on that delivery." As soon as the door opened, the brothers began entering.

"Brothers, take your seats so we can begin. Junior, sit here." Numbers motioned to the seat next to him.

"We have a shipment coming into the docks tomorrow that we gotta transport to different locations. We will head to the docks around nine. There will be fewer people working at that time. Plus, we need it to be dark. I need four vans, three brothers in each. Two in the front and one in the back with our passengers. This is our largest haul with our biggest payload. We aren't delivering drugs—we're delivering people." Numbers saw Junior flinch out of the corner of his eye. So, his little Junior was surprised. "If we can pull this off, our friends down south will set up future deliveries. We'll make a killing with this haul. I don't need to tell you all how important this is for the club. No mistakes and watch your backs. Are we understood?"

A round of "yes brother" was avowed as Numbers looked around the room.

"Smiley," Numbers pointed at him. "As our road captain, figure out the best route in and out of the docks. The fewer people see us, the better. Trigger, get ready to receive our payments. We need to clean that money quick. Brick, figure out who goes in what van, but you and Junior will ride with me. Butch, you're in charge of the prospects. Brothers, we will meet here tomorrow at seven for the final details before we head out. For today and tonight, drink, fuck, do whatever the hell you want," –Numbers paused as the brothers pounded on the table, hooting and hollering. When they settled down, he continued– "because tomorrow, I need all of you to bring your 'A' game. Now get the fuck out of here."

Junior moved to get up.

"Junior," Numbers grabbed his arm. "I need you to stay in the clubhouse today. Sit with Trigger and learn the ropes. Someday you'll need to know how to run the money side of this club."

Junior nodded. "Yes, sir." Then left with Trigger.

Numbers sat back and watched them leave. Checking his watch, he realized Red should call any minute now. He would get his answers about Angel soon. Then he would visit Reaper and let him know they were on schedule.

"Brother," Brick was standing in the doorway. "Do you need anything?"

Numbers' phone rang, and he saw Red's name–perfect timing.

"No, I just need a minute, in private. Please close the door on your way out." Brick nodded and followed directions.

Numbers answered his phone. "What did you find out?"

"I had to cross police tape. Her body's not there, boss."

"Fuck!" Numbers yelled.

"You okay in there, brother?" Numbers heard Brick's voice. He must've still been by the door.

"I'm fine!" Numbers hollered. "Stay there. I need to talk to you in a minute."

"You got it."

"What do you want me to do, boss?" Red asked.

"Take a photo of her grave, send it to me. I want to see it." Numbers put his phone on speaker and clicked on messages.

"Sending now."

Numbers pulled it up and took a screenshot. *Fuck! How did they know so quickly? Was there a mole in the club? Did Steele somehow call the cops?* "Delete this off your phone and keep this to yourself. I'll take care of it. Now get the fuck out of there."

"Got it." Red agreed before he hung up.

"Brick! Come in here." Numbers was seething inside. He should've checked for a pulse before he left Angel on the ground. Or better yet, shot her in the head. That was a rookie mistake. One he didn't intend to make if he ever caught up to her. That is, if she was still breathing.

"What's going on?" Brick scrambled into the room, shutting the door behind him.

"We either have a fucking mole or Junior betrayed us. We need to find out what the hell happened to Angel's body."

Chapter 28

Nightmares

Barrett

B arrett checked on Angel several times throughout the day and every time she lay there asleep. He wanted her to eat something, but didn't want to wake her. He got comfortable on the couch and settled in for the night. Sometime after midnight, something woke him up. He looked around, disoriented by the whimpering sounds coming from the bedroom. *Was Angel okay? Had someone gotten past him and was hurting Angel?* Barrett bolted into the room and saw no one with Angel. The sounds she was making were what had woken him up.

Barrett crawled into bed behind her and wrapped her up in his arms. "Shh, he whispered in her ear. It's okay. You're safe now."

Angel's body jerked. "Where am I?"

Barrett gently rolled her onto her back. "You're with me, in my bed."

"Barrett, why are you in bed with me?" Angel stared at his bare chest. Barrett had taken off his shirt to sleep, but kept his unbuttoned jeans on. He usually slept naked, but hadn't wanted to freak her out. "You promised you'd sleep on the couch."

"I was." Barrett ran his thumb over her cheek. "Until I heard you moaning, and I wanted to make sure you were okay. Are you hungry? Do you need anything?"

"Not what's poking me in my thigh," Angel squirmed.

With his fingers on her neck, Barrett felt her racing pulse. He didn't think she hated the thing that was poking her thigh, but he wasn't about to argue with her. "Sorry," Barrett murmured. "I won't force myself on you, if that's what you're worried about. You don't have to fear me."

"Okay." Angel's nostrils flared. Her body shifted closer to him, and her stomach grumbled.

Barrett smiled. "So, you're hungry, then?"

Angel grinned. "I guess so."

"Okay," Barrett released her and stood. "I have some soup I can heat for you. Stay here. I'll bring it to you when it's ready."

"Thank you." Angel whispered, staring at his unbuttoned jeans.

Barrett nodded and left the room, grinning. He would make Angel soup, but wished he could comfort her in other ways. Unfortunately for him, she wasn't ready for that type of comfort. She'd been through a lot, and he wasn't going to add to her trauma.

When the soup was hot, but not scalding, he poured it into a soup bowl and added crackers. After filling a glass with water, he placed the items, along with a napkin and spoon, on a serving tray. Angel was still laying down, so he placed the tray on the nightstand.

"Can you sit up or do you need help?" Barrett watched Angel wincing as she struggled to sit up. He helped her and added pillows behind her back for support. Then he placed the tray on her lap.

"Chicken Noodle?" Angel grinned at him.

"My favorite in the winter. Not that it gets that cold here." Barrett shrugged.

Angel spooned some into her mouth. "It's delicious."

"Don't give me too much credit." Barrett sat on the side of the bed in case she needed help. "It's from a can."

"It's still good. Thank you."

Barrett nodded. "Tell me about Steele. How old is he?"

"He'll be fifteen in a few days." Angel smiled for a few seconds before it became a frown. "He's had to grow up so fast. They're trying to turn him into a killer. He doesn't deserve that." Angel dropped her spoon into the bowl, picked it up, and drank the remaining liquid. "He's a good boy."

"A good boy who hit you." Barrett murmured.

"You don't understand how the LRs work." Angel slammed her empty bowl on the tray causing the water glass to shake. Barrett hurriedly grabbed it and the tray from her lap.

Angel laid back and covered her face. "They are monsters. If Steele had not hit me, they would have shot him and me."

Barrett placed the tray on the nightstand. "I thought you said they were grooming him to be president."

"They are, but Numbers would never accept his disrespect, especially in front of his brothers." Angel scooted down and rolled over, her body trembling as she cried into the pillow.

The heart wrenching sounds coming out of her were killing Barrett. When he couldn't take it anymore, he laid down and pulled Angel into his arms. She tried to pull back, but Barrett held her tighter against his chest and let her cry it out. Her painful muffled screams were killing him. Barrett always ran from crying women, but not Angel. He wanted, no, needed, to make her happy and feel protected. She was twisting him inside out.

Sure, he had friends that were girls, and he loved his sister, but he'd never felt this strong about anyone. To solely care for, love, and protect one special woman was uncharted territory for him. As he held her, thoughts of love and a future with her consumed him. *What was she doing to him?* Just a few days ago, he was a confirmed bachelor. Now all he wanted to do was hold her and make love to her.

But he'd promised her he'd sleep on the couch—and he would as soon as she calmed down. He was pretty sure that 'sleeping on the couch' meant no sexual passes or funny business. That was okay with him. He'd go slow and show Angel she could count on him—for anything.

Her sobs were slowing down. Barrett ran his hand over her hair, brushing it away from her face with his fingers.

"I'm sorry." Angel mumbled into his chest.

"Hey." Barrett pulled back and leaned down to look at her. "It's okay. Why don't you get some sleep? We'll talk in the morning."

Angel nodded and laid back down, curled up in a fetal position away from him. Barrett stood and grabbed the tray. He was almost out the door when he heard Angel and stopped.

"Can you come back and lie with me?"

"Absolutely," Barrett grinned. "I'll be right back."

Barrett quickly rinsed the dishes and put them in the dishwasher before getting back to Angel. He didn't want her to have too much time to second guess her decision to allow him into her bed. Or was it his bed? It didn't matter as long as they were in the bed together. Barrett dropped his pants and crawled into bed next to Angel. He laid on his back, arms behind his head.

Angel rolled over and placed her hand on his chest. Her actions surprised the shit out of Barrett. He lowered his arms and placed one behind her back and the other on his chest.

"Are you naked?" Angel whispered while she ran her hand down his chest.

Barrett's breathing became erratic as his cock grew hard. He was well-endowed, and she would soon feel it if she continued to keep her hand above his waistband. "No, I have underwear on."

"I see that," Angel chuckled when she reached for the elastic waistband and snapped it against him.

Barrett's body jolted. *What the hell? Was that her playful side?* He hadn't seen that before.

"Sorry." Angel chuckled and moved her hand up his chest. Barrett trapped her hand against his abs.

"Don't be sorry." Barrett mumbled. "You can run your hands over my body anytime."

"There's something you need to know."

"Okay." Barrett wasn't sure what she was going to say, but his body stiffened when her voice sounded scared.

*** Angel ***

"I...I didn't fight Numbers when he had sex with me, I consented." Angel closed her eyes and leaned her forehead deeper into his chest. She didn't want him to see her face.

Angel felt his hand on her waist make a fist. *Was he mad at her?* She had to make him understand she would've done anything to survive. She told him because she trusted him not to judge her, but maybe she was wrong, and he thought she was a slut.

"Angel, look at me." Angel removed her hand from his chest and stared into his eyes.

Barrett's face looked murderous. His eye was twitching, and he was clenching his teeth. But the hand he brought to her face stopped mid-motion because she flinched.

"I will never lay a hand on you in anger. I promise." Barrett slowly placed his hand behind her neck and stroked her cheek with his thumb. "Did you want him to touch you?"

"No." Angel whispered.

Barrett got up on his elbow and leaned over her. His eyes darting from her eyes to her lips. "Did you feel anything when he touched you?"

"Just pain and disgust."

Barrett looked away for a few seconds and took a hard swallow before looking at her again.

"Did you enjoy yourself?"

"No!" Angel pushed his chest. Now he was pissing her off. "I wanted him to leave me alone."

"Then, he raped you and I can't wait to get my hands on him. But you, Angel, did what you had to do in a fucked-up situation. I don't fault you for that and you shouldn't either." Barrett kissed her forehead. "As far as I'm concerned–he's a dead man walking."

"You don't think I'm a slut or that I asked for it?" Angel's voice wavered.

Barrett lifted her face to his and gazed into her eyes. "Never say that again. You did not ask for someone to abuse you or your body."

The corner of Angel's lip turned up in a partial smile. She was relieved that he didn't think the worse of her. She wasn't sure why his opinion mattered so much, but just that it did. "Thank you."

"No need to thank me. I think you're an incredibly strong woman and I totally understand if you want to take this," –Barrett motioned with his finger between them– "slow. I don't ever want you to do anything you feel forced to do. I will lie down with you if you want, or I'll go back out there on the couch. It's your choice."

"For tonight, will you just lay with me and hold me?"

Barrett laid back down and pulled her into his arms, her head resting on his chest. "Absolutely. Get some sleep. It'll be morning soon."

Angel wrapped her arm around his waist and prayed laying in his arms would keep the nightmares away.

Chapter 29

Morning of the Shipment

Steele aka Junior

Steele stayed in his room that day and avoided everyone at the club. He knew he was riding with Numbers and Brick tonight, and with the cover of darkness, he hoped to give them the slip. It would not be easy, and if they caught him, there would be hell to pay. But he had to try. Unfortunately, he wasn't sure where he would go. His mom was the only family he had, and he wasn't even sure she was alive.

He couldn't go to the cultural center because those people might hate him from when he got a tour there and treated Maggie like shit. School wasn't an option; they would wonder how he was doing after his mom's death, not to mention it was Saturday and he would have to wait somewhere for two days living off the streets.

Maybe if he showed up at a homeless shelter and gave a different name, no one would recognize him, and he could stay there for a few days until he could come up with a better plan. He would be fifteen soon and could get a job if they paid him under the table. God, he missed his mom.

By lunchtime, he was starving and headed downstairs. He should've stayed in the kitchen making his sandwich, but Cherry was in there with Sandy, and he didn't want to get stuck talking to her. Instead, he'd brought it all out and plopped it on the bar top. Bad move since most of the brothers were in the living area asking him to make them a sandwich.

Every time he finished a sandwich, another brother would ask for one. On the couch, he saw Brick and Numbers staring intently at him. It was making him nervous, and he was looking forward to returning to his room. He suspected something was up because Numbers immediately visited Reaper after their meeting yesterday. That was the second time Numbers had left him behind when they went to visit Reaper. It was weird because Numbers was constantly telling him that Reaper wanted to see him. Steele, wired and jumpy, knew he needed to compose himself before his brothers grew suspicious and questioned him.

After making the last sandwich, he put it on a plate and took it to his room. The looks that Brick and Numbers were giving him were wreaking havoc with his nerves. It's like they were daring him to tell them what he'd done with his mom. Or was it just his guilty conscious playing tricks on him? He wasn't sure, but he wasn't about to find out.

After eating his sandwich, he laid in bed, scrolling through his social media accounts in case his mom had posted anything. Which was stupid because if she was okay, that was the last thing she would do. The social media rabbit's hole took up all afternoon and by seven, he was ready to go. He'd dressed in all black, hoping to blend in with the night.

Chapter 30

Waking Up with An Angel in His Arms

Barrett

Barrett woke up to a sexy body lying on top of him. He stayed still, so he didn't disturb her. Although his cock was at full mast between her legs, he refused to take advantage of her. Most girls would call him a slut, but with Angel, he would be a gentleman–even if it killed him.

Today was the day the LRs got their shipment. George and the other officers were going to intercept them and grab Steele if he was there. Barrett was waiting for a call from George, letting him know the final details of the plan. George was well aware that Angel and Barrett wanted to be there.

He felt Angel stir.

"I'm sorry, I used your body as a pillow," Angel murmured into his chest. "You must be uncomfortable from being in that position all night. Although, I think someone is happy to see me."

Barrett chuckled, "I'm fine." He tightened his hold when she tried to roll away. "How did you sleep?"

"Good." Angel sighed. "Thank you. It was nice to not have another nightmare."

"I'm glad." Barrett rubbed her back.

"I think I should move before I hurt you." Angel giggled.

"Or you could slide on top of me and make me feel better." Barrett sat up and wiggled his eyebrows at her.

Angel smacked his chest and laughed.

"Wow, that's a first." Barrett stared at her.

"What?"

"A beautiful woman laughing at my hard on."

"Barrett!" Angel's cheeks turned pink.

"Good morning, beautiful." Barrett kissed her forehead. "What I really meant was, it was the first time I've heard you laugh since I met you. You should do it more often."

"I haven't had much to laugh about, so thank you."

"You're welcome. Now, stop tempting me. I have to shower." Barrett got up, walked into his bathroom, and shut the door.

Staring at himself in the mirror over the sink, he wondered what the hell he was doing. He couldn't tease her like that, or she might feel too much pressure and leave. But how was he supposed to not get morning wood with a sexy as shit woman laying on him? Hell, she was lucky he hadn't come just from being tucked between her legs. *Fuck!* He needed a cold shower to release some of the tension.

Barrett turned on the water and stepped in, hoping the cold water would have him shrinking. But the water turned hot quicker than he'd hoped and all he could think about was how good it would've felt to slip into her wet pussy. Thinking about Angel, he braced one hand on the tile while the other worked his shaft up and down. Thoughts of her perky nipples, luscious lips and perfect ass had him shooting his come all over the shower wall. *Fuck! That didn't take long.* He'd better not be that quick when he finally got her in bed for sexy time. Nah, he'd take his time and make sure she was wet and ready for him.

And just like that, he was hard again. Barrett dropped his head and sighed. It was going to be a long day.

*** Angel ***

Angel watched Barrett walk his sexy self into the bathroom. She woke up hot and bothered wanting to have sex with him, but it was too soon. Her ribs were still stiff, and parts of her body were sore. Stretching, she felt every twinge of pain from her head to her toes. As soon as Barrett finished, she planned on taking a nice, hot shower.

When she heard the shower stop, she slowly sat up and placed her feet on the floor.

Barrett swung the bathroom door open. "Wait, Angel. I'm filling the tub with some Epsom salt for you. It will be relaxing and relieve some of your pain."

"Oh, okay." Angel braced her hands on the bed and stood. Her ribs were screaming at her to lay her ass back down, but she managed to straighten before Barrett was in front of her, holding her hands and walking backwards. "Thank you."

"I would've carried you if you'd waited for me." Barrett guided her to the bathroom.

"I wanted to walk a little. Can I have some privacy to use the restroom?" Angel held the counter as she made her way to the toilet.

"Of course." Barrett stepped away. "I'll be right outside the door. Holler, if you need me." Barrett shut the door.

Angel relieved herself and watched the tub fill up. She couldn't wait to get in it. The water looked so welcoming with all the frothy bubbles.

Barrett knocked. "Do you need help getting into the tub?"

"No," Angel took off her clothes and stepped in.

Wow, that felt incredible.

"Can I come in for just a minute? I won't look. I promise."

"Okay." Angel covered her body with the suds.

Barrett walked in with his eyes closed. A towel in one hand, and a bath pillow in the other. "I forgot to bring you the bath pillow." He ambled to the tub and stubbed his toe. "Fuck!"

Angel laughed. "You can drop the pillow. I'll catch it. How do you have this nice Jacuzzi tub in a hotel bathroom?"

"My job is stressful and every once in a while, I take a punch to the gut and like to soak my body in a nice hot tub. Plus, I work out a lot and it helps my muscles." Barrett reached around, finding the counter, and stubbed his other toe. "Motherfucker!" He placed the towel on the counter.

Angel covered her mouth, but couldn't stop the laughter from coming out.

"Are you laughing at me?" Barrett spun around and placed his hands on his hips. His eyes opening and widening when he saw her in the tub. "Oh, shit."

"Uh…" Angel's laughter died when she saw his nostrils flare and his eyes heat up while they skimmed her body. She knew he couldn't see much beneath the bubbles, but it was still a heated situation.

"Don't you also give me shit about my tub," Barrett whispered while he stood motionless. His eyes wandering back to her face.

"I didn't mean to. I love that you have a bathtub and nice bubble bath." Angel smiled. "Few men have lavender bubble bath."

"As a fucking joke, all the security officers on staff get me bubble bath for Christmas every year. I have quite a stash." Barrett's voice was coming out choppy. He took several swallows. "Stick around long enough and you'll get to use it up for me."

Angel couldn't stop looking at him. She would love to invite him to soak with her, but was it too soon? Would he think she was a slut? It had been years since a man had loved her. The past few days with Numbers didn't count, and she wanted to wipe them off her mind. She loved having sex and being intimate with her man.

"Okay. Um. I'll leave you to it." Barrett turned around and left the bathroom, leaving the door ajar. "Call me if you need anything."

"Thank you." Angel placed the pillow behind her head and closed her eyes.

Chapter 31

They Had to Save the Kid

José

J osé had finally gotten Lola to open up to him. He was making progress, and he was so fucking happy. At least now, she would lay next to him in bed and place her hand on his arm. It was better than when she was afraid of him.

Those fucking LRs were going to pay for what they did to her. Their day was coming. As a matter of fact, it was tonight, and he hoped they all either got arrested or killed. He'd given Deputy George the information about the shipment and offered to have him and his brothers there for the arrests. José enjoyed working on the right side of the law for a change. Helping the FBI and police to take down the LRs was the best legal revenge for his parent's death.

José's phone buzzed with an emergency text from Machete.

"Sorry, Lola." Jose got up and sat on the edge of the bed. "I need to meet with Machete. I'll be back as soon as I can."

"Okay." Lola whispered.

Progress. How sweet her voice sounded. He hadn't heard her speak in several weeks except to scream at him when she was scared. Taking a deep breath, José got up and left the room. Walking into the main room, he looked for Machete, spotting him by the bar with Correcamino.

"What's going on, Prez?" José sat next to him.

"Correcamino, tell El Loco what you told me." Machete nodded.

"I was hanging out at the LRs clubhouse. They don't say much in front of me, but I caught Red before he entered the main room and he was spewing shit about how Angel wasn't really dead. They think they either have a mole or the kid saved his mom." Correcamino took a sip of beer. "If it was the kid, he's in for a world of hurt because Numbers hates traitors and Red couldn't wait to help him so he could earn his member's patch before his first year as a prospect is up."

"Fuck! I need to call Deputy George." José stood. "Correcamino, can you be there for the shipment? Do they trust you?"

"They don't trust me with information yet, but they asked me to go to bury the dead. They probably want me to dirty my hands, so they have something on me. I assume 'by the dead' they mean anyone who tries to fight them or doesn't survive the container ride. Those motherfuckers are animals."

"Correcamino, if you can, protect the boy tonight." Correcamino nodded. Machete pointed at him. "Go back quickly so they don't notice you missing for too long." Correcamino guzzled his beer and hightailed it out of there.

Machete slammed his beer down and motioned with his hand for José to follow him. "We'll go into my office and call the deputy."

Chapter 32

Unexpected Surprise

Barrett

B arrett couldn't stay in the bedroom, knowing Angel was naked in the tub, just a few steps away from him. Her sexy body all slippery and wet. The living room seemed a safer option. If he left the bedroom door open, he could hear her if she called out to him. Sitting on the couch, he grabbed the remote, clicking through channels, trying to find some bullshit show that would distract him from the desirable woman in his tub.

He went with the sports channel. Nothing sexy about watching grown men tackling each other on a field. He wasn't rooting for either team, so no stress there. When his phone buzzed, he saw George was calling him with an update. Checking the time before answering, he realized Angel had been in the tub for about thirty minutes. Her water had to be getting cold. He needed to check on her after he talked to George.

"Hey man," Barrett answered. "What's up?"

"We might have a problem."

Barrett sat up and muted the television. "What sort of problem?"

"José thinks Numbers suspects Steele of saving his mom."

"How the hell does he think that?" Barrett ran his hand over his head.

"Apparently, Numbers sent Red to check on Angel's burial site and he found the police tape and no body."

"Fuck!" Barrett screamed and bolted off the couch. "George, we need to get Steele out of there, now!"

"What happened?" Barrett spun around at the sound of Angel's voice behind him. She was dripping wet with a towel wrapped around her.

Barrett swallowed his groan. While maintaining eye contact with Angel, he said. "Just a second, George." Barrett covered the phone. "Let me get you something to wear." He brushed past Angel into his closet, where he grabbed a t-shirt and sweatpants. "Go ahead and get changed, then we can talk."

"Are you going to tell me what's going on?" Angel grabbed the clothes.

"After you get dressed...yes." Barrett stepped out and shut the door.

"Should I expect trouble here, George?"

"Not sure, but I would stay alert."

Barrett walked into the security office and checked all the monitors. "I don't see anything suspicious on any of our monitors, but I'll tell the other security officers to stay alert. Are we still on for tonight?"

"Yep. We will start setting up surveillance when night falls around seven. Any chance I can get you guys to stay home?"

"Not a chance in hell." Barrett murmured. "But I promise to do whatever you tell us to do."

George sighed, "Well, at least that's something. Though I'm not so sure I believe you."

"Oh, wow." Barrett turned to see Angel in the doorway, staring at all the monitors. He hadn't heard her enter the security office. "This is quite the setup," she mumbled.

"George, I gotta go. Text me the time and place for us to meet you." Barrett hung up and faced Angel. "This is another one of our security monitoring offices. Holt, Mark, and I use it when we want to stay up here instead of working the floor.

"That's a lot of camera angles for the resort and casino." Angel stated as she walked around. "No wonder you said you had good security here and it would be safe for me."

Barrett nodded. "We monitor the resort and casino from here and the office downstairs. Plus, we have security officers that walk around downstairs and check the perimeter."

Angel turned and walked to Barrett. "So, what was that call about? What's going on?"

Barrett wasn't sure how to tell her Steele was in danger, but he wanted to be honest with her. "Let's go sit on the couch."

"Okay." Angel squinted at him, but allowed him to lead her to the couch.

Barrett sat next to her, turned his body, held her hands, and blurted. "We think Numbers knows you're still alive."

"No!" Angel pulled her hands back and covered her mouth. "Do they think Steele was involved? Is Steele okay? Did they hurt him? We need to get him out." Angel bolted up, running toward the door.

"Whoa, there." Barrett wrapped his arms around her from behind, stopping her from leaving. "We're gonna get him tonight. George has a plan."

Angel spun in his arms and gripped his t-shirt with both hands. "You don't understand." Angel shook him. "If they think he's a traitor, they'll kill him."

Angel fought him, trying to get out of his arms.

"Angel, stop." Barrett grabbed her shoulders and leaned down to stare into her eyes. "We will not let anything happened to your son. I promise. Please, just listen to me."

"No, we need to go." Angel was slapping his chest.

"Dammit woman, stop hitting me and listen to me." Barrett grumbled.

"No, let me go. I need to go to my son."

"Fuck." Barrett wrapped his arms around her and pulled her tightly against his chest, trapping her hands between them. Not knowing what to do, he kissed her. He plunged his tongue into her mouth to shut her up. Her hands glided up his chest and around his neck. He could feel her fingers gliding through his hair.

One of his hands cupped her ass while the other held her head in place so his tongue could ravish every crevice of her mouth. Moaning into each other's mouths, Barrett released her mouth and ran kisses and licks from her jaw to her neck. Angel turned her head, giving him access.

Her skin tasted so damn sweet, and she smelled like the lavender bubble bath. His new favorite scent. Angel released his hair and unbuckled his jeans.

Barrett held her hands and looked into her eyes. "Are you sure about this?"

"Yes," Angel nodded, pulling him with her as she walked backwards into the bedroom.

"If you change your mind," Barrett watched her closely, "let me know and I'll stop."

Barrett would rather cut off one of his balls than stop, but he didn't want to rush her. She had been through so much, and the last thing he wanted to do was hurt her. He would let her set the pace, even if it killed him.

As soon as they entered the bedroom, Angel let go of his jeans and pulled her t-shirt over her head. *Jesus Fuck!* She wasn't wearing a bra, and she had the most beautiful tits he'd ever seen. They were more than a handful with hard as hell dark pink nipples ready for him to suck.

Next, she dropped the sweatpants and bared her beautifully trimmed pussy for him. He could die a happy man right now before even touching her. She was so fucking beautiful.

"Your turn." Angel said and stepped back.

So engrossed in watching her, Barrett forgot he was still dressed. Wanting to make her happy, he took off his clothes in record time. Angel grabbed his hand and pulled him toward the bed. Then she surprised him by turning them until the back of his legs touched the bed and she pushed him back. Barrett landed on his back and quirked an eyebrow at her. "Now what?" He was loving this sexy, bossy side of her. Barrett loved fucking a woman who knew what she wanted in the bedroom.

"Do you have a condom?" Angel's eyes roamed over his body.

Barrett pointed with his right hand toward his nightstand. "Top drawer." Barrett scooted backward to reach it when Angel straddled his thighs.

"I got it," she said before she leaned over him to open the drawer. Her tits near his mouth. Barrett licked her nipple before she pulled back with the condom. He'd hoped she would take longer so he could fill his mouth with her breast.

Angel grimaced when she sat upright on Barrett.

"Angel, are you okay?"

"I'm better than okay." Angel smiled, but her hand went to her ribs.

"We should wrap your ribs. This isn't a good idea." Barrett sat up. He didn't want to hurt her.

"This is a great idea." Angel stilled and stared at Barrett. "I need this, please," she whispered.

"Okay." Barrett watched her closely. "But if it hurts, you gotta tell me so we can stop."

"I will. Now lay down so I can have my way with you." Angel tore the condom wrapper with her teeth. Barrett gritted his teeth. He wasn't sure how much more torture he could take. She was killing him. All he wanted to do was drive into her wet pussy and fuck the hell out of her.

After wrapping his cock with the condom, Angel braced one hand on his chest while she used the other to guide him into her. Barrett glanced down and watched his cock get swallowed up by her pussy. Once she was fully seated on his cock, he closed his eyes and groaned. She was so fucking tight and felt so damn good. Barrett placed his hands on her hips but let her set the pace.

When she rocked against him, he opened his eyes just in time to see her open her mouth and moan.

"You are so beautiful," Barrett moaned. Reaching up, he ran his hands up her body to cup her breast. His thumbs running over her nipples before his fingers tweaked them. Angel arched her back and dropped her chest lower. Barrett couldn't stop himself from taking her luscious mounds into his mouth. His tongue swirling around her nipples.

Angel grabbed his head and held it to her breasts, her body thrust harder onto him. *Fuck! He wanted to be on top.* She released his head and leaned back. Her breast popped out of his mouth. They stared at each other, panting.

"Help me, Barrett. I'm so close," Angel whispered.

Barrett gripped her hip with one hand and moved his other hand to play with her clit. Angel leaned back and placed her hands on his thighs, giving him full access to her pussy and her pleasure. It only took a few swipes of his thumb on her clit for her to squeeze his thighs and release her orgasm. Barrett held still, letting her enjoy the moment and draw out her pleasure. He watched her face as she threw back her head and screamed out.

When her breathing returned to normal, she looked at him. He was still hard as fucking nails and ready to pound into her if she allowed it. She ground herself onto him while he watched her.

"Are you still okay? Can I get on top now?" Barrett asked between panting.

Angel smiled, melting his heart a little more. This woman was turning him inside, fucking out.

"Yes."

Barrett rolled her onto her back. Leaning down, he held her hands above her head, kissing the daylights out of her, while he pounded his cock into her wet pussy. He wasn't letting up until she came again. She felt so fucking good. He never wanted to leave her body. Grounding into her, she trembled as her second orgasm exploded before his.

"Fuck, Angel." Barrett released her hands and held her head, kissing her until he was drained.

"I'll be right back," Barrett scooted off the bed to take care of the condom and get a damp towel to clean her up. Angel lay on the bed unmoving while he wiped between her legs. He tossed the towel toward the bathroom and pulled her into his arms.

"Thank you for trusting me." Barrett whispered, while he ran his fingers through her hair.

*** Angel ***

Angel didn't know what to say. Of course, she trusted Barrett. He'd never done anything to hurt her. If anything, she was shocked that he trusted her. She was the one that left him to bleed out.

"It's hard for me to trust anyone, but I do trust you." Angel draped her arm around his waist and slid her leg between his.

"Tell me about your husband," Barrett asked softly.

"Really?" Angel leaned up and looked at him. *Was he serious?* They'd just had amazing sex, and he wanted to talk about her husband.

"Yeah." Barrett pulled her head back down to his chest. "I want to know everything about you. The good, the bad, and the ugly."

"Okay." Angel sighed and burrowed into him. "We met when I was fourteen. He was a prospect for the LRs. My dad saw I liked him, so he would invite him over for dinner all the time. Reaper always wanted me to be more involved in the club. When I was little, I adored my father. I was daddy's little girl and everything revolved around him. He treated me like a princess. But then my mom died, and he turned into a bitter, mean man."

"How old were you when your mom died?" Barrett's hand stroked her back.

"I was twelve. She caught pneumonia and never recovered. My dad took his anger out on me. If I disobeyed or disrespected him, he would hit me. If I didn't have dinner ready when he got home, he would hit me. I think he felt like he had to control me. I talked about hating his club and wanting to run away. He beat the shit out of me that day and I never said that again."

Barrett kissed the top of Angel's head.

"A couple years later, he started bringing Tools home. I guess in his twisted mind, he figured if I hooked up with an LR, he'd keep me close. He was right. I fell for Tools and got pregnant at fifteen. Tools was only seventeen and had been living on the streets when Reaper found him. His parents had died a couple of years earlier. I fell for him and wasn't sorry when Reaper made us get married. He made Tools a brother and paid him. I took my GED and went to night school to get my law degree. Reaper thought I was getting it to be the club's lawyer, but I was getting it to help my family and hopefully one day leave that hellhole. Tools knew I was unhappy and scared of the LRs. That's when he came up with the idea of the garage. He was an excellent mechanic who could fix cars, bikes, anything on four wheels. It's how he got his biker name. He loved his brothers and didn't want to leave, but he also wanted to make me happy. He begged me to hang in there until he could get the club to go legit. Then he died, and you know the rest," Angel sighed.

"I'm so sorry you went through all that." Barrett mumbled.

"Me too. Tools was a great husband and father. After we got married, Reaper never laid a hand on me again. He saved me from my father's wrath."

Barrett rolled them over and cupped her jaw. "I will not let your father or anyone else use you as a punching bag. Got that."

"Yeah." Angel grinned. "Thank you."

"It's my pleasure, my angel." Barrett kissed her and rolled her around to spoon her. "Rest. We have a long night ahead of us."

Chapter 33

Go Time

Numbers

Numbers had been watching Junior. So far, he had done nothing suspicious. But Numbers wasn't one to wait for shit to happen. They had an important shipment tonight, and he wanted to know everyone, including Junior, had their head on straight.

Junior was sitting on the couch talking to Red when he approached.

"Junior, I need to talk to you." Numbers motioned with his thumb. "Red, take a hike."

"Yes, boss." Red smirked and darted off the couch.

"Anything you want to tell me, son?" Numbers wanted to give him the chance to tell him if he was a traitor.

"No, sir. Why?"

"I know your mom's body was not in the grave." Numbers glared at him. "Do you know anything about that?"

"What?" Steele's body went rigid. He looked outraged. "What do you mean?"

"I mean, she's not there. Did you take her body? Is she alive?" Numbers stood and grabbed Steele by the shirt, pulling him up to his face. "Are you a fucking traitor like your mom? Are you lying to me and the club?" Numbers growled.

"No." Steele shook his head. His eyes widened with fear. Numbers glared at him, looking to catch him in a lie. Had the kid become good at lying, or was he telling him the truth? Had he grown balls of steel? Only time would tell, but for now, he wouldn't take his eyes off him.

Numbers released his shirt and shoved him back. "I better not find out you're lying to me." Numbers pointed his finger in Steele's face. "Or I'll fucking kill you. I don't give a shit that you're the prodigal grandson and future president. We do not want or need a fuckin' traitor as prez."

Steele nodded, "I understand."

"Meeting starts in a few minutes. Give me your phone." Numbers stuck out his hand.

"Sure." Steele placed his phone in Number's palm and sat down on the couch.

Numbers tucked it into his back pocket and went into the meeting room. He planned to search for all incoming and outgoing calls from the night of Angel's murder. Before they all left for the warehouse, he needed to know if the kid was clean; otherwise, Junior would die accidentally before nightfall. Reaper would be angry, but Reaper didn't want a liar or a snitch in the clubhouse, no matter who he was.

*** Steele aka Junior ***

Fuck! That was close. Steele wiped his brow. He could feel the sweat pouring down is back. He needed to get it together before anyone noticed.

"You okay, Steele?" Red sat next to him, drinking his beer.

"Uh, yeah. I'm good." Steele forced a grin. "Just not used to not having my phone."

"Yeah, I get that." Red nodded and took a swig of his beer.

Steele wanted to get away from Red, but didn't know how to leave without looking guilty.

"You're not lyin' to Numbers, are you?" Red glared at him.

"No, the last time I saw my mom she was dead, and I buried her before I went back to you guys." Steele stared at Red and did everything in his power, not to blink or hesitate.

Red nodded. "Okay, kid." Red got up. "I'm gonna get another beer. You want one?"

"No. I'll get a bottle of water."

"Drank too much last night, huh?"

"Yeah." Steele stood.

"Relax, I'll get you a water bottle when I get my beer." Red stood and waved Steele to sit back down.

"Thanks."

Steele's mind raced through all the recent conversations he'd had with Numbers, hoping he hadn't said or done anything to make Numbers or anyone at the clubhouse suspicious of him. Thank goodness he'd deleted anything he didn't want Numbers to see off his phone.

He knew at some point Numbers would take his phone if he thought Steele was lying to him about his mom. It was one reason why Steele hadn't called the hospitals looking for her. Any sign of weakness would've gotten him in trouble.

He had to see his mom as the evil, horrible woman who turned on the club. After everything Steele had witnessed, he just didn't see his mom that way—not anymore.

Steele didn't understand how anyone could beat another person like they had done to his mom. He could accept her being kicked out, but her murder was unacceptable. A bitter rage boiled inside him; the thought of his mother vulnerable to the Everglades' creatures fueled a furious desire for vengeance against Numbers. He had been excited to be a member of the clubhouse until that day. Now, he couldn't wait to get away from them and find his mom. Steele hoped she was safe, either in a hospital or in police custody. She deserved safety and distance from the LRs.

He regretted ever calling Numbers and putting them in the situation they were in. Glad that his mom was free, now he had to work on getting himself out of there. Tonight, during the shipment pickup, Steele planned to hide around one of the many containers at the dock. If he could give the brothers the slip, he might be able to get somewhere safe and ask for help.

Chapter 34

Let's Roll

Angel

"**A**ngel," Barrett whispered in her ear. "It's time to go."

Angel had been having the best dream. She had been at the beach lounging in a beach chair, watching Barrett and Steele playing in the surf. It was the first relaxing dream she'd had in a long time, and she hated waking up to reality.

"What time is it?" Angel rolled over to face Barrett.

"It's eight o'clock. George just called and said they were in place. He wants us to wait at 'Smitty's Seafood' near the docks." Barrett brushed the hair off her face.

"We're not going to the docks?" Angel sat up wincing from the pain in her ribs. She was upset that she wasn't going to be near Steele.

"It's not safe for us there and you're still in pain. George will bring Steele to us as soon as they get him away from Numbers."

"No, Barrett." Angel scooted to the side of the bed, whipped the covers off, and stood. "I need to be where the cops are. I need to make sure he's okay."

"Angel." Barrett grabbed her hand. "We can't be there. It's going to be a shitshow and you could get yourself or him killed if they see you. The restaurant was the closest location George could get us."

"We'll see about that." Angel pulled her hand out of his, stormed into the bathroom, and slammed the door. *What the fuck!* Didn't they understand that was her son? She didn't give a shit if her ribs still hurt. It was crucial for her to be there to support him. She could stay hidden.

Angel used the restroom and realized she didn't have any clothes. Swinging the door open, she shouted, "Barr...," but stopped because he was standing on the other side of the door with a set of clothes in his arms. "Who's are those?"

"Maggie came by earlier." Barrett shoved the clothes toward her. "She said you guys are about the same size and brought these over for you."

Angel reached for the clothes. "That was very nice of her."

"Yeah, Maggie's a little spitfire, but she can be nice when she likes you."

"You think she likes me?" Angel was puzzled. After everything her family did to her, she couldn't believe that Maggie would be her friend, let alone like her.

"She wouldn't let you borrow her clothes if she didn't like you. Maggie says it like it is. So, yeah, I think she likes you." Barrett pointed to the bathroom. "You can change in there; I'll change in the closet. Then I need to check the monitors one more time before we leave."

"Okay." Angel locked the bathroom door and changed her clothes. She was astonished by the events that unfolded in just a few hours. She hoped the LRs wouldn't figure out he'd helped her. Numbers was an asshole who wouldn't think twice about putting a bullet in Steele's head. Being Reaper's grandson only went so far. A traitor or liar to the brotherhood was not acceptable–it didn't matter who your parents were.

Angel left the bathroom and waited for Barrett on the couch. She didn't have to wait long.

"Yeah, I'm gonna take off now to meet George." Barrett pointed at the phone and mouthed 'Mark'. "Please tell Maggie thank you for the clothes for Angel. They fit her perfectly."

Angel smiled. Maggie must be her same size because Barrett wasn't lying when he said the clothes fit.

"Thank you for taking my shift." Barrett grabbed his wallet off the foyer table and waved for Angel to follow him. "I'll let you know how it goes."

Angel followed him to the elevator.

"Thanks." Barrett said before he pocketed his phone and turned to Angel. "Maggie's glad the clothes fit. She said you can look in her closet tomorrow and borrow anything else you might need."

Angel nodded and entered the elevator.

"How are you holding up?" Barrett draped his arm over her shoulder.

"I'm scared, but also excited to get Steele back." Angel grinned at him through the mirrored panels on the wall of the elevator.

"It's going to be okay. I'm not gonna let anyone hurt you or your son." Barrett held the door open for her when they exited in the lobby and led her to his truck.

Angel was glad no one stopped them in the lobby. She didn't want to waste any more time.

Barrett held open the passenger door for her, shutting it after she got in. He was such a gentleman. Not many men treated women like precious cargo.

Angel waited until he got in before she asked, "Can we call George and ask him if we can get any closer?"

"Angel," Barrett sighed, "we've already gone over this. It's not safe for you to go any further."

"I don't care about me. I want to get my son!"

"Dammit, I get it," Barrett sounded exasperated. "But I care about you. If you're not going to take care of yourself, then I'm gonna do it for you."

"Fine." Angel sat back with her arms crossed and stared out the window. He didn't understand that she was nothing without Steele. If anything happened to her boy, she would never survive the loss. Life would never be the same. Barrett didn't understand. He didn't have a child.

"Angel." Barrett reached over and pulled her hand, uncrossing them. He wound his fingers through hers and placed their hand on the center console. "I know you're worried. If it was one of my family members, I would be beside myself too, but we need to listen to the police."

Angel didn't answer, but she also didn't remove her hand from his. His thumb stroked her hand, soothing her anxiety. When they arrived at the restaurant, Angel threw the door open and would've jumped out of the car, except Barrett gripped her hand, holding her in place.

"Angel, please remember what I said."

"Of course." Angel nodded but knew if, given the chance, she would run toward the docks and look for Steele.

Barrett came around and placed his hand at her back as they walked into the restaurant. Deputy George was waiting for them in front of the hostess stand.

"Angel, Barrett." Deputy George held out his hand.

Angel and Barrett shook his hand. Barrett tucked Angel into his side.

"Angel, I know this is hard for you. Please know we have a lot of officers out there on the lookout for Steele. We will get him and bring him to you here as soon as we arrest the LRs." George stared at Angel.

"Thank you."

"I gotta go, but I'll call you," Deputy George looked at Barrett, "as soon as I know anything. Hang tight."

Barrett nodded. They watched Deputy George leave before Barrett turned to the hostess and asked for a table for two.

"Let's get a drink to calm your nerves. What do you say?" Barrett kissed her cheek.

"Sure." Angel followed the hostess to a table. Barrett was close behind her. When they reached the table, he pulled out her chair for her. Angel sat down and took the menu from the hostess.

"Your server will be with you in a few minutes." The hostess said before leaving them alone.

"I need to use the ladies' room," Angel put her menu down. "Could you order a glass of white wine for me, please? I'm not picky. Whichever you choose will be fine with me."

"Sure." Barrett smiled.

Angel got up and walked to the hallway, which led to the restroom. She never entered the ladies' room. She turned around and peeked at Barrett. He was staring at the menu so intensely she went around the other side of the restaurant and slipped out the front door.

It was a short walk to the docks. As long as she kept to the shadows and stayed hidden, she would be okay. Suddenly, she heard the roar of motorcycles coming her way. Quickly, she found a large dumpster at the entrance to the docks and she crouched behind it. When Barrett figured out what she had done, he was going to be furious with her, but saving Steele was her first priority.

*** Barrett ***

Barrett wasn't sure which wine Angel would like. Did she like a dry white wine or a sweet white wine like Moscato? He knew he should've asked her to pick it out before she left.

"Have you decided on what you want to drink?" the waitress smiled at him.

"Um, can you give us a few more minutes?"

"Sure, take your time."

"I just don't want to order my girlfriend the wrong wine." Barrett looked back at the list.

"Wasn't your girlfriend the one that just left?" The waitress pointed out the front door.

"What do you mean, left?" Barrett frowned.

"Blonde lady in a black blouse and jeans?"

Barrett nodded.

"She just left in a hurry."

"Shit!" Barrett stood up so fast his chair fell backwards. "Sorry." Barrett picked it up and pushed it under the table. "I gotta go."

Dammit Angel. He knew exactly where she was headed, and he had to get to her before the LRs spotted her. Running full speed, he ignored the pain shooting up his ankle as he looked left and right for anywhere Angel might be hiding.

"Angel," Barrett whispered harshly. "Angel. Where are you?"

"Shh," Angel stepped out from behind a dumpster. "I'm over here. How did you find me?"

"The waitress said you ran out, and I left. I told you not to come here."

Barrett heard the roar of motorcycles coming closer. Angel grabbed his arm and pulled him with her behind the dumpster.

"You can yell at me later. For now, stay quiet and let's see where they go."

"Fuck, Angel." Barrett glared at Angel when she placed her hand over his mouth.

As soon as the sound of the motorcycles flew past, Angel moved to go around the dumpster.

Barrett grabbed her hand and pulled her behind him. "Stay behind me."

Angel nodded and gripped the back of his jeans. They had run for just a few minutes before Barrett ran smack into a gun being pointed at his face.

Chapter 35

Oh Shit!

Steele aka Junior

Numbers made Steele ride on the back of his bike with him. Brick rode next to Numbers and all the other brothers rode in a "v" formation behind them. The vans which were transporting the shipment followed behind the bikes. Steele looked around the entire time they were riding through the docks, looking for good hiding spots. He found several and was making a plan when they reached a blue container, and Numbers stopped.

"Brick." Numbers waited until Steele got off the bike before he dismounted. "Open it up."

Brick strolled to the container and took the lock off. When he pulled the door open, Steele saw a bunch of Hispanic men, women, and children crammed inside. They were all staring at them. Some were sitting on the floor and others were standing, but they all shared the same look of fear on their faces. Steele had heard rumors about the LRs taking part in human trafficking, but he'd never actually seen it.

He thought they were picking up a shipment of guns or drugs—not that a drug or gun shipment was good, but trafficking people was horrible. He had to get away from them. His mom was right. They were bad people, and he didn't want to have anything to do with them. He wished he'd listened to her when she wanted to run. Instead, he'd called Numbers and messed everything up. That had been a stupid mistake that might have cost his mom her life and could still get him killed.

As Steele stood in shock, the brothers pointed their guns toward the open doors, and Numbers walked to the people and spoke to them. They looked scared as they clung to each other.

"You will all come out in a single file line. If anyone runs or tries anything, we will shoot you. *¿Comprende?*" Steele saw them look at each other until a woman tending to an elderly man on the floor spoke up.

"*¿Agua, por favor?*" the woman pleaded with Numbers.

"Get out, then we'll give you water." Numbers motioned for them to get out.

Steele knew Numbers spoke a little Spanish. Besides, they all knew the words for water and please. He looked in Numbers saddle bags for a bottle of water.

Numbers turned to him and shouted, "What the fuck are you doing?"

Steele withdrew his hands from inside the saddlebags and turned to Numbers. "Looking for some water."

"Get the fuck away from my bike. They can get water when they get in the vans." Then Numbers turned to the people and screamed, "Get the fuck out of there, now!"

The men helped the women and children exit the container. One man draped the older man's arm around his shoulder to help him up and out. Steele watched as they walked past him. The powerful smell of urine clung to them, and he gagged. He wondered where they came from and how long they had been in that container? The LRs opened the van doors and waited for Numbers to sort them. It clearly looked as if they knew the drill–they had done this before. They didn't seem to be offended by the smell or the look of hopelessness on the people's faces.

Steele saw several containers near the open blue one. If he could make it behind the open door of the container, he could run and hide. As the Hispanics shuffled toward the vans to get in, he took several steps back. He was halfway there when he heard, "Police, freeze!" And all hell broke loose.

Some LRs shoved Hispanics into their vans while others took cover and fired shots in the direction of the police. Their blinking lights partially blinding the LRs and causing their shots to go wild. Steele ducked as bullets flew everywhere, ricocheting off the containers. Numbers grabbed the back of Steele's shirt and pulled him toward a container. Brick followed them.

"Brick." Numbers ducked behind the container. "How the fuck did they know we were here?" Numbers pointed his finger in Steele's face. "Did you call the police?"

"No." Steele shook his head profusely.

"Don't fucking lie to me." Numbers grabbed a fist full of the front of Steele's shirt and pulled him up to his face. "Did you fucking call them?" He growled at Steele.

"Nn...nn...no," Steele stuttered. "Numbers. How could I? You had my phone." Steele was scared shitless. Numbers' eyes were shooting daggers at him.

Numbers had never looked at him like that before. It was pure evil. While still staring him down, Numbers said, "Brick, watch him," then turned to go to the end of the container and began shooting at the police. Or what Steele assumed was the police, because he sure as shit wouldn't be shooting a brother or a Hispanic. That was his payload.

Steele took a few deep breaths and leaned against the container. Brick watched him but kept looking in Numbers direction. He was twitchy. Steele could tell he wanted to get into the fight. Steele looked around for his chance to run. Lucky for him, it came sooner than he thought.

"Brick, I'm out," Numbers hollered, "give me your gun or another round!"

Steele waited until Brick ran closer to Numbers and when he pulled the extra cartridge out of his pants, Steele turned and ran. He heard Numbers curse behind him and yell at Brick to follow the little fucker. Steele knew he had to make his way around the back of the containers, hoping to reach the cops. He couldn't run straight to them, or he might get shot by either them or the LRs.

He could hear Brick running behind him. "Junior, stop. I can help you."

Steele didn't believe him for a second. Brick was loyal to Numbers and the club; he wouldn't do anything to help him. Suddenly, out of nowhere, a hand came out and pulled Steele behind one of the many containers. Steele felt another hand cover his mouth and heard a low voice in his ear.

"Shh. It's Correcamino."

Correcamino, shit, that was a new prospect for the LRs that had been a Los Lobos member. He would, for sure, turn him into the brothers so he could become a fully patched LR member. Steele struggled in his arms, but Correcamino held tight. I mean shit; he was twice Steele's size and just because he was lean didn't mean he wasn't all muscle. He'd heard from Red that Correcamino was a star soccer player in college, but when he got caught with drugs, everything went south. Steele knew he couldn't outrun him.

"Listen to me. I'm gonna help you. I'm on your side. I only infiltrated the LRs to hear about their drops and keep you safe."

Steele didn't know what to believe. Everyone in the club had their secrets. What if Correcamino was a great liar and was going to take him back to Numbers? Then Brick appeared in front of them and pointed the gun at them.

"Good job. I see you found Junior." Brick lowered his gun and grabbed Steele's arm. "Let's take him back to Numbers.

Correcamino released him and allowed Brick to pull him along. He'd been right. Correcamino just wanted the glory of the member patch. Hell, capturing him might even get him a leadership role in the club. He should've fought harder and not believed the lies spewing from Correcamino's mouth when he grabbed him. Suddenly, Brick released his arm and dropped to the floor. He lay crumpled in a heap. *What the fuck?*

Steele spun toward Correcamino, who lowered his gun. "Come on kid, we gotta go, now!"

So Correcamino was helping him and must've hit Brick over the head with his gun. Correcamino was waving him to follow. Steele had no other choice but to follow him and pray he was leading him to the police and not to his death.

Chapter 36
Twisted Turn of Events

Barrett

"**F**uck!" Barrett placed his hand over his heart. "You scared the shit out of me." Barrett never expected to see José with a gun pointed at his face.

"Sorry," José pointed the gun at the floor. "I thought you were one of the LRs. What the hell are you doing here? With her?"

"I couldn't keep her the fuck away."

"Women," José smirked.

"Yeah." Barrett nodded.

"Hey," Angel smacked Barrett's chest. "I'm standing right here."

"Yup, and I wish you weren't." Barrett turned to José. "Why are you here?"

"Assisting the police, have been for a while. I gotta go, but stay out of trouble."

"Copy that," Barrett said as he watched José run closer to the containers.

"Who was that?" Angel demanded.

Barrett couldn't let her know that was José. She would go batshit crazy and blow the entire operation...with reason, but this wasn't the time. He needed to distract her long enough for her to forget who she had seen.

"Is he an undercover cop?" Angel insisted on asking questions about José.

"Yes," Barrett hated lying to her. But was he really lying? José was working with the police. He could wait to feel her anger after they saved her son. "We need to find George or a deputy." Barrett mumbled loud enough for Angel to hear, but low enough for his voice not to travel.

They were quietly making their way deeper into the docks when they heard the sounds of automatic gunfire. Angel suddenly bolted from behind a container and took off in a dead run. *Shit! So much for her listening to him.* "Angel," he growled, "get back here." Barrett shot off after her. Barrett ran all the time. It didn't take him long to reach her and push her behind a police car.

"What are you doing?" Angel panted and shoved at him. "I need to find Steele."

"I know." Barrett held her head in his hands and made her look at him. "Angel, we will get him, but running into a gun fight unarmed is a good way to get shot. Let's find an officer, preferably George," Barrett looked around, "and see what we can do." Then he gave her a quick peck on the lips and grabbed her hand, pulling her along.

Angel tried to pull out of his grip, but Barrett stopped and pulled her into him. He glared at her and said, "Don't make me fucking zip tie your wrist to mine. It'll hurt, but I'll fucking do it."

"Why do you have zip ties?" Barrett couldn't believe those were the words she heard.

Barrett quirked a brow. "Don't look at me like that. I'm not kinky or a fucking serial killer. I use them at the casino when our guests need to be detained for the police."

"Oh," Angel's eyes widened, and Barrett felt her nipples harden against his chest. His little Angel liked the idea of exploring some kink with him. Interesting and something he would have to plan out at a later date.

Barrett's smile widened. "I see being tied up turns you on. We'll have to explore that the next time we get in bed."

"There won't be a next time if we die standing here." Angel grumbled.

Barrett belted out a laugh. "Okay Tiger, let's go find Deputy George."

Barrett couldn't believe she'd sidetracked him so much that he was laughing at a gun fight. Damn, he needed to get his head on straight because this girl was going to be the death of him. Suddenly, Angel smacked his back repeatedly, and Barrett stopped and turned to her. "What now, Tiger?"

Angel was jumping up and down, pointing to the right, trying to pull him in that direction. Barrett looked at where she was pointing and saw a man running behind a boy with his gun out, moving it around, looking for a target. The boy saw Angel and screamed, "Mom!"

The man with the gun was so intent on watching them, he never noticed the LR that shot him in the back. Before hitting the ground, the man turned and shot LR in the forehead.

"We need to get the hell out of here." Barrett wrapped his arms around both Angel and Steele and led them behind a police car. Several officers came to their aid. They must've heard Steele's cry for his mom or seen him. A couple of officers pulled the man who had run with Steele to another safe location and radioed for an ambulance.

"Shit, are you guys okay?" George appeared out of nowhere. "I told you to stay in that damn restaurant."

Angel was crying and holding Steele so tightly, she was gonna suffocate the kid. But he didn't seem to mind. He was trembling and holding her just as tight.

Barrett stood and stepped away from them to talk to George. "I couldn't keep her away. She ran from me, and I had to keep her safe." Barrett looked around to make sure no one was heading their way to hurt Angel.

"That must've been strange for you." George was scanning the area, too.

"What?" Barrett quirked an eyebrow at him.

"Usually, girls are running to you not away from you." George burst out laughing. "I think you've finally met your match."

"Fucker." Barrett smirked at George. "I'd ask if you need any help, but I don't hear much shooting."

"Thank God, that's how I heard him scream for his mom." George holstered his gun. "We are arresting the ones still standing and getting ambulances for the ones that are down." George nodded to Angel and Steele. "How are they doing?"

"Better now, don't you think?" Barrett grinned as Angel rubbed her hand over Steele's face and body, checking him over.

"Yeah, sure looks that way. Let me see if I can take off and drive you guys back to the restaurant so you can get your car." George looked around. "I'll be right back."

Angel helped Steele off the floor, wrapped her arms around him, and led him to Barrett.

"Barrett, this is my son, Steele." Angel turned to Steele. "This is the man I was telling you about that helped us."

"Hi, Steele," Barrett stuck out his hand. "It's nice to meet you. I'm glad you're okay. Your mom was going crazy worrying about you."

"What do you want from my mom?" Steele pulled her away from Barrett.

"Steele," Angel's mouth dropped.

Clearly, Angel didn't expect Steele to be rude. She probably thought he was going to thank him. But Steele was a teenager caught up in a lot of bad MC shit. Barrett could tell it was going to take some time to get Steele to trust him.

"It's okay." Barrett put his hands in his pockets. "Steele's been through a lot. I care about your mom, and I want to make sure you are both safe." Steele didn't look like he was buying Barrett's shit. This kid would need a lot of time to heal from this ordeal.

George interrupted them, "Okay, the captain said I could take you guys to the restaurant. Follow me to my car."

"After you guys," Barrett waved his arm in George's direction.

"Why is he coming with us?" Steele glared at Barrett.

"Steele, stop." Angel wrapped her arm around his shoulder and guided him to follow George. "He drove me here and we are staying with him." Then she looked over her shoulder and mouthed "sorry".

"What do you mean, we're staying with him?" Steele turned around and gave him the evil eye before looking at his mom. "Why can't we stay at our house?"

George stopped and turned around. "Because your house isn't safe until we find Numbers."

"What?" Angel froze and pulled Steele into her arms.

Barrett couldn't believe with all the officers here, Numbers had given them the slip. *Fuck! He was a slippery son of a bitch.*

"We know at least one bullet hit him. We'll find him." George turned back. "Let's go."

"What about those people that were trapped in the container?" Steele tapped George on the back.

George turned around again. "We got all of them. The ones that were hurt in the crossfire are being taken to the hospital. The others are being processed."

"Come on." Barrett nudged Angel and Steele to follow George. "I'll keep you both safe at the resort."

"Yeah, right?" Steele mumbled. "Like you can protect us from the LRs. We're a dead mother and son pair walking."

Barrett would've found the comment witty and morbidly funny if it wasn't for the fact that it was true until they found Numbers. Angel's face had gone pale, and she stumbled at his words. He placed his hand on the small of her back for support. *Fuck him!* He was gonna have to have a little man-to-man talk with the kid and the kid hated him. *That should be fun—said no one ever when dealing with an angry teen.* But it had to be done. Angel had been through enough, and Steele needed to watch his mouth.

*** Numbers ***

From his hiding place, he'd watched Junior and that bitch walk away with that asshole Barrett from the casino, with the officer living at the cultural center. He would get them all even if he had to blow up that fucking cultural center or resort with them in it. Looking down, he saw the blood running down his leg from the bullet he took to the thigh. Thank fuck it didn't hit his femoral artery, or he'd be dead lying beside Brick.

An officer shot him in the thigh as he ran after Junior and stepped away from the container. With all the bullets flying, no one noticed Red dragging him to where the dock met the water. Red had done his research because now they sat in a small wooden hidey hole under the dock, away from the water. Unless someone knew these docks, Numbers didn't think anyone would find them.

"How did you know about this place?" Numbers whispered to Red. He was being quiet because the police were still searching for any other LRs.

"I used to play on these docks as a kid," Red smirked. "I know all the hiding places down here."

"You just saved my life. There's a member patch waiting for you at the clubhouse. Unfortunately, we can't go there right now. Got a place we can go hide?"

"I have a cousin in Hialeah." Red shrugged. "We could crash there."

"That's a little too close to Los Lobos. Tonight, we'll head north and lay low. I'll think of something." Numbers tore off the bottom of his t-shirt. "Wrap this around my thigh."

Red crouched in front of Numbers and wrapped his thigh. "I don't think the bullet is bouncing around in your leg cause I feel an exit hole."

"Shit!" Numbers gritted his teeth. That fucking hurt. "After you tie this off, get me some meds."

"Where should I go?" Red sat back, waiting for instructions. Wasn't he an eager beaver?

"I don't give a fuck where you go, but get me antibiotics, pain meds, cash, and some fucking alcohol."

"You want a drink?" Red looked confused.

"Yes, asshole, this fucking hurts. Then I want to pour it on my fucking bullet hole to disinfect it. Now go and be careful." Numbers pushed him and laid back against the wall. He heard Red scrambling out of their hiding spot. He didn't know where Red was going to find all the items he asked for and he didn't give a shit as long as they showed up quick. *Motherfucker!* He wanted that drink, now. Feeling himself getting drowsy from the loss of blood, he closed his eyes and prayed the police didn't find him.

Because if they found him, there was absolutely nothing he could do.

Chapter 37

Their Safety is My First Priority

Barrett

Even though Barrett wanted Angel beside him, he knew Steele needed her more, so he sent her to sit with Steele in the backseat for the drive home. She'd thanked Barrett for understanding and kissed his cheek before she got in the back. Barrett smiled, knowing he'd made the right decision until he looked in the truck and saw Steele glaring at him—his smile turned upside down and he sighed. How was he going to get Steele to accept him in their lives?

From the front seat, Barrett could hear them whispering to each other. Occasionally, he heard his name or the resort's name, but he stayed quiet, trying not to intrude on their conversation. When they arrived, Barrett escorted them through the lobby to the elevators. He saw his mom behind the lobby desk, but shook his head and waved her off. This wasn't the time to question any of them. She nodded her understanding and stayed behind the desk, helping a guest. He knew she would text him as soon as she finished with that guest.

He also saw a couple of officers and again nodded, but kept walking. One of the officers followed them and stood behind them until they entered the only elevator that went to their floor. As the doors closed, he nodded at Barrett and stood guard.

Barrett was grateful they were all aware of what was going on. George must have called them on his drive over. When they got off on their floor, Maggie was waiting for them on the couch of their family floor lobby. She rushed to Angel.

"Are you all right?" Maggie put her palm on Angel's shoulder. "Steele, right?" Maggie put out her other hand for him.

"Why are you here?" Steele probed. "Mom, she doesn't like us." Steele backed up until he ran into Barrett's chest. Bouncing off, he moved around to face all of them.

"Steele." Angel reached for his hands. "I know what this looks like. But the LRs also hurt Maggie. She understands our situation. She's a friend. You can trust her."

Steele looked shocked and pointed at Maggie. "But it's because of us that Numbers fou...found you." Steele stuttered.

"Your mom and I have talked about that. We were all doing what they wanted so they wouldn't hurt us. I don't blame you for anything." Maggie stepped forward, still holding her hand out. "Friends?"

Steele looked at Angel. When she nodded, he shook Maggie's hand. "But why are you here?"

"I'm in hiding from the LRs, too." Maggie pointed to a door across the hall from Barrett's room. "I live there temporarily with Mark and Sky for now."

"Who are Mark and Sky?"

Barrett couldn't blame the kid for wanting to know who all the players were. It was smart of him to ask as many questions as possible about his new living arrangements, especially since he didn't know how long he would be staying.

Maggie released his hand and stepped back, giving Steele some space. "Mark is the security officer at the cultural center. You met him when you came in with your mom that day to see the exhibit. Do you remember him?"

"Yeah," Steele nodded. "Big guy with the dog."

"That's him," Maggie smiled. "He's my boyfriend, and Sky is his dog."

"Hey, buddy." Barrett rested his hand on Steele's shoulder. "Are you hungry?"

Steele shrugged Barrett's hand off his shoulder and stomped away from him. "I'm not your buddy."

"Steele." Angel placed her hand on Barrett's arm. "Barrett's trying to help us. Please show him some respect."

"It's okay," Barrett nodded and stayed in place while Maggie approached Steele.

"No," Angel glared at Barrett and Steele, "it's not okay."

"Steele." Maggie crouched in front of him. "Barrett's a good guy. He's not gonna hurt you or your mom. You can trust him."

Steele swallowed and continued to glare at Barrett.

"Okay," Barrett sighed. "How about you and your mom go in my apartment? I'll go downstairs and grab some snacks and drinks for everyone. Here's," –Barrett took his key card out of his pocket– "my key card so you can get in. I'll be back soon."

"Thank you," Angel kissed his cheek and Barrett nodded. God, all he wanted was to hold on to her and let her know he had their backs. He would die protecting her, but now wasn't the time. Right now, she had to have some time with her son, and he needed to leave before he dropped to his knees, begging them to include him.

He knew Angel and Steele were a package deal, which was fine with him. But how was he going to bond with a young man that didn't want anything to do with him? Barrett was going to have to find a shared interest. A tall order since Steele didn't want to talk to him.

"I'll go with you." Maggie walked to Barrett and grabbed his wrist.

Barrett didn't leave with Maggie until Angel and Steele were both safe in his room.

As soon as the door shut, Maggie squeezed his wrist and said, "You got it bad, my friend."

"Tell me about it." Barrett rubbed his hand over his jaw. "Got any advice?"

"Always," Maggie beamed at him.

"Of course you do." Barrett rolled his eyes and followed her into the elevator.

*** Angel ***

"Steele, we need to talk." Angel led Steele to the couch. "I know you don't know Barrett, but I wouldn't be safe if it wasn't for him."

"How long have you known him?"

"Since I interrupted the wedding." Angel answered sheepishly. She knew it had only been a couple of weeks.

"That's not long enough. Especially since you weren't with him that entire time."

"You're right." Angel sat down.

"What if he's like Numbers? Has he hit you?" Steele fisted his hands.

"He's nothing like Numbers and No, he hasn't hit me," Angel smiled and opened his hands, pulling him down to sit next to her. "Barrett would never hit me. He's not that kind of man. He's like your dad."

"But my dad was an LR." Steele frowned.

"He was, and I'm sure he did a lot of bad stuff. But the minute you were born, he wanted a better life for all of us. I mean, sure, he stayed with the LRs, but only because he wanted to show them with the garage that they could do good things. His club brothers were like real brothers to him, and he wanted to help them. He thought he could change them, and maybe he could've, if he hadn't been killed. We'll never know." Angel squeezed his hands and raised her eyes to look at him. Trying to read the thoughts behind the pensive look.

"But it was that lady "Maggie" that killed my father. How could you be friends with her?" Steele pulled his hands away from her.

Angel sighed. "Your father was collateral damage from Reaper, killing her parents at their home. She didn't kill your father, her brother did, because he was seeking revenge."

Steele's head snapped up. "What? Why didn't anyone tell me?"

"You were just a little boy when it happened. I was trying to protect you. Not that I did a good job since you've had to grow up fast." Angel brushed his hair from his forehead. "But I promise, from now on, no more secrets. I will tell you anything you want to know. I don't condone what Reaper or El Loco did, but at some point, we need to stop the fighting or get the hell out of the way. Because it won't end well."

"I...I don't know what to say." Steele fell back onto the couch and closed his eyes.

"I know it's a lot to process, but I need you to know that the rivalry between the LRs and Los Lobos hurt Maggie, just like it's hurt us. She lost both her parents."

Steele sat forward and opened his eyes, staring at his mom. "So, Maggie's brother is a member of the Los Lobos MC?"

"Yes." Angel held up her hand. "To answer your next question. No, I haven't met him. I'm not sure how I feel about that right now. I loved your father, and he took him away from me. I don't think I can ever forgive that. But, please, be nice to Maggie because she had nothing to do with any of this revenge nonsense."

"She lost her mom and dad because of Reaper?" Steele urged.

"Yes." Angel noticed that was the first time Steele referred to his grandfather by name.

"Okay," Steele sighed. "I'll try."

"Why don't you go shower?" Angel saw Steele nod. "I'll try to find something for you to wear." Angel stood. "Follow me."

Angel showed him the bedroom and the bathroom. Leaving him to shower, she walked into the living room just as Barrett came back loaded with bags of snacks, drinks, and who knew what else.

"Hey," Barrett set everything on the table and beelined it to her for a hug. "How are you?"

"I'm okay." Angel stood on her tippy toes and whispered against his mouth. "Thank you for today."

"Anytime." Barrett kissed her back. "It was a good day. I got you and you got your son."

Angel felt her cheeks get hot.

"Oh, don't go all shy on me now, Tiger." Barrett smiled and gave her a quick kiss. "Anyway, look at my stash. Sam, our head chef at Rush, our casual dining restaurant, loaded me up with food. Then my mom gave me hygiene stuff for both of you, and Maggie gave me these clothes for Steele."

"Wow," Angel opened every bag he pointed to glancing at his stash, as he called it. "How did Maggie know Steele's size?"

"She guessed. Besides, it's easy to buy sweatpants, t-shirts, and sweatshirts for a teenage boy," Barrett smirked.

"But she's not supposed to leave the resort. When did she have time to buy this stuff?"

"She called her bestie Isa and asked her to shop for her. The two of them are thick as thieves." Barrett pulled everything out of the bags. "You'll meet Isa. She's Thunder's wife."

"I've heard their names when Reaper talked about them. Thunder owns the cultural center, right?"

"Yup. Maggie, Mark, Tori, and Alex work for him."

Angel had heard horrible things about all of them, yet the ones she'd met so far were helping her and her son. She should've known better than to believe anything that came out of Reaper or Numbers' mouths. Barrett's friends and family's generosity and kindness were overwhelming. Other than Angel's mom and Tools, no one had accepted her 'no questions asked' during her entire life. Barrett was lucky to be surrounded by such caring people.

"I'm so sorry my family has cost your friends and family so much pain." Angel grabbed the pack of underwear and a set of pajamas from the clothes pile.

"Hey, hey." Barrett pulled her into his arms. "None of this is your fault and they know that."

Barrett leaned down and kissed her, deeply this time, until they heard Steele's voice screaming for her from the bathroom. Barrett ended the kiss and rested his forehead on hers.

"I need to get these clothes to him." Angel gave him a quick peck on the lips. "Thanks again."

"Of course." Barrett mumbled.

Angel left Barrett by the table sorting the rest of his stash.

Chapter 38

Another Good Man

Angel

Angel stayed with Steele in the bedroom until he fell asleep. She was glad he didn't object to Isa's choice of tighty whities underwear or plaid pajamas. He'd never been picky before, but after having several sexual encounters, he might prefer something else. Ugh...she did not want to think about that.

The only positive aspect of Steele's clubhouse stay was avoiding the uncomfortable conversation about the physical details of sex. Though she still needed to reiterate the importance of using protection. Which seemed strange coming from her since she had him at fifteen, his age right now...ugh. She should've practiced what she would preach to him, except then she might not be looking down at her beautiful boy.

Change of plan. When she talked to Steele about his sexual activity, she would try to steer the conversation towards his deep affection for the other person. She needed to stress the importance of caring about someone before you did the deed. She would make it very clear to Steele that she and Tools were in love when they first slept together. From now on, Steele needed to understand that he would need to treat the girls he wanted to date with respect and not like he probably treated sweet butts at the clubhouse.

Once his breathing evened out, she went looking for Barrett. The television was still on low, but he was lying on the couch asleep. She didn't want to wake him, but she also wanted to curl up with him. He made her feel loved, even though he hadn't said those words to her. His actions showed how much he cared for her. But it was too soon to make such a declaration. For heaven's sake, they'd only known each other a week. How could she feel so strongly about him so fast?

Angel sat on the edge of the couch and stared at him from head to toe. He was such a handsome man. His face was sexy with his chiseled jawline, brown eyes you could sink into when they looked at you, and a lock of hair that always dropped over his forehead in such a sexy way. Her gaze travelled down his eight-pack abs. He'd told her he worked out a lot, but damn, his broad shoulders tapered down to his smaller waist. He'd opened the button on his jeans, so they rode low, and she got a good look at his V-shaped muscular physique.

As her gaze drew lower, she moaned and saw the head of his cock peak out from the waistband of his underwear. Licking her lips, she watched it grow until the head was totally out and slick at the top. She knew from earlier today that he knew what to do with his hard cock. Angel couldn't wait to put it into her mouth and give him pleasure.

"See something you like?" Barrett grumbled. "Cause it definitely likes you."

Angel gave him a wickedly sexy smile.

"You're killing me. Come here." Barrett spread his arms out, inviting her to snuggle with him. But she didn't want to snuggle. She wanted to take control of him and thank him at the same time. Watching his reaction, she crawled between his legs and lowered his zipper.

"Angel," Barrett's breathing was deeper. "Is this a good idea?" He motioned with his head toward his bedroom.

"He's sound asleep, and I know for a fact that when he snores, he's not getting up for a long time." Angel pulled his pants and underwear down to his thighs. Barrett helped her by raising his pelvis so she could continue with her plan.

"Angel," Barrett held her head and brushed her cheeks with his thumbs, "you don't need to do this."

"For the first time in a long time," –Angel licked her lips again– "I want to."

"Go for it, Tiger." Barrett softened his hands on her face. Still gazing into his eyes, she dipped her head and slid his engorged cock into her mouth. His eyes blazed with hunger and his breathing increased. When she took him all the way down her throat, he moaned and closed his eyes. Angel knew he was enjoying it as much as she was.

One of her hands slid down to cup his balls while the other continued to stroke the part of his cock that didn't fit into her mouth. Creating suction, she pulled her mouth up to the tip of his cock and licked the head. He tasted salty and all man. Angel looked down as she licked and sucked all around his dick. His hands left her head and now gripped the couch cushions. Angel grinned because his body didn't lie. She knew she was taking him to the brink of his patience.

Angel glanced up and saw Barrett staring at her mouth as it nibbled on him. His nostrils flared and his panting increased. She had him right where she wanted him. Looking down as she fisted him in a tighter grip, his cock grew even longer and thicker. As come leaked from the head, it pulsed in her hands. His hands were now fisting the couch cushions as she placed her mouth over him, moving her head up and down.

"Fuck!" Barrett groaned. "Angel, your mouth feels so good. Take your clothes off, turn around, and sit on my face."

"Uh, uh," Angel murmured. "This one's for you to enjoy."

"Your enthusiasm shows that you're enjoying this, too...shit," Barrett moaned. "I bet if I touched your pussy, you'd be soaking wet."

"I am." Angel licked his underside on the way up. "He's so hard and beautiful."

"Fuck, Angel, please don't call my cock beautiful." Barrett groaned.

"Sorry," Angel sucked his head. "He's sexy," she said before taking him to the back of her throat.

"Angel, Tiger, baby, fuck, if you don't want me to come in your mouth, pop off."

Angel wanted to swallow every ounce of come he gave her, so she continued until his body stiffened and burst into her mouth. Most of his orgasm rushed down her throat, but some overflowed into her mouth and out the sides. She wiped the sides of her mouth with her tongue and fingers before looking up into his eyes.

"That was so fucking hot," Barrett grumbled and pushed her onto her back. "Your turn."

Kissing her breathless, his hands made quick work of undressing her. His lips left hers and between his hands and mouth, he didn't leave any part of her body untouched.

Barrett sucked on her neck while his hand ran over her sensitive breasts. He tweaked and pulled on her nipple before continuing down to her pussy. She was so ready for him.

"I was right, you're soaked." Barrett glided his lips from her neck down to her breast. "You like sucking my cock?" Latching on, he rolled his tongue around her nipple before sucking as much as he could fit into his mouth.

"Yes," Angel panted. "It was sexy and delicious."

Barrett moaned, releasing her breast. Using his tongue, he licked his way down to her throbbing pussy. "No, Angel. You are the sexy and delicious one."

Oh my word, Angel thought, *how did I find another perfect man?* The things Barrett was doing with his tongue felt so incredibly good. Angel thrust her hips into him, wanting more.

Barrett slipped a couple fingers into her while his lips sucked her clit. *Holy Shit!* Angel's body bucked and writhed in earnest. When she couldn't hold back her orgasm, her mouth opened to scream. Only the first bit of sound came out before the hand that had been playing with her nipple slammed over her mouth. Her body trembled with aftershocks as Barrett slid up her body and replaced the hand covering her mouth with his mouth.

"I want to fuck you so bad right now," Barrett moaned against her lips.

"We can wait if you're not ready." Angel knew it took men several minutes to harden after an orgasm.

Barrett chuckled and pulled her hand down to his lengthened, stiff cock.

"Nevermind, I guess you are ready."

"Unfortunately, my condoms are in the bedroom."

Angel gazed at him while she continued to stroke him slowly. "I haven't been with anyone willingly since Tools." Her eyes watered. "Numbers wore a condom, and I was on the pill. But after he left me for dead, I haven't had them to take them." She hated what Numbers did to her. He made her feel dirty.

Unlike Barrett, who made her feel special. She regretted not having her birth control pills because she would love to feel Barrett without a condom. His bare skin inside hers would feel wonderful. The only other man to be inside her bare was Tools.

"Angel, where did you go?" Barrett brushed the hair off her face and stroked her cheek. "None of that was your fault. When you're with me, it's only the two of us in this bed," Barrett smirked, "or couch. Besides, I'm a big boy. I can handle blue balls."

Angel smiled, knowing he was trying to cheer her up. "Lucky for you, my hand can help you out."

"Shit," Barrett dropped his head onto her shoulder while her hand got him off. "You're so fucking perfect."

Barrett grabbed his shirt off the floor and wiped them both before snuggling on the couch under the blanket.

Angel knew she should get up and go back into the bedroom with Steele, but it felt wonderful being the little spoon to his big one. A sense of peace that she hadn't felt since Tools death washed over her. She would always love Tools, but maybe it was time to make room in her heart for Barrett.

Chapter 39

Where the Fuck is He?

Numbers

Numbers fell asleep during the night and into the day. It was quiet on the docks, probably because it was Sunday. Red had been gone a long time. Numbers wasn't sure if he'd ever see him again. His body was trembling and he was freezing, which meant he had a fever. *Fuck!* He tried to stand, but his leg wouldn't hold his weight, and he dropped back down.

Numbers curled up into a fetal position and continued to doze on and off until he heard Red say, "Numbers, drink this." He felt a hand rolling him over.

"What the fuck is that? And where the fuck have you been?" Numbers mumbled.

"Sorry." Red held a bottle of water and pills in the palm of his hand. "It took me longer than I thought to sneak pills out of the clinic without being seen."

"We need to get out of here by tonight." Numbers swallowed the pills and guzzled some water. "What time is it?"

"It's almost five."

"AM or PM?" Numbers had totally lost track of time.

"PM."

"Is anyone out there snooping around? Can we leave now?" Numbers was eager to get the hell out of dodge before more cops came snooping around. Tomorrow was Monday, and the docks would be packed with workers.

"There's nobody around. You don't have to walk far because I stole a car and parked it near us."

"Fuck! You idiot!" Numbers scooted up into a sitting position, leaning against the wall. "Help me up. We gotta get the fuck out of here before someone calls the cops to report their stolen car."

"Boss, it's my cousin's car. I left him passed out from a drug induced haze provided by yours truly." Red pointed to himself. "He won't notice it's missing until he wakes up." Numbers put his arm around Red's shoulder and used the wall behind him to help him stand. Pain shot up his leg when he put weight on it. He would have to limp to the car.

"Besides," Red continued, "he always forgets where he parks it. He won't notice it's missing until sometime tomorrow. We'll be long gone by then. The fucker won't call the cops or I'll anonymously turn him in for dealing narcotics."

"Okay. Did you get me some alcohol?" Numbers closed his eyes, bracing himself for the painful trek to the car.

"Yeah, it's in the car."

Numbers was going to take a swig, but he'd have to wait until he got to the car. "Let's do this. Check and make sure no one's around. I'll wait here."

"I didn't see anyone when I got here, but I'll check again and come back for you."

Numbers leaned against the wall, keeping the weight off his leg. He hoped the pills Red gave him would help his fever and pain. He needed to get somewhere and clean his leg before infection set in, if it hadn't already.

"All clear boss." Red went to Numbers and helped him off the wall.

"How far is the car?" Numbers limped beside Red, hoping it was the white, non-descript, four-door sedan just a few steps away.

"That white one." Red pointed to the one Numbers was hoping he was talking about.

"Thank fuck," Numbers groaned and sat in the front passenger seat with Red's help. He saw a paper bag in the back seat. "Is that my shit?" he asked Red when he got in the car.

"Yeah." Red reached over and placed it on his lap before asking, "Where to?"

"Head North, I'll tell you when to stop." Numbers grabbed the bottle of whiskey, took a swig, and then poured some on his wound. "Fuck me!" He screamed as pain shot up his body. He knew it was going to hurt, but shit, that fuckin' burned.

"I got us some money, too."

"Let me guess, your cousin?" Numbers glared at Red with a raised eyebrow.

"Well, yeah. He had some lying around."

"Did you just fucking steal money and a car from a drug dealer? Is someone going to come after us?" Numbers was livid. That asshole had now put a bounty on their heads and he didn't know how many brothers were around to help them out of the mess Red had just created.

"I had to." Red's fingers were tapping incessantly on the steering wheel. "How else was I going to get us enough cash to get out of town?"

"Fuck! Did you go by the clubhouse? Were any of our brothers there?" Numbers had to know if they were alone or could call on anyone for help.

"Only the sweet butts and Sandy were there. The cops had come by with a warrant but left by the time I got there. Sandy said no one had come back from the night before. She wasn't in good shape, boss. The cops told her Brick was dead."

"Fuck! I was hoping he was hurt and not dead. Let's hope some of our brothers are alive and hiding, because the ones in the hospital are going to be sent to jail as soon as they recover. Reaper is going to lose his shit, if he hasn't already, when he sees how many of our brothers are joining him in jail. Great, just fucking great." Numbers sighed and laid his head back on the headrest. "I'm gonna take a nap. Keep driving north until I wake up. Then I'll call around and see who I can reach."

"Boss, if they're arrested, then the cops have their phones."

"Motherfucker. You're right." Numbers must be getting tired and not thinking straight because a fucking prospect had just corrected him—and he was right. He wouldn't be admitting that to Red. Numbers hated any signs of weakness even within himself. He only bowed down to Reaper because he was his president. *Fuck!* Reaper was going to be pissed as shit. "Just drive North."

Chapter 40

Fuck Me

Barrett

B arrett woke up with a sense of being watched–because he was. Steele was standing in front of him and Angel with his arms crossed, glaring angrily at him. If looks could kill–he'd be dead.

"Good morning." Barrett mumbled and pulled the covers tighter around Angel. It was awkward enough having Steele catch him with his mom, let alone if any part of her beautiful naked body was showing. Barrett squeezed Angel and kissed her temple. "Angel, wake up," he murmured against her skin. "We fell asleep on the couch and Steele is in front of us." Barrett felt her body stiffen before he saw her eyes blink open.

"Hey, Steele," Angel whispered.

"Hey, mom," Steele glared at her. "I'm hungry."

"How about you turn around and let your mom and I go into the bedroom to get dressed? Then I'll make us all breakfast."

"How about you stop fucking around with my mom and leave us the hell alone?"

"Steele!" Angel shouted and grabbed the covers before she sat up.

Barrett laid a hand on her shoulder. "It's okay. He's been through a lot and is allowed to be angry."

"Don't fucking tell me how to feel, motherfucker!" Steele blurted.

"Hey!" Barrett pointed at him. "Watch your mouth. Show your mom some respect."

"I will when you will." Steele smirked at him.

"Okay, that's enough. You both need to go to your corners." Angel stood, pulling the blanket with her as she grabbed Steele's arm and pulled him into the bedroom.

"Fuck." Barrett groaned. He'd slept like a baby only to face a furious teenage boy who wanted to kill him. Deep down, he couldn't blame Steele. He would've hated catching his mom in a compromising position even if it was with his father. Barrett was also very protective of his mom, so he understood Steele's dilemma. He would do the only thing he could do—get dressed and make them breakfast.

*** Steele ***

"What the fuck, mom?" Steele whirled on Angel as soon as they entered the bedroom, and she slammed the door.

"Don't you dare talk to me like that." Angel pointed to the bed. "Sit."

Steele could tell his mom was royally pissed at him. He didn't know why he was talking to her like that, but the words just kept flying out of his mouth. He felt so much anger inside and he didn't know what to do with it. Steele stomped over to the bed and sat facing her.

"I know you have been through a lot and I'm so sorry, but Barrett has done nothing to you. I need you to give him a chance. He was on that couch with me because I wanted to stay with him. He was not forcing me."

"What about dad?" Steele crossed his arms and stared at the floor.

"What about your dad?" Angel sat next to him. "I loved him with all my heart, but he's in heaven. If I could bring him back, I would. We had a wonderful life planned with you and maybe other children, but the LRs ruined that with their anger and vengeance. This," Angel used her finger to turn his jaw toward her, "is what's important. You and me. I love you, Steele. Your father loved us, and he wouldn't want either of us living half a life. We can talk about him and think about the fun times we had any time you want. We had so many wonderful years together and you brought us so much joy from the moment you entered this world. But I can't close myself off from Barrett when I have strong feelings for him."

Steele swallowed. He wasn't sure he was ready to see his mom with another man even though he'd seen her with Numbers. But that was different. He had to accept that because that's what the MC had taught him to do. He was so fucked up. Steele dropped his head into his hands, frustrated with all the feelings of love, hate, and emptiness floating inside of him.

"Steele, I know this is a lot to take in." Steele felt his mom's hand on his shoulder. "I'm just asking you to give Barrett a chance and let's take it one day at a time. If at any time Barrett makes you feel uncomfortable, we'll leave, and I won't see him again."

Steele raised his head and stared at his mom. *Was that all he had to do?* Prove to her they didn't need Barrett and they could leave. It seemed like such an easy solution. "Okay, mom. I don't like him. Let's go."

"Give him a chance." Angel shoulder bumped him. "Please?"

"Okay. I'll try to like him." Steele grumbled.

"That's all I ask." Angel pulled him into a tight embrace.

Knock, knock.

"Come in," Angel said and stood.

Barrett opened the door and peeked in. "I made breakfast. Why don't you guys come eat while it's hot?"

"Sure, let me get dressed and we'll be right out."

Barrett nodded and shut the door. Angel grabbed some clothes and went into the bathroom. Steele waited for his mom. The last thing he wanted was to make small talk with Barrett.

After his mom came out of the bathroom dressed, Steele reluctantly followed her to the dining room table. Barrett must be kissing ass because there were eggs, bacon, and a stack of pancakes on the table. It smelled delicious and Steele's stomach growled.

"What can I get you guys to drink?" Barrett asked when they sat down.

"Coffee." Angel smiled at him.

"Do you have juice?" Steele asked as he piled food on his plate.

"Yeah." Barrett walked into the kitchen and opened his fridge. "I have orange juice. Is that okay?"

"Sure." Steele answered.

"Why are there only two plates?" Angel asked Barrett when he placed a heaping glass of orange juice in front of Steele. "Are you not eating with us? There's plenty."

"Uh, no." Barrett shook his head. "I'm gonna work a double and give you guys some time alone."

Angel's hand shot out and grabbed his wrist. "You don't have to."

Barrett looked at Steele, who was watching their interaction intently.

"I think I do." Barrett grinned at Angel. "Besides, I've been off for a few days, and I need to give some of the other security officers who helped me out a day off. You guys enjoy your breakfast. I'm gonna shower and go."

"Wait." Angel bolted out of her seat and grabbed Barrett's hand before he reached his bedroom. Steele noticed his mom looked agitated. "You're gonna leave us?"

Barrett turned and looked at them both. "You're safe here."

Angel kept shaking her head. "Please don't leave us."

What the hell? What was I chopped liver? I could protect my mom. Steele swallowed and watched Barrett embrace his mom. *Why couldn't he keep his hands off her?*

"Okay." Barrett rubbed her back. "How about I work from the security office up here during the day, but at night I have to make my rounds on the casino floor?"

Angel nodded, pulled out of his embrace, and kissed him. Steele wanted to puke. He turned away and continued to eat his breakfast, wondering what Barrett meant by 'security office up here'.

Chapter 41

Step One

Barrett

After his shower, Barrett cleaned up all the dishes from breakfast and went to work in the security office connected to his room. He wanted to give them space after being caught naked by her son, but after Angel's mini panic attack, he compromised and stayed upstairs.

Holt and Frey would be back from their honeymoon in five days, and he couldn't wait to talk to them about Angel and Steele. They were his sounding board, and he needed their advice. Except for the time a few months ago when they were all arguing, he always went to one or the other whenever he wanted to talk something out. So much had happened in the past week after their wedding that they didn't know about.

"What is this place?" Steele's voice jolted him from his thoughts.

Barrett spun his chair to face him. "Hey, Steele. This is one of two security monitoring rooms." Barrett watched Steele walk around the room, looking at all the monitors. They had an impressive setup. All the monitors displayed every camera angle within the resort and casino.

Osceola had this room installed when Holt and Barrett were teens because they would sneak into the casino, checking for anyone cheating. Barrett remembered the last straw that broke the camel's back.

Barrett, Holt, and Frey snuck into the casino, hiding from security behind the slot machines. They had repeatedly been told not to go into the casino, because it could be dangerous, especially when someone was losing or cheating, but they never listened and would sneak in several times a week.

The security officers would catch them and either send them out or call Osceola, who kept having 'the talk' with them about stranger danger. Osceola promised them when they turned eighteen, they could go in. But the three musketeers, what they called themselves, never listened. Holt and Barrett liked to walk around and catch anyone cheating while Frey would hang out by the blackjack table to watch the game. She was an expert at catching cheaters, but mainly she watched the dealer and the customer's reactions to their cards.

That crazy night, as they were making their way around the slot machines, a man reached out and grabbed Frey, pulling her onto his lap. Holt and Barrett went ballistic, trying to pull her away from him, but the man was much taller and stronger than them. Needless to say, they caused enough of a commotion that the security officers ran to them and led the man away in zip ties. Osceola banned them from entering the casino again and promised to build a monitoring room on the family floor so they could watch everyone inside the casino from the safety of their floor.

"Do all these monitors show everything?"

"Sure do." Barrett leaned over and pulled a chair out for him. "Sit here. I'll show you."

Steele immediately sat, his eyes darting from monitor to monitor.

Barrett pointed to each monitor as he spoke. "This one cycles through our lobby and restaurants. This one does the different floors in the resort and the pool area. The two in front of me go through the first and second floor of the casino, and this one to my right focuses on the perimeter of the casino and our new conference center slash wedding venue."

"How can you watch all of these at the same time?"

Barrett chuckled, "I don't. I mainly focus on the casino, although lately I've also been watching the perimeter. We have other security personnel that sit in our other monitoring room, bigger than this one, downstairs behind the lobby and also watch for any suspicious activity."

"Hey man, who are you telling all our secrets to?" Barrett heard Travis' voice over the earpiece.

He'd forgotten to mute it when Steele came in. Barrett grabbed the headphones that were connected to a console so Steele could hear Travis.

"Give me a sec, Trav."

"Who are you talking to?" Steele's forehead scrunched in confusion.

"Put these on." Barrett handed Steele the headphones. "My earpiece," Barrett tapped his ear, "allows me to communicate with our security team. You can hear them through these headphones. I was talking to Travis. He's ex-military and working the casino floor right now."

Steele put on the headphones and said, "Hello?"

"Travis, this is Steele, Angel's son. Steele, this is one of our security officers and a good friend, Travis."

"Hey there, Steele." Travis immediately responded. "You helping Barrett. I mean, he's not as good as me and could use all the help you can give him."

Barrett smiled when Steele chuckled and answered, "Hi, Mr. Travis."

Barrett pointed to one screen monitoring the inside of the casino. "That's Travis."

Steele nodded, and Travis did a two-finger wave into the camera.

"I'm just Travis, not Mr. Travis. That just makes me sound old."

"You are old," Barrett bantered back.

"Shit, son, just cause I'm older than you doesn't mean I'm old. I'm not even forty yet." Travis walked away from that camera, but they spotted him on another a few seconds later. "Sorry for cussing."

"I've been around the LRs for a long time. I can handle cussing." Steele mumbled as he watched the monitors. "What are we looking for?"

Barrett grinned. "We are looking for anyone who is trying to steal either from the dealers or other customers. We are also looking for anyone agitated by losing who may want to retaliate against a staff member or another customer. They need to be escorted out immediately."

"What happens if they begin a fight or have guns?"

"Since guns aren't permitted on our premises, anyone with a gun is breaking our rules, and we'll confiscate them. Every officer carries a gun and a taser, and while we are trained to use them, we always try talking things through first. We can't arrest them, but we can restrain them with zip ties until the police get here. Do you remember the deputy who walked us to our vehicle at the docks?" Steele nodded in agreement. "That's Deputy George Smith. He and his partner, Deputy Sean O'Reilly, are two of the deputies assigned to this area who respond to our calls.

"Hey," Steele pointed at a monitor. "That guy just stole a couple of chips from the lady next to him."

"Good eye," Barrett saw it at the same time Steele said it. "Travis, table five."

"Copy that," Travis whispered.

Barrett kept his eye on the man so he could provide Travis with a detailed description and inform him about the amount that was stolen. "Black button down, black dress pants, brown hair, medium build, sitting next to a blonde lady with a tight blue dress." Barrett continued until he saw Travis approach the man.

"Check his pockets. He took two red chips off the blonde. She's clueless."

"Sir, please collect your items and come with me." Travis grabbed his arm, assisting him off his seat.

"Why, who are you?" the man asked.

Travis was standing so close to him; Barrett and Steele could hear the entire conversation.

"Hi, I'm Travis, a security officer at this casino. Please, come with me." Travis escorted him to a private room between the casino and the resort, with a door to the outside parking lot.

Barrett pointed to the room Travis, and the man were in. "That's one of our holding rooms until the police arrive. When my dad and our tribal council built this place, they didn't want the police going into the casino and disrupting or scaring our other guests. So, whenever we have to question someone, we take them to one of the holding rooms."

Barrett tapped his earpiece to mute him and hit the mute button on the console to mute Steele. "We're now muted so we don't bother Travis, so you can speak freely. No one can hear us. Good job, by the way, that was a good catch seeing that man pocket the chips."

"Thanks," Steele smiled at him. "Watching all this is sooo cool. But what did you mean by a tribal council?"

"My family and I are part of the Seminoles of Florida Tribe. The tribe receives most of the money we earn from running the resort and casino."

"Wow. I've never met anyone that was an Indian."

Barrett grinned. "We like to be called either Native Americans or American Indian."

"Oops, sorry." Steele winced.

"Nothing to be sorry about. You wouldn't understand that without exposure to our culture."

"Yeah, but I kinda remember Maggie telling me about that when I got the tour of the cultural center." Steele looked down, using his toes to swing his chair.

"Probably, but on that day, you were on a fact-finding mission." Barrett nudged his foot. "Not really listening to her giving you a history lesson."

"That's true." Steele suddenly sat up. "Hey, you think you can take me there and teach me?"

"I would love to. We'll talk to your mom and make a day of it."

It was the first smile Steele had sent his way, and he had to admit it felt pretty fucking awesome. Just as he was getting ready to explain what else to look for, the door swung open, and Angel burst in soaking wet with a towel wrapped around her.

"Oh my God, Steele!" She ran to him and dropped to her knees, hugging his waist. "I didn't know where you were. I was so worried."

Barrett watched Steele's eyes widen while his mom clung tightly to him and cried. The boy looked like he didn't know what to do, but finally awkwardly pat her back.

"Hey, Angel." Barrett rolled his chair to her and pulled her off Steele. She was so distraught the knot holding her towel together was unravelling. Barrett quickly grabbed it and pulled her onto his lap, holding her tightly against his chest. "Shh," he whispered into her wet hair as he ran his hands down her back, attempting to calm her down.

"I'm sorry," Angel wiped her face. "I didn't see him, and I panicked."

"It's okay." Barrett brushed her hair off her face. "He's here with me. We were working. He's helping me find cheaters, right Steele?"

Angel grabbed her towel and jumped off his lap. She turned her head just in time to see Steele nod.

"Oh, okay, sorry." Angel walked backward, scurrying to the door. "I didn't mean to interrupt."

"You're not interrupting anything." Barrett frowned.

"I'll go put some clothes on." Angel whirled and hurried out the door.

Barrett didn't understand her about face and the fear he saw briefly on her face before she ran out. *What the hell was that about?*

"Steele, stay here and watch for any more cheaters. If you want to talk to Travis or anyone else on the security team, push this button to unmute yourself. I'm gonna go talk to your mom." Barrett stood. "I'll be right back."

Steele's mouth dropped. "You trust me to sit here." Sitting up straight with his chest puffed out, he asked, "What if I call the LRs and tell them all about your setup?"

"Are you?" Barrett raised his eyebrow at him.

"No," Steele deflated. "I couldn't get away from them fast enough after they made me hurt my mom."

"I'm sorry about that. I would've stopped it if I could."

"Thanks," Steele nodded. "So, I can stay here. You believe me?"

"Yeah," Barrett patted his shoulder. "I do. Give us a few minutes, okay?"

"Sure."

Chapter 42

All Shook Up

Angel

Angel was lying on the bed crying when she felt Barrett pull the towel out from under her and dry her.

"What are you doing?" Angel said between cries.

"Drying you and tucking you in." Barrett rolled her over, got her under the sheets, and climbed in behind her, holding her tightly against his chest. Angel loved when he was the big spoon.

"But my hair's all wet and I'm soaking your pillow," Angel cried harder.

Barrett chuckled, "Angel," Barrett brushed her hair back and kissed her cheek, "I don't give a shit about my pillow. I just want to make sure you're okay." Barrett held her until she stopped trembling. Then he rolled her over to face him. While keeping her in his arms, he cupped her jaw, lifting her face to his and kissed the tip of her nose. "You want to tell me what happened in there?" He whispered.

Angel raised her eyes to his and sighed. "When I didn't see him, I was afraid they found him and took him. I know you said we were safe here, but for that moment, I lost it."

"Angel, you are safe here." Barrett ran his hand behind her neck and pulled her into his chest. "My security team and I are watching those cameras and walking the perimeter constantly. We won't let anything happen to you while you're here. What about when I said we were working, and you ran out almost losing your towel?" Barrett chuckled.

"Stop laughing at me," Angel smacked his chest. "It's not funny. I was scared."

Barrett grasped her waist and scooted her up, so her face was on the pillow next to his. "You're right, there's nothing funny about seeing your beautiful body naked, but what I really want to know is why were you afraid?"

"Because growing up whenever I was at the clubhouse and I did something Reaper didn't like, he would hit me without warning. When I saw you teaching

Steele about the monitors, I thought you were going to hit me for interrupting you guys and creating a spectacle of myself."

"Oh, my sweet, beautiful, Angel," Barrett sighed and held her face while he placed a loving kiss on her lips. "I will never hit you. I love you."

Angel felt Barrett stiffen. Did he not mean what he said? She needed to know because she knew she loved him, but was afraid of taking that leap until Steele was comfortable around Barrett. If not for that, she would've already told him she loved him. She knew she was being a coward, but giving your love to someone was like giving a part of yourself to them. She needed to be sure he would guard that part of her and Steele would accept Barrett.

"Are you okay?" Angel stared at him. "Do you mean that? You have a faraway look on your face, and I can't tell if you are happy or sad that you just told me you loved me."

Barrett smiled, "I'm good. And for the record. I meant it. I know it's soon; we haven't known each other that long, and I was a man whore before you. But now all I think about is you. You're the only person I want to be with. I know in my heart I love you."

"A man whore, huh?" Angel grinned. "How did I not know about this?"

Barrett laughed, "that's all you heard from my heartfelt speech?"

"Well, you caught me by surprise. I mean, you are hot as hell, and I assumed you weren't celibate since you are excellent in bed. I just didn't know you were that active."

"So, you think I'm hot as hell and excellent in bed?"

"You know you're good in bed." Angel loved this teasing side of him. "How many women have you been with twenty, fifty, a hundred?"

"I do not want to talk about this while I have you naked in my arms."

"Why not?" Angel pouted. She really wanted to know.

"Uh, because it doesn't matter." Barrett rolled on top of her. "You are it for me."

"I am?" Angel murmured.

"Mmmhmm," Barrett kissed her neck and licked his way down to her breast.

"As good as that feels," Angel moaned. "We can't do this right now."

Barrett released her breast with one final swipe of his tongue to her nipple. "I know, but I needed a taste. Lavender is becoming my new favorite scent."

"You are becoming my new favorite scent," Angel moaned.

Barrett growled, "Fuck! I want you so bad right now. Where can we send Steele?"

Angel laughed and shoved him away. "Stop, you're driving me crazy."

"Okay." Barrett kissed her lips once more and said, "You are so fucking beautiful when you laugh. I'm gonna go check on Steele." Barrett got out of bed and pointed at her. "Get dressed, my little temptress." With a wicked grin, he held his hand out to help her up.

"How is he doing in there?" Angel took his hand and stood before him. "Does he like it?"

"He's taking to it like a duck to water. Watching him brings back memories of Holt and I when we were young. He's a quick learner. He already caught someone stealing."

"Really?" Angel didn't realize Steele was that observant. All this time she'd hoped he didn't catch on to what was happening within the MC. Clearly, she had just been deluding herself and he had been holding everything in.

"Yep, he's a chip off the old block, just like his mom," Barrett kissed her.

"Thank you for helping him." Angel hugged him.

"Of course." Barrett groaned and cupped her ass. Angel wasn't sure if he was a leg, breast or ass guy because he was always copping a feel wherever and whenever he could get one which made her smile. She loved their intimacy.

"Get dressed before I toss you on that bed and fuck you–hard." Barrett growled.

"Okay." Angel stepped out of his embrace. "But just for the record, if Steele wasn't in the other room, I'd let you throw me on the bed and fuck me–hard."

"Woman," Barrett placed his hands on his hips and dropped his head in defeat. "You're fucking killing me."

Angel laughed and walked into the bathroom.

*** Barrett ***

Barrett waited until she closed the door to the bathroom before he adjusted himself. He would've given anything to sink his cock into her and stay there forever, but he had to think about Steele. Right now, it was important to build trust with him and getting caught fucking his mom was not the way to do it.

He strolled into his closet and leaned against his shoe rack, taking a few deep breaths and thinking about what to teach Steele first. Turning on his earpiece and listening to the banter between Steele and the guys helped calm his throbbing cock. Steele was quick with the responses. If he didn't know better, he would've thought Steele was older.

Chapter 43

Friends Arise from Tragedy

Angel

After her shower, Angel sat on the couch channel surfing. Barrett and Steele had come out for lunch and then gone back into the security room. Wanting to be sure everything was fine, she looked into the room multiple times that day. Barrett's kindness to her son meant a lot to her, especially following Steele's earlier bad behavior. She never imagined they'd bond over security cameras, especially so quickly. Angel was happy they were getting along, but she wished they were with her on the couch. She wanted some relaxing family time.

Wait, had she just thought about family time? They'd only known Barrett a short time, and she already considered him a part of her family. They were moving so fast, but she hadn't felt this loved and safe in a long time. She knew she would have to go to her house and get her computer and work files, but for now, she would enjoy the quiet and comfort of Barrett's couch.

When she got her law degree, she became a defense attorney because Tools asked her to help his brothers. She hated it, but did it for her husband. She'd become very good at finding loopholes and getting criminals off. Angel would come home upset whenever she defended someone who confessed their guilty to her, but she still had to defend them. She would always pray that the prosecutor was better than her or that the jury would convict.

It sucked when the wrong person was found innocent, but Tools always helped her cope. On the flip side of her job, she loved when she helped an innocent man or woman go free. After Tools died, she didn't want to be a defense attorney anymore. She thought back to the day she told Reaper about that.

"Are you fucking stupid?" Reaper stood so fast from her kitchen table; the chair toppled over.

Steele had just left after finishing his dinner to go to his room to do his homework.

"Lower your voice," Angel hissed. "And no, I'm not stupid. I'm tired of representing murderers and thieves." Angel got up and began clearing the table. Stacking the dishes on top of each other to carry them into the sink. She had thought about this conversation so many times after Tools died and was proud of herself for finally facing her father and standing up for herself. What she hadn't planned on was the slap that came out of nowhere and caused her to drop her favorite glass dishes she had picked out with Tools.

Angel dropped to her knees and picked up the pieces, wishing she could glue them together, but knowing it was yet another memory about Tools that was also shattered. Steele must've heard the loud crash because he came out running.

"Mom, are you okay?"

"Don't come in!" She hadn't wanted him to step on the glass shards and cut himself. But more importantly, she didn't want him to see the painful, reddening handprint on her cheek. "I dropped some plates. Everything is fine."

"She's fine." Reaper yelled at him. "Go back to your room."

Reaper had hit Angel before, but not since she married Tools. His back-handed slap had surprised her, but she didn't want her son to see her crying. *Why she tried to protect her father, she never knew.* Maybe if Steele had seen the type of man he was back then, he wouldn't have idolized him. But she didn't. Instead, she let her hair fall in her face and wiped her tears before she looked up at Steele with a fake smile on her face.

"I'm so clumsy, I tripped and dropped all the dishes. It's okay. Go finish your homework. I'll be in after your grandfather leaves to tuck you in."

"Okay." Steele hesitated, but glanced at Reaper and ran out of the room.

Reaper then turned to her. "The club paid for your fucking school and set up your practice. You fucking owe us."

That night had been the beginning of future beatings from Reaper to keep her in line. He was right. The LRs had paid for everything with the condition that she would represent them whenever any of them got in trouble—which she did for all these years. She believed she had repaid her debt many times over, as the LRs' illegal activities constantly landed them in trouble.

Her end game was always to save enough money to run away with Steele. She planned to work for the prosecutor's office once she found some place where Reaper couldn't find them. If that place even existed. So, for the past few years, she represented the LRs, saved her money, and followed all of Reapers' plans and rules like a lamb led to slaughter. He was so pleased with her that the beatings stopped.

Her dreams of being on the prosecution's side were put on hold until he was arrested. She'd thought that was her chance to get out from under the club, so she refused to be his lawyer. Naively, she'd thought she was free from Reaper and his club, but she had been mistaken. Hindsight is an incredible thing. She should've run away with Steele right after Tools died. She was so stupid in letting Reaper help her. Had she known he didn't give a shit about her and just wanted to groom Steele to become a future president, she would've made different choices. Now she had to play the cards she was dealt from her crappy choices.

The time had come to make another decision. It was time to reach out to the prosecutor's office and see if she could get a job with them. They'd be happy to hear from her because she would be a key witness for them against Reaper, but would they hire her after his case went to trial–or before?

She knew prosecutors earned less than defense attorneys because the private sector could sometimes offer higher pay than the government, but she wanted to advocate for victims and play a larger role in upholding the law. She needed to have some peace of mind. Being a lawyer was a tough job and if the prosecutor's side was too much, she would consider another law career path.

Knock, knock.

Angel wasn't expecting anyone, and she didn't want to interrupt Barrett, so she walked to the door and peeked through the peephole. Maggie was standing on the other side, holding two ice cream sundaes.

Angel loved ice cream. She swung the door open and smiled at Maggie. "Hi."

"Hey, Mark told me Steele was helping Barrett in the security office, and they needed someone on the casino floor until Barrett could get down there later tonight. So, he went down there to help and I figured you might be going as stir crazy as me. So, I went into the restaurant and made these for us."

"You read my mind." Angel stepped back and opened the door, letting Maggie in. "Are you going to get in trouble for taking the ice cream?"

"Nah, they have several flavors down there. Besides, Sam helped me make them." Maggie stepped inside and walked to the couch. "Grab some spoons."

"What flavor did you get?" Angel saw Maggie set the sundaes on the cocktail table and grab the remote.

"Cookies and cream and mint chocolate chip."

Angel grabbed two spoons, sticking one in each sundae before she sat on the couch next to Maggie. "Which is your favorite?" Angel was eyeing the yummy desserts. They both had hot fudge dripping down the sides of the ice cream, topped with crushed nuts, whipped cream, and a cherry.

"I like them both, so you pick one."

"Okay," Angel sighed. "Decisions, decisions...I'll take the cookies and cream."

Maggie smiled and grabbed the other one.

"What do you want to watch? I just had the TV on for background noise. I wasn't paying attention to that show." Angel took a bite and was in heaven. The ice cream was creamy, and the toppings were delicious.

"What do you like?" Maggie ate her cherry first.

"Anything you want. I don't watch a lot of television." Angel dipped her spoon for another bite. "I'm always working from home, but all my files are at my house."

"Hmm, how about something with a little less adventure?" Maggie wiggled her eyebrows. "I think we've both had enough of that to last us a lifetime."

"Agreed." Angel laughed and Maggie found a home improvement show.

"Let's watch this. They're just one-hour episodes, so if we get bored, we can always change the channel." Maggie pointed her spoon at Angel. "But I warn you, I gotta watch it to the end. My favorite part is the reveal."

"Deal." Angel and Maggie clinked spoons, then sat back to watch the show and eat their ice cream.

They commented on what they liked and didn't like, as if they were builders and designers. After about the fourth show, Maggie received a text and checked her phone.

"Well, it's time for me to head back to my room. Mark is done and is on his way up." Maggie grabbed her empty bowl from the cocktail table and stood.

Angel followed suit. "Thank you for this, Maggie. I really appreciate it."

"Of course, we'll do it again." Maggie gave Angel a quick hug.

"Hey, Mags," Barrett said from behind Angel. "Mark's on his way up."

"Yeah, he texted me."

"Mom, were you eating ice cream?" Steele walked to Angel and peered into her bowl. "Did you bring me some?"

"Uh, no." Angel winced. Barrett crossed his arms and quirked his eyebrow at her.

Well, they caught her red-handed, and now she had to find a way to get ice cream for Steele.

Maggie was laughing at her and texting something. "I just texted Mark to pick up an ice cream sundae for Steele and bring it on his way up. What flavor do you like, Steele?"

"What did you get, mom?"

"I got cookies and cream with hot fudge, crushed nuts, whipped cream, and a cherry." Angel beamed at them.

"That sounds great." Steele looked pleadingly at Maggie. "Can I get one of those?"

"Sure," Maggie smiled and typed it quickly. "He said he's on it. Barrett, do you want one?"

"No," Barrett chuckled. "I gotta get dressed and go downstairs. I'll eat something later." Barrett turned and headed back into the bedroom.

"I'll be right back." Angel put her bowl down and hurried after Barrett. She wanted to know when he would be done. He hadn't worked yet while they were together, and she had no clue about his schedule.

Barrett was already in the closet, changing into his dress pants. "Hey."

"Hey," Barrett pulled off his t-shirt and grabbed a white shirt off a hanger. "Everything okay?"

Angel leaned against the frame of the doorway. "Yeah, I just didn't know when you would be done. Sorry, I don't mean to pry." Angel looked away when he unzipped his pants to tuck in his buttoned shirt. She didn't want to bother him with incessant questions. "Should I wait up for you?" Suddenly, her socked foot looked very interesting. How could she be embarrassed watching him get dressed when she had seen him undress twice already? Then his feet appeared in front of hers and he lifted her face up to look at her.

"Angel, you are not prying. I usually work a nine-hour shift from five to somewhere between one or two in the morning. Please don't wait up for me. It'll be late." Barrett gave her a quick kiss.

"Do you want me to bring you dinner?"

"No," Barrett grinned. "As sweet as that sounds, I don't have a set time when I eat. I try to cover everyone else's dinner breaks."

"But you will eat something?" Angel was worried about him. He needed to eat and stay healthy.

"Yeah," Barrett hugged her. "I'll eat something. Thank you for worrying about me." Barrett released her and grabbed his socks and shoes.

"Okay." Angel wrapped her arms around herself and stepped out of the doorway back into the living room.

Barrett went into the bathroom, and when he came out, he was fully dressed. He walked toward her, gave her a hug, and said, "See you later, my Angel."

Angel got on her tippy toes and gave him a quick kiss. He smelled incredible. His woodsy, cologne sent tingles down her body. Had they been alone, she would've climbed him like a tree and got in a quickie before he left.

Barrett leaned down and whispered in her ear, "Stop thinking dirty thoughts, woman." Then he gave her a kiss on the cheek and headed toward Steele and Maggie. "Mags, thanks for keeping my Angel company. Steele, thanks for the assist today. I'll see you guys later."

Then Barrett headed to the door, opened it, and said, "Well, look who's here? Perfect timing. Thanks, man. I love ice cream." Barrett moved his hand to grab the sundae.

"Not for you, asshole." Mark moved the sundae out of Barrett's reach. "Go to work, lazy ass."

Barrett stepped aside, laughing as he left. Angel loved the easy banter Barrett shared with his friends.

"Are you the lucky recipient of Sam's perfect ice cream sundae?" Mark held it out to Steele.

"Wow, that looks great!" Steele took the sundae and looked at his mom. "Did yours look this good, mom?"

"No, buddy, I think yours looks better." Angel knew they both looked the same, but why burst her son's bubble? There wasn't much he got excited about lately. If having that delicious-looking ice cream sundae made him this happy, she would make sure he could get one anytime he wanted.

"Well, we gotta go, but we'll see you soon." Maggie hugged Angel again. How much hugging did these people do? "Bye Steele, enjoy your sundae."

Angel walked them to the door and heard Maggie whisper to Mark, "Surfer Smurf, I got some extra whipped cream in our room."

"You read my mind, Smurfette."

Then Mark picked up his speed, practically dragging Maggie out the door to their room. Angel wondered what that was about. Did Maggie have a fetish with the Smurfs? Angel remembered her mom collecting the little blue figurines when she was young. She'd have to talk to Barrett about that.

Chapter 44

Time to Take Shit from His Team

Barrett

B arrett knew the minute his feet touched the casino floor, Travis and his team were going to give him shit about Angel and Steele. He loved those guys, but nothing got past them, especially since Steele had been talking to them all afternoon. ·

"There's the man of the hour." Travis was the first to approach him and slap his back. "I'm shocked you left that beautiful woman unattended to come play with the big boys?"

"You are such an asshole," Barrett grinned.

"I got eyes on your floor and the elevators," Chris, another officer working from the downstairs security office, piped in through the earpiece.

"Thanks man, I appreciate it." Barrett mumbled. "Not gonna lie. If we weren't so short staffed, I would've stayed with her upstairs."

"We'll be okay if you don't feel right being down here." Travis was all business now.

"It's fine. Mark is up there now, too." Barrett scanned the room for trouble. "How's it been going down here the past few nights?"

"Same ole, same ole." Travis nodded, and they spoke lowly as they made some rounds. "George came and got the guy Steele spotted cheating. Steele's got a good eye."

"Yeah," Barrett nodded, and they walked for a few more minutes together before they split up to cover more ground.

"Bachelorette Party at the roulette table is getting a little rowdy," Chris said. "You want to take this one, Slick?"

Barrett sighed. Slick was the nickname the guys gave him because of his behavior with the ladies. Now that he had Angel, he hoped to get rid of it quick.

"Fuck. Yeah, I'll head over there." Barrett could hear them as he approached. "Travis, stand by. They love to see the big, strong, military cut, tatted guy."

"Pussy, you just don't want to handle a bachelorette party because you got a woman now."

"You're not wrong." Barrett stepped behind the loudest woman, twirling her purse around. "Ma'am, I need to ask you to please keep it down."

"Slick, I don't think that's going to work." Chris laughed. "She's eyeing you like a wolf eyeing her next meal."

Barrett wanted to reply with a smart-ass remark, but she was standing too close to him and would hear it. Then she leaned into him and ran her hands over his chest.

"Oooh, sexy and muscular. Just how I like my men." The woman said in a throaty voice and then licked his jaw.

"Barrett, can I stay on the line and watch the monitors even if you're not up here with me?" Barrett heard Steele's voice in his earpiece at the same time as Travis laughed.

"Sure, Steele." Barrett gave consent.

Shit, his night was gonna suck if Steele could see how some women behaved toward him. Tomorrow, after his shift, he needed to discuss privacy and inappropriate behavior with Steele. Maybe the night shift wasn't the best shift for him to watch?

Barrett grabbed her hands, pulled them away from his body, and held her still. Fuck, what if Angel was with Steele and she saw the woman lick him? Angel would be furious.

"Ma'am...," was as far as Barrett got before Angel shoved the woman away from him. Barrett was so surprised by Angel's presence he wasn't quick enough when the woman slapped Angel.

"Did you just fucking slap me, bitch?" Angel screamed before she punched the woman in the face. "That's my man, so lay off!"

"Oh Shit, Travis!" Barrett grabbed Angel by the waist and pulled her back just as Travis did the same with the other woman.

"Oh, my God!" One of the woman's friends shrieked and tried to grab Angel.

Barrett swung her around him and held her behind his back. "I need backup here, now." Barrett screamed into the earpiece.

"Let me go," Angel tried to get around Barrett.

"Take them out of here, now," Barrett told Travis, who was trying to control two drunk women.

"I got this." Travis grabbed each woman by their biceps and dragged them out of the casino.

Barrett spun around, grabbed Angel in a fireman's carry and stormed out of the casino, taking Angel to the first holding cell that had an open door. Once inside, he slammed the door and said, "cut the feed" into his earpiece before he turned off his earpiece and threw them on the table. He didn't have to say which cell, because anyone in the monitoring offices could see every room. Since they had all heard Steele on their earpieces, Barrett knew they would cut the feed really quick.

"I can't believe you carried me out of there with my ass hanging out." Angel was pushing her tight dress lower. He was so busy trying to get her out of there he never stopped to see what she was wearing. Where the fuck did she get that outfit? Fuck, it had to have been Maggie.

"Well, if you weren't wearing that scrap of a dress, your ass wouldn't have been hanging out." Hell, why the fuck was he complaining? She looked hot as hell. The little black dress was tight as shit and had a plunging neckline that showcased her beautiful tits.

Angel was still yelling at him, but he wasn't listening to her words, he was tuned into her body language. Her nipples were hard, her neck was flushed, and her eyes glittered with desire as they kept darting up and down his body while she swept her tongue over her lips. Oh yeah, she might pretend to be mad at him, but what she really wanted was for him to fuck her–now. Barrett took off his shirt as he stormed toward her. With every step he took forward, she took one backward until she bumped into the wall.

"What are you doing?" Angel was panting.

"I'm gonna fuck you against that fucking wall." Barrett pointed at the wall behind her and dropped his pants. He placed his hands on either side of her head and leaned down to kiss her. Angel held his face as he ravished her mouth.

Slowly, he pushed her dress straps down and groaned when he realized she wasn't wearing a bra. He crouched and slid her dress up to her waist. Fuck! She wasn't wearing panties either. Running his hand around to her pussy, he noticed she was soaking wet. "Angel, why did you come down here looking like this?" Barrett pushed his finger inside her folds.

Angel moaned. "I wanted to see you and I needed to talk to you about something, but when I saw that woman touching you, it pissed me off, okay?"

"You wanted to see me, or you wanted to see me lose control and fuck you?" Barrett licked her nipple and played with her clit.

"What if I say both?" Angel was fucking his finger at a frantic pace. He couldn't wait for her to fuck his cock. Jesus Fuck, she was so sexy.

"Mmm," Barrett grabbed her ass and picked her up. She immediately wrapped her legs around him, sinking onto his cock. "Then I guess I'm giving you both. We'll talk later."

"Harder," Angel yelled.

Barrett kissed her to keep her screams from travelling outside the room while he fucked her hard against the wall. Soon they were both coming, and Barrett realized he hadn't worn a condom.

"Fuck, Angel." Barrett slowly lowered her and fixed her dress. "Please, promise me you won't come down here without underwear again."

"You didn't like it?" Angel pouted.

"I fucking loved it, but only if you're hanging off my arm the entire night." Barrett pulled his pants up and zipped. "What did you want to talk to me about?"

"Deal." Angel smiled, then went to get his shirt. Holding it out to him, she said, "Do all drunk girls throw themselves at you like that?"

"That's what you wanted to talk to me about?"

"No, I'm getting sidetracked." Angel crossed her arms. "But answer that question, anyway."

"Sometimes, but it doesn't mean anything." Barrett put on his shirt, but before buttoning it, he wanted to reassure her. "I only want you. I could give a fuck about anyone else. I hope Travis gets that girl to not press charges."

"She slapped me first." Angel looked outraged.

"You're a lawyer, Tiger." Barrett pointed at her. "You know she could still press charges."

"Fine." Angel sat in the chair while Barrett finished getting dressed. "Do you know where she is?" Angel used her toes to spin the chair left and right while Barrett finished getting dressed.

Barrett grabbed his earpieces, put them in his ear, and turned them on.

"Steele mute your headset for a minute."

"Travis, which room are you in?" He knew Travis would take the ladies into the back to give them water and calm them down.

"The one that shares the wall you fucked your girlfriend on."

"Asshole," Barrett ran his hand over his jaw. Shit, he'd tried to keep Angel quiet. "We'll be right there. Angel wants to apologize."

"That's good cause the slapper is still riled up. I had to get her ice. Your Angel packs quite the punch." Travis chuckled. "I like her."

"Of course you do." Barrett sighed. "We're on our way."

"Can I listen again, Barrett?" Steele piped in.

Damn, the kid really liked this job. "Sure." Barrett gave in and muted his earpiece. "Angel, Steele is on the line and can hear everything you say, so be good."

"I feel left out. Why can't I have one of those ear thingys?" Angel pouted.

"Uh, maybe because you would be in more of these situations?" Barrett raised his eyebrow at her.

"Fine," Angel stormed to the door. "Let's just go see the touchy feely bitch."

Barrett led Angel to the room next door, but before knocking he whispered in her ear, "behave," and turned his earpiece back on.

Angel nodded and waited for the door to open.

"Hey, the gang's all here." Travis stepped back and motioned for them to come in.

"You have something to say to me, bitch," the girl with the black eye stepped toward Angel.

Barrett bent down and murmured in her ear. "Easy. She's not worth it."

Angel straightened and stuck out her hand. "I'm sorry, truce."

"No," the woman slapped her hand away. "I'm gonna press charges and sue your ass."

Barrett wrapped his arm around Angel's waist. He was afraid she was going to hit the woman again. With his other hand, he stopped the woman from getting any closer to Angel. "Can we all please calm down and talk like adults? What's your name?"

"Kendall." The woman strutted closer to Barrett—a big mistake. "You want my number, handsome."

Barrett could feel Angel's body trembling with anger. He turned to her and said, "let me handle this." But he could see it on her face that she wasn't listening to him as she stared daggers at Kendall. "Angel?"

Angel shoved him aside and stood directly in front of Kendall. "You stupid, spoiled rich bitch. You think you can go anywhere you want and proposition any man you want." Angel pointed a finger at Kendall's face. "Well, let me make myself clear. He," Angel then pointed her finger at Barrett, "is fucking off limits to you or any other skank that comes into this casino. I'm a trial defense lawyer and I can keep you in litigations for years until your daddy runs out of money. I have people too and believe me, Kendall," Angel spit her name out, "you won't like my people coming after you."

Barrett watched Kendall's face slowly drain of color. She looked scared shitless, and so did her friend behind her.

"Kendall," her friend pulled her back away from a furious Angel and said, "just drop it. Let's go."

"Okay ladies, it's time to go." Travis stepped between them. "The casino doesn't condone your behavior, but we are not pressing charges for your fight. In the future, please be aware of how much you are drinking and remember, no means no." Travis winked at Barrett. "I'll escort you ladies to your car." Then he put one arm behind each of them and walked them out. Stopping before he walked out to lean back in and point at Angel to say, "she's a keeper."

Barrett slammed the door shut and locked it. "Turn this camera feed off." Barrett said, before he muted his earpiece. "That was fucking hot. I can't say I've ever had a woman fight for me like that."

"Well," Angel crossed her arms and glared at him. "She had to know your ass is mine."

Barrett smiled. "Just my ass?" Barrett approached her and pulled her with him onto a chair. She straddled him, her dress riding up, and fuck, he remembered she had no panties. "Is that all you want?"

"No," Angel unzipped his pants and got his cock out. "I want this too." Then she impaled herself on Barrett's dick.

"Fuck! I love you," Barrett let her set the rhythm, but as she got wetter and louder, he grabbed her waist and thrust into her harder and faster. Angel grabbed his head and kissed him while she exploded on his lap. Barrett gripped her hips and held her in place when he climaxed. "You wreck me." Barrett mumbled into her neck and held her tight. His cock pulsed with aftershocks and relaxed after emptying inside her. *Fuck! He didn't wear a condom again.*

Barrett held her to his chest, stroking her hair until their breathing returned to normal. "I have to get back to work."

"I know," Angel squeezed him and stood. "I'm sorry if I got you in trouble tonight."

Barrett chuckled and zipped up his pants. "I'm not in trouble. I'm just glad she didn't press charges. You're too beautiful to go to jail and be someone's bitch."

Angel smacked him on the shoulder. "Watch it, or I'll make you, my bitch."

"Oh Angel, I'm already your bitch." Barrett kissed her and guided her out of the room.

She needed to leave so he could finish out his shift. When he got home tonight, he'd show her just how good of a bitch he could be.

Chapter 45

Party for My Baby

Angel

Angel walked into the room to find Mark and Maggie on the couches watching a movie. When she left, it was just Maggie with Steele, but Mark must've wanted in on the movie night action.

"Where's Steele?" Angel looked around but didn't see him. "Did he go to bed early?"

"No," Mark pointed toward the bedroom. "He's watching the monitors. That kid's a natural at security."

"So, how'd it go?" Maggie wiggled her eyebrows at her. "Wait." Maggie grabbed the remote and stopped the movie. "Come closer. Is that a red mark on your cheek?"

"Oh, no!" Angel covered her mouth. "Did Steele see me hit that girl after she hit me?"

"Yep," Mark chuckled. "Nice punch, by the way. But before you pass out, he didn't see or hear what happened in the holding cells. I cut the camera feed and turned off his headset like Barrett asked us to do."

"Oh, thank goodness." Angel slipped out of her heels and walked to the couch. Angel was glad now when Barrett had spoken into his earpiece to cut the feed. She did not want Steele to watch her and Barrett during their rendezvous.

"So." Maggie wiggled her eyebrows at her. "What happened that Mark had to cut the camera feed and Barrett's microphone?"

"A girl was touching my man. She slapped me, and I punched her." Angel rolled her eyes. The shocked look on their faces were funny, not funny. She shouldn't have lost her temper like that. It was wrong to hit anyone, hadn't she learned that from her father and Numbers.

But something inside her snapped when she saw the woman running her hands over Barrett. It was like a declaration of war, and she had to defend her territory. She was tired of being the one that lost everything, and she'd taken it out on the rich drunk girl. She had to be better than that for her son and for Barrett.

"Mark looked at Maggie, "I can see you two will be great friends."

"Mom, are you okay?" Steele ran into the room.

"I'm okay." Angel rubbed his back. "I shouldn't have stepped in. Barrett was handling it just fine."

"Of course he was," Mark mumbled. "What?" he hollered when Maggie slapped his shoulder, glaring at him. "All I'm saying is that Barrett's been putting up with women hitting on him for years. He knows what to do." Mark shrugged.

"You are not helping," Maggie said through gritted teeth. "We're gonna go now." She stood, pulling Mark's arm until he stood. "See you tomorrow."

"What?" Mark mumbled as Maggie dragged him to the front door.

Angel followed. "Thank you for coming over and hanging out with Steele."

"You're welcome, anytime." Maggie smiled.

"See ya later, Steele," Mark hollered from the hallway.

Angel shut the door and turned to Steele. "I'm gonna go shower."

"What happened with that lady?"

Angel sighed and stood in front of the bedroom door. She wanted to get this over with so she could shower and relax with Steele. "I lost my temper, but I apologized and neither of us are pressing charges. Barrett and Travis calmed us all down. Travis escorted them out, and I came upstairs. It's all good."

"Okay." Steele smirked, "but mom?"

"Yeah?"

"That was a good punch."

"Yeah, it was," Angel laughed. "But don't lose your cool like I did. It wasn't the right thing to do. Violence doesn't solve problems—communication does. I should've just let Barrett handle it from the beginning. I'm gonna go shower. Are you okay?"

"Yep." Steele followed her. "Can I keep watching the monitors while you shower?"

"Sure, just let them know you're there. Apparently, crazy women's fights happen at night."

Steele laughed, "Okay mom. I'll let them know."

"Hey," Angel grabbed one of Barrett's shirts and some pajama pants from the dresser. "How about we watch a movie when I'm done?"

"Sounds good. Come get me." Steele pointed at her. "But don't look at the monitors."

"Yeah, yeah, yeah, smart ass. You got it." Angel grinned. "One fight a night is enough for me."

While washing up, Angel was thinking about how nice it would be to develop her friendship with Maggie. Who would've ever thought they would be friends, not her. The last time Angel was friends with a girl was in grade school.

Stephanie had been her best friend in second grade until their last sleep over. Usually, her mom picked her up from sleepovers, but this time, Reaper showed up on his bike.

As Angel waved goodbye from the back of Reaper's bike, she remembered the frightened expression on Mrs. Allen's face and the way she clasped her daughter against her. Angel didn't understand why Stephanie became distant at school, playing with other kids and ignoring her. Although Stephanie continued to have sleepovers with classmates, she was never invited back.

All seven-year-old Angel remembered was how much fun they had during their sleepovers. They would play with their barbies, draw, and laugh while they played outside. Mrs. Allen always made them a home-cooked meal, which she didn't get at home very often because their money was tight, so they mostly lived off of peanut butter and jelly sandwiches. Then after dinner, the Allen family, along with her, would curl up on the couch to watch a child friendly movie. Mrs. Allen would hand out freshly baked chocolate chip cookies and hot chocolate with mini marshmallows for everyone to enjoy.

It wasn't until years later, when she heard her parents yelling at each other. Their screeching was so loud she followed the sounds until she was just outside the kitchen. That fight was worse than their normal shouting matches. Angel crouched on the floor just outside the kitchen doorway and did what any normal middle schooler would do–eavesdrop.

"We're leaving." Angel's mom, Cathy, screamed at Reaper. "This is not the life I want for my daughter and me. She can't even keep any friends because their parents are all afraid of you and they tell their kids to stay away from her. It's not right."

"Bitch." Angel heard a loud slap and then a thump. "The only way you're leaving me is in a fucking body bag."

Angel peeked into the room and saw her mom lying on the floor. Reaper kicked her stomach and when Cathy balled up, he kicked her legs. "Don't even think about taking my daughter with you. Now get your ass up and make my dinner."

Angel saw her mother grab the kitchen table to stand while Reaper sat on his ass in a chair at the table, just inches away from her. All he did was watch her struggle to stand up. He never even attempted to help her. Once she stood, she placed her hand over her stomach and stumbled to the stove, tears running down her cheeks.

Angel later found out her mother had been pregnant at the time and lost the baby. The beatings got worse after that until one night when he beat her to death and had the brothers bury the body.

Angel heard her mother's screams but was afraid of her father because every time she would try to help her mother; Reaper would beat them both harder. Whenever her father was enraged, her mother urged Angel to stay in her room. *Her mom told her it hurt her more when she saw Reaper hitting Angel.*

Angel loved her mother, so she stayed in her room, curled up on the bed. Knees to her chest with her arms wrapped around them and her hands covering her ears. That was the worst fight. She could hear objects crashing against the walls. She wasn't even sure what they were arguing about, but it took little to anger Reaper. Why is there dirty laundry? Where's my dinner? Why are there dirty dishes in the sink? It could be anything that set him off. Suddenly, it became eerily quiet before she heard the roar of motorcycles.

Angel was afraid to leave her room, but she wanted to check on her mother. The LRs had arrived, so maybe her father was leaving with them, and she could help her mom. That's usually what happened. Reaper would beat her, then leave with his brothers and stay at the clubhouse. Then the next morning he would come home sober and apologize. It was a vicious cycle that she wished would end so that Angel and her mom could leave.

But when she got up and peeked outside her door, Numbers saw her and walked toward her.

"Go back inside." Angel nodded, but before Numbers could shut her door, she looked behind him and saw her mom's body being carried away. Her body was limp. She wasn't moving. Overwhelming fear and sadness consumed her. She ran to her bed, got under the covers, and cried herself to sleep.

Her sweet mother was gone. She was her champion, her protector, her sounding board, her best friend. Who would hold her when she needed a hug or a shoulder to cry on? Her world came crashing down on her. That was the last time she saw her mom.

Angel snapped out of her thoughts as tears rolled down her face, mixing with the water. The day her mom died was when Reaper turned his anger out on her. If she didn't do exactly what he wanted, she was the one that got the beating. Lucky for her, she met Tools a couple of years later.

Angel turned her face toward the shower head and washed her face. That part of her life was over. She was never letting another man lay a hand on her or Steele. Finishing her shower, she put on Barrett's shirt, which fell to her knees and her pajama bottoms. She went into the security room looking for Steele, but it was empty. *How long had she been in the shower?*

Walking into the living room, she found Steele curled up under the covers, asleep.

Angel smiled to herself. He was too big for her to pick him up and carry to the bedroom. She had to wake him up.

"Steele?" Angel sat on the edge of the couch and stroked his shoulder. "I thought you were going to watch the monitors?"

"I was, but I started getting tired and wanted to set up a movie for us." Steele yawned.

"Why don't you go into the bedroom?"

Steele mumbled, "I'm good here. You and Barrett take the bedroom. But, please, close the door so I don't hear my mom and her boyfriend going at it."

"Steele, what are you talking about?" Angel felt the heat rise in her cheeks.

Steele rolled over and closed his eyes. "Mom, I'm not a baby. Thanks to Numbers, I'm not a virgin either. I know what you two are doing and I'm okay with it. Barrett is a good guy."

Angel was shocked how in just a couple of days Steele had bonded with Barrett enough to be okay with their living arrangements. "I don't know what to say."

"You don't have to say anything. I'm good," Steele sighed. "Good night."

"Good night." Angel stood and bent down to kiss his temple. Her little boy was growing into a man, but she wanted to stop the clock because time was racing by too fast. The LRs lifestyle made everyone grow up too soon. Angel dragged herself into the bedroom, took off her pajama pants, and curled up under the covers. The last few hours had drained her emotionally.

***

Hours later, Angel felt the bed dip and muscular arms wrap around her, pulling her into a solid chest.

"Hi," Angel whispered.

"Hey," Barrett kissed her cheek. "Why is Steele on the couch? Is everything okay?"

"Yeah, he fell asleep out there waiting for me while I was in the shower. When I asked him to go to the bedroom, he said we could have the bedroom as long as we closed the door."

Barrett chuckled into her neck. "Smart kid. I knew I liked him."

"He likes you too if he offered you the bedroom with me."

"True." Barrett licked and sucked the sensitive spot on her neck that always drove her crazy. "So, let's not let this opportunity go to waste. Are you wearing one of my shirts?"

"Yes." Angel answered breathlessly. His soft lips and sexy voice could get her going from zero to a hundred in no time.

Barrett grunted before he slid one of his hands under her shirt and played with her nipple while the other parted her legs and glided into her wet pussy. "Fuck. I love when you don't wear panties. I couldn't stop thinking about you after you left. I think I walked around with a permanent hard on all night."

Angel moaned and rocked back against his cock. He was definitely hard and naked.

"Help me out, my sweet Angel," Barrett groaned and licked her ear. "Guide me in."

Angel reached back and felt his cock wrapped up in a condom.

"You came prepared."

"I hoped, yes," Barrett groaned when she pumped his cock twice and placed him at her entrance.

Barrett rolled them over, so he was lying on her back, pressing her body to the bed. He continued massaging and tweaking her breast while his cock pumped into her. Angel pushed back into him so hard, he pulled her up doggie style and gripped her hips. Sinking and rising to a slow, steady beat as he moved in and out of her. Angel fisted the sheets. He was so deep inside at this angle, and she loved it.

Remembering what Steele had said, she asked, "Did you lock the door?"

"Yes," Barrett fisted her hair and angled her head toward him for a kiss. "But you are loud, Tiger. Grab a pillow if you need to scream, cause I'm not stopping." Barrett nudged her head down into the pillow with her ass up.

Angel wrapped her arms around the pillow and sunk her mouth into it. Her climax mounting while Barrett relentlessly pounded into her. Then his fingers slid around her hips to play with her clit, and her orgasm detonated as she screamed into the pillow. Barrett pushed into her harder and her body collapsed on the bed as he exploded inside her.

"Fuck, Angel," Barrett panted. "I love you. I'm gonna get cleaned up. I'll be right back."

When she heard Barrett come back, she was still in the same position as when he'd left. She felt a damp, warm towel between her legs, but she didn't have the energy to move.

A few minutes later, Barrett came back to bed and rolled her onto his chest.

"Was I quiet? Did the pillow work?" Angel murmured.

"Let's just say it's a good thing he's a heavy sleeper." Barrett chuckled. Angel could feel his chest moving from his laughter. "It's not funny."

"It's not," Barrett pulled her closer into him and Angel draped her leg between his. "It's sexy as hell and I absolutely love all your sounds."

"Hm."

"What did you want to come talk to me about when you came downstairs earlier?" Barrett rubbed her back.

"I wanted to ask you if we could have a sixteenth birthday party for Steele. He's been through so much, and I just want his life to feel normal again. It doesn't need to be anything big. He's not a little boy, but…"

"Angel," Barrett kissed her, which stopped her rambling. "You don't need to convince me. I would love to be a part of his sixteenth birthday. We can do it in the lobby of this floor. That's where we have all our Christmas parties, birthday parties, and bridal showers. When is his birthday?"

"January eighteenth."

Barrett leaned over her. "Are you shitting me?"

"No, why?" Angel watched his eyes widen, then he smiled.

"Because that's my birthday with my twin."

"You have a twin?" Angel frowned. She didn't think she could handle another Barrett walking around.

"My sister, Frey, who tells everyone she's older than me." Barrett dropped back down.

Angel ran her hands over his chest. "Let me guess, by a minute?"

"Yep," Barrett sighed. "How about we have it the Saturday after our birthdays? I would love to do a joint party. We can have the celebration here and then enjoy the pool. Bryce will live here by then, so we can also invite the shelter boys. Those boys love coming over for parties and to swim in the pool. Plus, I think some of them are Steele's age so he could make some new friends."

"Whoa," Angel leaned over Barrett. "Who's Bryce, and who are the shelter boys?"

"Actually, you've seen them before."

"What are you talking about?" Barrett was confusing her. She didn't recall being around a group of boys.

"That day you went to the cultural center to get info on Maggie. The boys were there. I remember because you were so fucking beautiful, I asked them if they knew who you were."

"You thought I was beautiful?" Angel smiled.

"Abso-fucking-lutely," Barrett gave her a quick peck on the lips. "You are the most beautiful woman I've ever seen."

"Okay, okay," Angel swatted his chest. "You already have me in bed. You don't have to lay it on so thick."

"Angel," Barrett cupped her face in his hands. "I'm not laying it on thick. I mean it. You take my breath away."

Angel blushed and dropped her head back onto his chest. "Stop." She had a hard time taking compliments and even thought she didn't want to talk about her beauty as seen through Barrett's eyes. Her heart swelled just thinking he found her beautiful.

Barrett chuckled, "I will not. I will continue to tell you every day how beautiful you are and that I love you."

"I love you too. I hated I had to do that to Maggie. That was during the time Steele still wore rose-colored glasses toward Reaper and Numbers. They told us to go in there and find out anything we could about Maggie. I'm so sorry we ever did that."

"You never have to do anything like that again." Barrett continued to rub her back.

"The boys were also at the weddings, not that you would've noticed. Anyway, Thunder, who owns the cultural center, started mentoring a few boys from a local orphan shelter. The boys go to the cultural center all the time and Mark, my older brother Alex, my brother-in-law Holt, and myself have mentored them too. As a matter of fact, Holt and my sister are adopting one of them, Bryce. He's the youngest, but they range from six to eighteen when they age out. Deputy George was the first boy that Thunder mentored, which is why he's so close to us."

"That's incredible. I can't wait to meet them, properly." Angel sighed. "Do you think they'll remember how rude Steele and I were that day?"

"Even if they do, all those boys have been through so much, they'll understand once they get to know you both." Barrett rested his hand on top of Angel's head and ran his fingers through her hair. "Let's get some sleep. You've worn me out."

Angel smiled. "Good night, Slick."

"You heard that, huh?"

"Yep," Angel kissed his chest.

"Great."

Chapter 46

Honeymoon's Over

Barrett

By Tuesday, Steele was going stir crazy at the resort and wanted to go back to school. After everything Numbers told his previous school, Angel and Barrett agreed it was best to transfer him to the school zoned to the resort address. At first, the district gave Angel a hard time, but once they heard her full story, they agreed it was best for the safety of the child.

They developed a routine where Angel drove him to school, since Barrett was usually asleep when they left, and Barrett would pick him up if Angel was working at the office. She still had to close out several ongoing cases. Angel also applied at the prosecutor's office and had an interview the following week. On the days that she worked from home, Barrett loved waking up with her in bed for a little sexy time before either of them had to leave to pick Steele up from school. They all ate dinner together before Barrett went to work.

Sometimes after homework, Steele would go into the security room to watch the monitors. He would put on the extra headset and check in. Barrett enjoyed teaching Steele all about the resort and casino security as much as Steele enjoyed taking it all in. The kid had a sharp eye for catching thieves.

Today, Barrett woke up in a great mood. Not only was Angel wrapped around him, but his sister and brothers came home from their honeymoon.

"Good morning, my angel," Barrett rolled over and kissed her mouth.

"You woke up happy," Angel stretched.

"I am," Barrett smiled at her. "Not only do I get the honor of waking up with a beautiful, sexy angel, but the happy married couples come back today."

Angel covered her face and groaned.

"What's going on?" Barrett pulled her hands away from her face.

"Do you not remember that I ruined their weddings?"

"You," Barrett kissed her, "didn't ruin anything. The LRs ruined their wedding. You," –Barrett kissed her again– "warned them."

"I don't think they'll think of me as their wedding savior."

"They will after they meet you. I mean, you won Maggie over, and she really hated you."

Angel playfully smacked his chest. "Thanks for reminding me."

"I'm gonna shower and then I'll make you guys breakfast." After another quick kiss, Barrett got up and headed toward the shower. Although he was glad it was Saturday and Steele was home, he couldn't help but miss Angel washing his back and other areas in the shower.

He needed to tell Angel and Steele about their weekly Sunday brunches. Alex's return meant brunch was back on its regular Sunday schedule. Barrett knew his mom couldn't wait to hear all about their honeymoon adventures.

Making quick work of showering and dressing, he walked over to Angel, who was still under the covers, and pulled the covers off.

"Hey," Angel pulled them back over her, "you were fast."

"That's because I was alone." Barrett wiggled his eyebrows. "I'm gonna start breakfast, time to get up, sleepyhead."

"Yeah, yeah, yeah." Angel mumbled.

Barrett strolled into the living room and sat on the couch opposite Steele. "Good morning. You want some pancakes?"

"Is mom awake?"

"Yeah, why?"

"Cause I gotta pee like a racehorse." Steele bolted up and ran into the bedroom.

Barrett sure as shit hoped Angel was still under the covers. Steele hadn't answered him, but he always ate a lot of pancakes when Barrett made them. He headed into the kitchen and started on the pancake batter and bacon. Eggs always tasted better when they were warm. He'd do those last.

Barrett was whistling away when Steele came in and stood next to him. "Can I help?"

"Hell, yes," Barrett passed the batter to Steele. "Stir this until it's not lumpy."

"Barrett?" Steele stopped stirring and stared at Barrett.

Barrett turned around to face him. Steele looked so serious, Barrett wondered what he was thinking. "What's up, big guy?"

"Mom just told me you agreed to give me a birthday party here."

"Yep, is that okay?" Barrett leaned back against the counter giving the impression of a casual pose when deep inside he was hoping Steele wanted to include him. "Or would you rather celebrate the day just with your mom?"

"No," Steele's eyes widened in surprise. "I'm glad we can have a party here, especially since it's you and your sister's birthday, too. I think it's cool we share a birthday."

Barrett relaxed and raised his hand, waiting for a high-five from Steele who didn't disappoint, and smacked his hand. "I think it's pretty cool, too. Let's get this food cookin' so we can have it ready when your mom comes out to join us."

"You got it."

Barrett started frying the bacon.

"Is this good?" Steele asked.

Barrett turned and looked in the bowl. "Yep, let me heat the pan and you can start making them."

"I've never made pancakes before."

"Really?" Barrett placed the flat pan on the stove and turned it on. "My mom taught my brother, sister, and I to cook at an early age. My sister, Frey, and I know how to cook the basics, but my older brother, Alex, took it to another level when he became a chef."

"Wow, that's cool. Is his food good?"

"Oh, yeah. He can cook anything, and it tastes great. If you ate fry bread that day you visited the cultural center, then you ate his cooking." Barrett grabbed his tongs and turned the bacon.

"That was an awful day. I already apologized to Maggie because I felt so bad. I remember liking the bread. It's called fry bread?"

"Yup, it's a Native American tradition and my brother makes the best fry bread I've ever eaten. And trust me, I've eaten a lot of fry bread. Okay, now," –Barrett stepped to the side and motioned Steele to the stove–"you know not to touch the burner, right?"

"Duh, I'm not a baby. I've cooked some stuff, just not pancakes."

"Perfect," Barrett grinned. "Let me show you about how much to pour so you can do the rest." Barrett poured one in the middle of the pan. "You can do a couple at a time, but for your first time, I'd start with one. You're looking for when you see the bubbles pop." Barrett pointed with the spatula. "When it looks like this, you slide the spatula as far as you can underneath it and flip. Give it a few seconds before you flip it again." Barrett gave the spatula back to Steele. "Now, you do the rest while I finish cooking the bacon."

They were working in unison until Steele finished the pancakes. Barrett turned on the coffeepot when he spotted Angel leaning against the doorframe to the kitchen.

"Hey," Barrett walked over and kissed her. "How long have you been standing there?"

"Long enough to watch my two favorite people making breakfast."

"Hi, mom. Barrett taught me how to make pancakes." Steele's voice was brimming with pride and excitement.

"Wow, I can't wait to taste them." Angel hugged Barrett and whispered, "thank you."

"You can thank me properly, later." Barrett whispered in her ear.

Angel laughed and pushed him away. "What can I do to help?"

"You can set the table. I'll make the eggs while you guys get everything set up."

"Sounds good." Angel grabbed some plates from the cupboard while Steele picked up the plate with the stack of pancakes and took it to the table.

When Barrett brought the eggs to the table, everything was ready. Angel had made him a plate and poured him a cup of coffee. Barrett loved how they all worked together like a family. He couldn't wait for this to be their Saturday morning ritual.

"So, Tori, Alex, Frey, and Holt come back from their honeymoon today. Steele, do you know who all those people are?" Barrett looked at Steele.

"You've told me about Frey and Alex, but who are Holt and Tori to you?" Steele fidgeted with his fork. "I know the LRs were after Tori, and I know she was the one that got my grandfather arrested, but I don't know how you know her."

Barrett nodded. He knew this was hard for Steele, but he was just a kid, and no one was going to hold anything against him. He would make sure of that.

"Tori works at the cultural center and is married to Alex, my older brother. Alex works as a chef here and at the cultural center. Holt is my best friend since grade school who married my sister. The three of us were like the three musketeers running around here, like we owned the place. I can't wait for you guys to meet them. I volunteered to pick them up from the airport. If you guys want to come with me, you can. I'll be driving the resort van, so there's room for all of us."

Angel cleared her throat. "I think it might be best if we wait here."

"Okay, sure," Barrett sighed. "I understand." He'd so hoped they would go with him. He knew they'd be safe. According to George, the LRs had dispersed or were in jail. They hadn't found Numbers yet, but no one had seen him lately. Reaper was so pissed, they didn't think Numbers would show up anytime soon.

"Mom, I think we should go." Steele blurted. "It would mean a lot to Barrett."

Shit. That kid was smart and so fucking observant.

"Does it mean a lot to you?" Angel placed her hand on his forearm.

"Yeah," Barrett swallowed and nodded. "It does."

"Okay, then we'll go with you."

"Thank you, Angel." Barrett grabbed her hand and pulled it to his mouth for a kiss. When he looked at Steele, he had a shit-eating grin on his face. Barrett winked and mouthed a thank you.

While everyone was in an agreeable mood, Barrett dropped the Sunday Brunch Day Bomb on them. It was best for everyone to meet Angel and Steele. Once they got to know them and got the hard questions out of the way, Barrett knew his family would love them just as much as he loved them. After everything that happened between Barrett and Holt a few months ago, he was a firm believer in ripping the band aid off instead of letting something fester.

"By the way, now that Alex is back, we'll be going back to our Sunday Family Brunches starting tomorrow."

"Cool. I love brunch." Steele dug into his stack of pancakes.

"What?" Angel gasped.

"My family all gets together downstairs in our sit-down restaurant 'Savor' for brunch every Sunday. It's nothing fancy; we just love to catch up on our week and enjoy Alex's cooking."

"Do we need to bring anything or dress a certain way?" Barrett could see Angel fidgeting with her fork, fear shining in her eyes.

"No." Barrett grabbed her hand and held it on his thigh. "It's very casual, and Alex and my mom take care of all the food. We just go down and eat it."

"Okay."

Angel didn't sound convinced. *Maybe he should've eased Angel into Sunday Brunch.*

Chapter 47

Frey Hates Her

Angel

Angel couldn't believe when Barrett sprung Sunday Brunch on them. She was already nervous about meeting the happy honeymoon couples, as Barrett called them, at the airport. What if they hated her? I mean, she did interrupt their wedding, and she got Barrett shot. It would make sense for them to not like her. But she loved Barrett, and he loved his family, so she had to get along with them, even if it killed her. Who knows, maybe they would talk it out and they could all be friends.

She had met Barrett's parents, Sehoy and Osceola earlier in the week. They'd kept their conversations in the hotel lobby brief because of her safety. Angel was surprised that Barrett's parents hadn't approached her, but perhaps Barrett had told them not to. He was very protective of her. Or maybe he was just waiting for everyone to be back, so she wouldn't have to repeat her side of the story.

After breakfast, they all worked together to clean the dishes before relaxing on the couch to watch movies. They'd been like this for the past couple of hours until Barrett paused the movie.

"Are you guys ready to go?"

"Yeah, let me use the restroom." Angel stood and turned to Steele. "Get your shoes. I'll be back in a minute."

Angel really needed to use the restroom, but she also wanted to take a minute to prepare for Barrett's siblings. She knew from this past week how much Barrett's family meant to him. *Would she be able to walk away if they hated her?*

Angel heard a soft knock on the door before it opened.

"Hey." Barrett stepped in and hugged her. "It's going to be okay, I promise."

Angel held on tight, but her stomach felt queasy. She pushed Barrett away, quickly dropping to her knees in front of the toilet, and promptly threw up.

"Shit. Angel," Barrett bent down behind her and pulled her hair back into a ponytail. "I'm sorry, if my wanting you to go is upsetting you this much you don't have to go, you can stay home."

"No, it's okay." Angel stood and flushed. "I feel better. It's just nerves. I'll be okay." Angel turned on the faucet. "Let me brush my teeth. I'll be right out." *Had Barrett just called his apartment their home?*

"Are you sure?" Barrett never left the bathroom. He continued to rub her back, watching her every move through the mirror.

Angel nodded and spat out the toothpaste. "Yeah." After she wiped her mouth, the corner of her mouth curved in a partial smile. "I'll be okay, let's go."

Barrett didn't look convinced, but she had felt better after she emptied her stomach. It was either her nerves or she was coming down with a stomach bug. They got Steele and headed downstairs.

"Barrett, are you leaving?" Sehoy came around the lobby desk. "Your father already moved the van to the front."

"Thanks, *chatski*," Barrett gave his mom a kiss on the cheek.

"It's good to see you Angel, Steele." Sehoy turned to them. "Did Barrett tell you about our brunch tomorrow?"

"Yes, ma'am, he did. Thank you for inviting us."

"No need for such formal talk." Sehoy hugged Angel. "You can call me Sehoy. Steele, I saved this one just for you." Sehoy pulled out a zippered bag with a cookie inside out of her blazer pocket and held it out to Steele. "Chocolate chip, I hope you like it."

"Thank you, ma'...," Sehoy pulled the cookie away from Steele and made a tsking sound while her pointer finger swayed from side to side in the universal sign for no.

"Miss Sehoy?" Steele corrected.

"Okay, I'll accept the miss since you are a young man." Sehoy pulled him into a hug and gave him the cookie. "But please don't call me ma'am or Mrs. Panther."

"Okay, Miss Sehoy." Steele grinned at her. "Thank you for the cookie."

"My pleasure."

"What about me?" Barrett held out his hand.

"What about you, *chakpootsi*?" Sehoy frowned.

"Where's my cookie?" Barrett pouted.

"Really, you're going to pout because I didn't give you a cookie?" Sehoy crossed her arms and tapped her foot.

"Yes, you know how much I love those cookies." Barrett grumbled. "Nevermind." He grabbed Angel's hand. "Let's go." Barrett pulled Angel behind him.

"Wait," Sehoy shouted. "These are for you."

Barrett spun around and saw a large, zippered baggie filled with cookies. He released Angel's hand and ran to his mom. He lifted Sehoy, twirled her around, and planted a loud kiss on her cheek when he set her down. "I love you, *chatski*. I knew you wouldn't forget about your baby boy."

"Funny, how when you want a cookie, you're my baby boy." Sehoy smirked at him.

"I love you, *chatski*," Barrett winked at his mom.

"Yeah, yeah, yeah." Sehoy looked at Steele. "You make sure he doesn't eat them all. They are for everyone."

"I will, Miss Sehoy." Steele smiled.

"I see your mother was pulling your leg with the cookies." Osceola came from Rush, their quick service restaurant with a small cooler. "Take these waters to wash down the cookies."

"Now, go get my other kids and bring them home." Sehoy wrapped her arm around Osceola. "Drive safely."

"I will," Barrett grabbed the cooler from his father. "I promise."

Angel waved to Barrett's parents and followed him and Steele to the van.

"You are such a mama's boy," Angel said when Barrett helped her into the front passenger seat of the van.

"Yep, and proud of it."

Angel chuckled. She loved the way he treated his mom. The ride to the airport was quiet while they ate the cookies. Angel only had one. She didn't want her stomach to act up and have to make Barrett pull over with everyone in the car. That would be a horrible second impression. Of course, nothing was going to be as bad as her interrupting their wedding as their first impression. Angel leaned her head back and placed her hand over her stomach.

"Hey." Barrett reached over and squeezed her leg. "It's going to be okay."

Angel nodded and closed her eyes. She must have dozed because next thing she knew, Barrett was at the passenger door, waking her up. "We're here Sleeping Beauty."

Barrett walked into the airport holding Angel's hand on one side and Steele's on the other.

They didn't have to wait long until Angel saw a woman come flying out of the exit terminal and barrel into Barrett. Angel recognized her as one of the brides and assumed it was his twin sister. Barrett immediately let go of their hands and caught Frey in a big hug, spinning her around as they laughed like two crazy loons.

Angel moved behind Steele and placed her hands on his shoulders.

"God, I missed you." Barrett set her down before hugging the other woman and the two men.

Frey smacked his shoulder. "Then you should've driven us to the airport when we left or called more than once while we were gone. Where were you?"

"Sorry," Barrett looked at her sheepishly. "I'll fill you in on the drive home. Do you guys remember Angel?" Barrett placed his arm around her back.

"Hi." Angel smiled and gave a little wave.

Barrett continued, "and this is Steele."

"Hi." Steele stepped back into his mom's embrace.

Barrett pointed to the group in front of him and said their names from left to right. "That's Tori, Alex, Frey, and Holt."

"Hey," Frey pointed to Angel, "You stopped our weddings."

Shit, were they going to get into it at the airport? "Yeah." Angel looked down and cleared her throat. "I'm sorry about that."

"Well, I'm exhausted and I can't wait to get home, so can we finish this conversation later?" Alex grinned at Angel.

"Yup." Barrett draped his arm around Angel and led them to the luggage area. "Let's get your stuff and head out."

Angel stood back with Steele while they all crowded the luggage carousel, ready to grab their bags. She was grateful for the reprieve Alex gave her. It would be best to discuss the past two weeks in private. From the sounds of it, Barrett never told them about being shot. Her stomach cramped, and she was afraid she was going to throw up again.

Steele grabbed her hand. "It's gonna be okay, mom."

"Thank you." She was so blessed to have him back to his normal self. When Numbers made Steele hit Angel, she feared he'd enjoy it and change, but it disgusted him instead and now she had her sweet boy back. Thank goodness. She didn't know how she could live her life if her son hated her. Angel squeezed his hand. "I love you."

"I love you too, mom."

Between all the men and with the help of Steele, they rolled all the luggage to the van and headed home.

"So, how was Hawaii?" Barrett blurted.

"Fantastic! How was it here while we were gone? Why didn't you see us off? How is the wedding venue after the shooting? Was anyone hurt from the shooting?" Frey bombarded them with questions. "I have others, but I'll ask you later."

Angel cringed. Barrett's sister was endearing, yet scary.

*** Barrett ***

Barrett glanced at Angel, who was staring at him like a deer caught in the headlights. He reached over and grabbed her hand, placing it on his lap. *Damn Frey and her bossiness. He missed her but couldn't she have waited a few more minutes before she began her interrogation?* Out of the corner of his eye, Barrett saw Alex stare at her with a look that said, 'what the hell are you doing'.

"Aren't you glad we're home?" Holt chuckled.

"Start at the beginning, please." Frey gave him a sarcastic smile.

Barrett sighed. He wanted to tell them everything, but with Steele in the car, he ended up giving them the short version. "Someone shot me while I was protecting Angel at the wedding...,"

"What the fuck?" Frey interrupted.

"Frey, let him finish." Alex blurted in his don't fuck with me voice. Barrett, Frey, and Holt had all heard Alex's stern voice growing up when he was in charge, because their parents were working. That voice usually followed a slap to the back of the head for Holt and him. Frey was lucky she only got the voice with a look.

"Which was why I wasn't there to say goodbye. I was at the hospital. And to answer your next questions, yes, mom and dad knew. George waited with me until the paramedics got me to the ambulance. I asked mom, dad, and George not to tell you guys so you could go on your honeymoon and enjoy yourselves. The bullet had gone through, and it didn't hit any vital organs, so I was going to be fine. I didn't want you worried about me."

Barrett heard Frey snort, ready to say something, but from the rearview mirror he saw Holt drape his arm over her shoulder and whisper something in her ear. Frey shut her mouth and nodded.

"After the hospital sent me home, George helped me find Angel. We also saved Steele from the LRs." Barrett finished.

"Why do I get the feeling you've left a lot of stuff out of your story?" Alex quipped.

"He'll tell us when he's ready." Tori kissed his cheek. "Steele, I'm Tori. How are you doing?"

Barrett loved Tori. Of course, she would've been the first one to address Steele to make him feel comfortable around them.

"I'm doing okay, ma'am." Steele nodded.

"Please, call me Tori. I remember you from when you came to visit us at the cultural center. I hope you come to see us again. Did you like Alex's fry bread?

Tell him the truth because if you didn't like it, he's been known to create a special one for you, like he did for Bryce."

"Absolutely." Alex nodded at Steele. "I cater to all my picky clients."

"Except me," Frey shoulder bumped him.

"Hey, who makes you your favorite turkey and cheese sub?" Alex pointed to himself and mouthed 'me' at Steele.

"It was great. I loved it." Steele grinned. "But I'm happy to taste test any samples."

"Get in line, kid." Holt laughed. "We all love his fry bread, especially Bryce."

"Bryce is one of the shelter boys, right?" Steele asked.

"Yes, but he'll soon be our adoptive son, joining our family as soon as we get home." Frey clapped her hands and kissed Holt.

Through the rearview mirror, Barrett glimpsed Frey smiling like a loon. Barrett and his sister were close. She told him everything, well except when she had been secretly dating Holt—that had been a shitshow—but that's an entirely different story.

Frey immediately bonded with Bryce the minute she met him at the cultural center. She then introduced Bryce to Holt and her entire family. Bryce reminded the Panther family of Holt when he was young.

Following the loss of their unborn child, Frey and Holt's relationship had taken a turn for the worse and they broke up. But after some family assistance, and interference, they found their way back to each other and decided they wanted to be parents. Frey once told Barrett they missed their baby, but they loved Bryce as if he were their own. Barrett was glad they got their shit together and proceeded with the adoption of Bryce. He loved Bryce from day one and couldn't wait to spoil his nephew.

"I'm so happy for you guys," Tori said.

"It'll be good to see kids running around on our family floor." Alex glanced at Tori and smirked. *Did Alex and Tori have an announcement to make?* Barrett wondered.

"Actually," Barrett glanced at Angel. "Angel and Steele are living with me. It's not safe for them to go home yet." In for a penny, in for a pound. "And Steele has been helping me monitor the security from the room on our floor."

"What?" Frey blurted before Holt gripped her shoulder.

"Would you look at that? We're home." Barrett stopped in the front loop of the resort where guests temporarily park to check in. Everyone got out and went to the back of the van, except Angel and Steele. They stood by the lobby doors.

Holt slapped his back and murmured, "We got a lot to discuss, bro."

"Yeah, we do." Barrett pulled all the bags out and set them on the ground.

"So, Steele, how do you like being a part of our security team?" Holt glanced at him.

"I really like it." Steele nodded enthusiastically. "And I've already caught several people stealing."

"Wow, that's great." Holt grabbed his and Frey's bag. "Frey, Barrett, and I used to watch those monitors when we were about your age and catch cheaters and thieves all the time."

"He's got a great eye and really focuses when he watches the monitors. We're gonna have to put him on the payroll." Barrett winked at him.

"Really?" Steele puffed up his chest and beamed at Barrett.

"I'll talk to my dad and see what I can do." Barrett closed the doors.

Everyone grabbed their bags.

"I'll park the van and be back." Barrett looked at Angel and Steele. "Can you guys go with them? I don't want you out in the open like this."

"Okay," Angel looked unsure and hesitated, but Steele grabbed her hand and pulled her along.

Barrett hurried into the van and parked it in record time. He wasn't trying to throw her to the wolves, well, Frey, but he didn't want her alone outside or in the lobby either. He knew Alex and Holt could read between the lines and would keep her safe until he got upstairs.

Chapter 48

What the Hell?

Frey

Frey was ready to scream her head off as soon as they got on the elevator, away from their resort guests. But there was so much luggage. They rode up in two shifts. Alex told Frey and Holt to go first. Frey knew Alex could tell she was seething and wanted to get her away from Angel. He and Tori stayed with Angel, waiting for the next elevator.

As soon as the elevator doors closed, she pivoted to Holt and pointed toward the closed doors. "What the fuck was that?"

Holt held up his hand to stop her. "Hold that thought until we get to our room."

"Fine." Frey turned to the doors and crossed her arms. There were cameras in all the elevators, and she knew Holt was trying to keep her from saying something others would hear, and she would regret.

They rode the elevator in silence. Frey was still in shock that Barrett had hooked up with the bitch who not only interrupted her wedding, but was Reaper's fucking daughter. *Had he lost his mind?*

As soon as the elevator doors opened on their floor, she grabbed her bag and stormed to her room. Holt reached around her to slide the key card and open the door. Taking a few steps into their room, she dropped the bag again and screamed.

"What the hell is she playing at?" Frey began pacing while Holt stared at her, arms crossed, and a smirk on his face. "Why are you laughing at me?"

"I'm not laughing at you." Holt shrugged. "I just think you're very cute when you're mad."

"I'm not cute! I'm angry!"

"Okayy."

"What is he thinking? How can he trust Reaper's daughter?" Frey stopped and pointed at Holt. "Did you catch how he said George was with him when he got hurt. Where the fuck was she?" Frey threw her hands up in the air.

"Easy there." Holt approached Frey and held her tightly against his chest. "I'm sure there's an explanation for everything you are thinking. But bottom line, if he loves her, then you need to back off. Look what happened to us when Barrett stepped into our relationship demanding promises. It wasn't pretty, and it took us what felt like forever for us to forgive each other." Holt held her head against his chest with one hand while he rubbed her back with the other.

Frey knew he was right, but she didn't want her brother to get hurt. Their circumstances were different. Holt, Barrett, and Frey had been the best of friends for years. This bitch just strolled into their lives and turned everyone upside down. And what was the deal with her son? If she was Reaper's daughter, then the Steele kid must be his grandson. Everything started clicking, and she stepped out of Holt's embrace.

"Oh, shit. If she's Reaper's daughter, José, Maggie's brother, killed her husband, after Reaper killed Maggie's parents." Frey gasped, a hand flying to her mouth. "How the hell could Barrett bring her anywhere near Maggie? How is Maggie feeling about all this?" Frey's chest felt tight. She couldn't seem to get enough air.

"Sweetheart, you gotta calm down before you pass out." Holt led her to the couch and sat next to her. In a calm voice he said, "clear your mind for a second and think about the beautiful ocean waves in Hawaii. That's it. Take a few deep breaths and let them out slowly."

"But I have to talk to Maggie?" Frey bolted up, but Holt pulled her back down.

"Not now, you don't." Holt laid down on the couch, pulling her into his arms. "Just like me, keep breathing. It's going to be okay." Holt continued to stroke her hair until her breathing became normal.

"I love you." Frey murmured into his chest.

"I love you, too. Are you calm now to talk about this without hyperventilating?" Holt glanced down and smirked at her.

Frey loved how he could cheer her up in seconds and put a smile on her face when, minutes ago, she was going ballistic and almost passed out.

"Yeah, but let's stay like this while we talk it out."

"How about we stay like this in our bed?"

"Okay, I'll unpack later." Holt got up, bent down, picked her up bridal style, and carried her into the bedroom.

"What are you doing?"

"Well, you were so wound up when we entered our home that I wasn't able to carry you over the threshold, so I'm gonna do it now."

"You are so romantic and sweet." Frey kissed his neck.

"Yeah, well, only for you."

Then Holt threw her onto the bed and Frey bounced, "Hey, what happened to romantic and sweet?"

"Can't have you expecting that all the time, can I?" Holt laughed and jumped on the bed next to her. "I mean, what will the guys think?" Frey laughed while he grabbed her, wrapped himself around her. "Now that I have you where I want you, talk to me."

"I just don't want Barrett to get hurt. I don't trust her. I mean, her son seems nice, but we don't know anything about them except that they're related to terrible people."

"I know." Holt kissed her forehead and stroked her cheek. "But you trust your brother. He's been around the block a time or two with women and he knows how to spot a liar. He seems to really like this girl and her son if he's already brought them into his home and taught Steele about our job."

Frey rose and leaned over Holt. "That's another thing," she pointed at him, "what secrets has he been telling Angel or teaching Steele about our casino?"

"Oh, sweetheart." Holt rolled her onto her back, pinning her down and holding her arms above her head with one hand as he leaned over. His other hand trailed down her body, playing with her breasts through her clothes. "Maybe he's teaching the boy how to calm a crazy woman when she's about to go nuts again."

"Pervert, that's not funny," Frey groaned with more desire than anger in her voice.

Holt chuckled before he unbuttoned her shirt, spread it open, and eased her left breast out of her bra cup. Frey loved when he sucked her breasts. It heated her up and shot a direct line of heat down to her pussy. Which, if he continued to suck and bite her, would be soaking wet in seconds.

"I love when your bras unbutton on the front." Holt made quick work of the snap and ran both hands to her breasts, massaging her, tweaking her nipples. His mouth trailed to hers for a heated kiss. Their tongues dueling before Frey broke the kiss to take a deep breath. Holt continued his exploration with his mouth to her breasts and her belly button.

Releasing her breasts, he scooted down and pulled her skirt and undies off at the same time.

"Damn, you look so fucking beautiful with your shirt open and your heels on."

Frey pouted, "I would say you look fucking beautiful with your shirt open, but you're still dressed."

"I can remedy that real quick." Holt jumped off the bed and stripped naked in seconds. "Better?" He quirked an eyebrow at her.

"Oh, yeah." He was so fucking fit and sexy. "Come here, big boy. Show me all your tricks for calming down a crazy woman."

Holt burst out laughing before he pounced on her. After he pleasured her pussy with his tongue drawing out the first orgasm, he slid into her. He changed his tempo several times, but always holding his weight on his elbows and holding her head as he gazed into her eyes.

Missionary style was her favorite because she could see his love for her reflected in his eyes.

"I love you so much," Holt murmured against her lips while still watching her.

"You are my everything. I love you." Frey blurted before they both climaxed at the same time.

After their breathing returned to normal, Holt got up and cleaned them up. Crawling into bed with her, he wrapped her up in his arms and they both fell asleep.

Chapter 49

What Now?

Angel

Angel could've killed Barrett for leaving her alone with his family. She was grateful for Steele's support. Angel was relieved when Alex sent Frey off in the first elevator. Because Angel was getting uncomfortable with the looks Frey kept throwing her way.

Once inside the elevator, Tori turned to her. "I'm glad both of you are okay." Tori touched her shoulder. "If you need anything, we are in the room through the adjoining door."

"Thank you, that's very nice of you to offer." Angel glanced down before she looked at Tori. "About your wedding. I'm truly sorry for showing up the way I did. I was only trying to help. I would've told you all sooner, but when I went to the cultural center, it was closed and I didn't know where any of you lived."

The elevator doors opened, and they all stepped out, heading toward their respective rooms. Just as Angel was getting ready to swipe her key card, she felt a gentle touch on her arm and turned around. Tori hugged her, shocking the hell out of Angel. After a couple of seconds, she hugged her back before Tori stepped back and smiled.

"Thank you for trying to help us. Frey will come around. She's just very protective of Barrett, them being twins and all. Please, let us know if you need anything."

Alex came up behind his wife and pulled her into his arms, kissing her cheek. "Go on in Angel." Alex nodded toward the door. "We'll wait until you are safely inside."

"Thank you." Angel opened the door and followed Steele inside.

"Mom, can I watch some TV?" Steele sat on the couch and held up the remote.

"Sure," Angel smiled. "I'm gonna go lay down for a bit." Steele handled meeting Barrett's family better than she did. Kids were resilient..

"Okay." Steele had already started channel surfing.

Angel was tired and out of sorts. Her mind kept replaying the conversations in the car. Tori was so nice and accepting, but she wasn't sure Frey liked her. She had to get along with Frey if she was that important to Barrett. There was no way she would ever make him choose. She would leave before she tore his family apart.

"Hey." Barrett came into the bedroom and curled up behind her. "Are you okay? I know my family can be a lot, especially Frey."

"I don't think she likes me."

"She's just overly protective of me. We're very close, much closer than we are to Alex. I mean, we love Alex, but our twin bond is strong."

"That's what Tori said."

"Alex was more of a parent to us since our parents were always working to make this resort and casino profitable. One thing you'll learn about Frey is that she speaks her mind, but that's also one of her best qualities. You always know where you stand with her. She doesn't pretend to like you and then stab you in the back. And when she trusts you, she will have your back forever." Barrett kissed her cheek.

"You seem close to Holt, too."

"Yeah, Frey and I met Holt in grade school when Frey stood up to his bullies. We all became close after that. Holt had a shitty family life, so he spent a lot of time with us. Then, around the time of our high school graduation, my parents gave him a home here with us. I never saw it, but Holt and Frey loved each other for a long time before they secretly dated. Then Frey lost their baby. I was a dick to them during that time because I was afraid of losing either of them, but when I realized I wasn't losing anyone, just gaining my best friend as a brother, I wised up and gave them my blessing."

"Wow," Angel turned to face him. "That must've been hard for everyone."

"It was, but I'm so glad now that they're together and are adopting Bryce." Barrett grinned and kissed her forehead.

"Tori was really nice to me on the ride up."

"I'm not surprised. She's the kindest person I know, even though she went through a lot with Reaper and Winston." Barrett leaned his forehead against hers.

"Yeah, I heard all about it from Reaper when he wanted me to be his lawyer."

"Are you his lawyer?" Barrett's face jolted back.

"No!" Angel cupped his jaw. "I could never defend him after I heard about everything he did to all of you. I'm positive, that's why he's so mad at me and set Numbers on me. He wanted me to keep my mouth shut and fall in line like a good little soldier."

"Well, he can't hurt you anymore."

"Have they found Numbers?" Angel asked before pushing Barrett onto his back and resting her head over his chest, listening to his steady heartbeat.

"No." Barrett wrapped his arms around her and kissed her temple. "But George said he's heard through the grapevine that Reaper is furious with him and put a bounty on his head. Rumor is, he drove up north hoping Reaper calms down."

"I'm surprised Reaper would want his best friend killed." Angel sighed.

"Why?" Barrett squeezed her tighter. "He wanted his daughter killed."

Angel shivered at the thought. How can a father put out a hit on their own flesh and blood? That explains the fact that Reaper isn't a father. He's a monster with a vengeance. She hoped he never got out of jail.

"So, we have a brief reprieve?" Angel yawned.

"Looks like, but we'll stay vigilant, just in case. You sound tired. Let's take a nap and when we wake up, I'll order food for dinner. We can get together with the fam tomorrow at brunch."

"Sounds good." Angel hugged his waist and draped her leg between his. This was her second favorite position. Her first was him as the big spoon.

Chapter 50

Praying for a Calm Brunch

Barrett

Last night Barrett put his phone on silent. When he checked it this morning, he had tons of texts from Frey. He answered as many as he could while he hung out with Steele on the couch and let Angel sleep. He hoped his answers would calm Frey down so she would be civil to Angel at brunch. Frey could get mean if she thought someone was taking advantage of anyone in her family. Hell, he hoped Frey'd talked to Maggie because Maggie had time to get to know Angel and they had worked their problems out.

He was so nervous he told Steele he was going to go to the gym.

"Can I come with you?" Steele asked.

"Can you stay with your mom? I trust you to keep her safe." Barrett hated saying no to Steele, but he really needed to blow off some steam alone. "I'll take you to our gym later. Is that okay?"

"Sure." Steele puffed out his chest. "I can take care of my mom while you're gone."

"I knew I could count on you. Thanks." Barrett grinned and left.

He knew running was impossible, but maybe a slow, supported walk, holding the treadmill's sides, would work. But once he stepped on, he realized his mistake. It sucked to stroll on a treadmill. Just fucking boring. He needed something to relieve stress, and the treadmill was not it.

Getting off after a few minutes, he rolled his shoulder. When he didn't feel too much pain, he headed toward the weights. He would work out his upper body and focus on the lower body later. Or better yet, work out his lower body with Angel. Barrett smiled.

"What are you so happy about this morning?" Holt entered the gym.

"Feels good to lift some weights. I haven't been able to for the past couple of weeks. I wanted to make sure everything healed properly."

"Yeah, about that. Where was Angel when you got shot? Why was it George that stayed with you?" Holt grabbed a couple of other weights and sat on the opposite weight bench.

"She was worried about her son, so she left me with George." Barrett wasn't totally lying. She had left when George got to him.

"Why do I sense a lie?"

Barrett sighed, "okay fine. She left me bleeding on the floor of my room, but George showed up just in time before I passed out."

"Fuck! Why the hell didn't she stay with you?" Holt stopped lifting his weights and glared at Barrett.

"Before I took her to my room to protect her, we were in the lobby, and she saw her son on the back of Numbers' bike. She wanted to get to him ASAP."

"Shit, was he okay?" Holt walked over to the bench press and loaded up the sides of the bar with weights. "Spot me, will you?"

"Sure," Barrett dropped his weights and walked toward Holt, ready to grab the bar if he struggled with one of his reps.

"Let's just say Steele went through a shit load of emotional stuff including having to hit his mom and help bury her."

"What the fuck!" Holt placed the bar on the rack and bolted upright. "He fucking hit her and buried her?"

"According to Angel, he had to, or they were going to kill him. He didn't bury her deep, and he called 911 when the brothers weren't looking, giving them the location of her burial site."

"Holy fuck! That's fucking harsh. She's a strong woman to deal with that." Holt stood up and pointed to the bench. "Want a turn?"

"Yeah." Barrett and Holt lifted the same amount on the bench press, so he didn't have to change out any weights. "Angel is strong. Hell, she put up with beatings from Reaper her whole life except when she was married to her husband."

"The one José shot?"

"Yep." Barrett finished his reps and switched again with Holt. They normally did three reps.

"How is Maggie taking it?"

"Fucking awesome." Barrett wiped his face with a towel. "She forgave Angel, and that shocked me."

"Really." Holt raised an eyebrow. "Our Maggie?"

"Yep. They talked and realized they were both brutalized by Reaper and his club and decided they would rather be called survivors than victims."

They switched again. "Holy shit. Frey was worried about Maggie. She wants to talk to her." Holt wiped his face with another towel. "We really missed a lot."

"Yup." Barrett finished his set. After getting up, he said, "You think you could talk to Frey, so she won't be so mean to Angel at brunch today?"

"I'm on it." Holt did his last set. "But you know your sister. She's like a dog with a bone until she is ready to let the subject drop. Maybe I'll get her and Maggie together before brunch so Frey can see Maggie's okay with Angel."

"Yeah, Frey can be stubborn, but please talk to her. Her and Maggie talking sounds like a good plan."

"I'll talk to her. I'll use my magically special Holt skills to calm the beast." Holt wiggled his fingers at Barrett and rotated his hips. Barrett swung at him, but Holt ducked and ran to the door. "I'm gonna go shower with your sister and conserve water. You know, do your sister. I mean...do my part for the environment."

"Motherfucker!" Barrett threw the towel at him. "That's not fucking funny. She's my sister. I don't need to hear about that shit."

Holt laughed at Barrett and hollered, "See ya later," on his way out.

"Asshole," Barrett grumbled before he picked up his used towel and left the gym. He needed a shower. Thank fuck, his bathroom looked nothing like Frey and Holt's. Thinking of his best friend fucking his sister was the last image he wanted in his head.

When he entered his room, Steele was still on the couch, dressed and ready to go.

"Hey, is your mom up?"

"No, she's still snoring. Didn't even get up when I went into the bathroom." Steele shrugged.

"Wow," Barrett grabbed a bottle of water from the fridge. "Well, I'm gonna shower. I'll be out and then we can wake up your mom."

"Sounds good. Shut the door."

Barrett laughed, "okay, will do."

Barrett chugged the bottle of water on his way to the bathroom. Glancing over to the bed, Angel laying on her back snoring, just like Steele said. She looked so fucking cute. Barrett didn't want to disturb her. She'd had a hard day yesterday and if Frey didn't calm down, today would be worse.

Barrett was in the shower, rinsing the soap from his body when he heard the toilet seat slam against the lid right before the retching began.

"Angel?" Barrett whipped the curtain aside. "Are you okay?"

Angel slumped over the toilet, her head in her hands and elbows on the sides.

Barrett glanced up to make sure the door was closed before he picked her up and held her against his chest in the shower. She clung to him. Barrett washed her hair and body. After rinsing her, he pushed her hair off her face.

"I'm worried about you." Her face looked pale, and she looked so tired. "I think you should make an appointment to go see your doctor."

Angel nodded and laid her head back on his chest.

This wasn't like her. "Do you want to stay in bed? I'll go to brunch for a few minutes and bring you back some food."

"No," Angel murmured. "This is important to you and Steele is so excited. I'll be okay. Just give me a few minutes."

"Okay." Barrett gave her another squeeze before he stepped around her and got out.

He didn't leave the bathroom for fear of her falling in the tub, so he brushed his teeth and piddled until she turned off the water. He handed her a towel and stepped back, letting her get to the sink to brush her teeth.

"Better?" Barrett stood behind her and held her hips when she bent down to spit. He wanted to make sure she was steady and wouldn't fall.

"Yeah." Angel leaned on the sides of the sink.

"Stay there, I'll dry your hair." Barrett plugged in the blow dryer and made sure her hair was dry before he left the bathroom.

Angel smiled. "Thank you."

Barrett nodded and walked into the closet to get dressed. When he finished, he waited for her in the bedroom. Maybe she had a stomach bug because last night Barrett had brought up steaks with a side salad and she'd barely touched her food.

She finally came out of the bathroom wearing minimal makeup and a sundress with sandals.

"Let's sit on the couch for a few minutes." Barrett led her into the living room.

"I'm okay, Barrett, really."

"Mom, what's going on? Are you sick?" Steele jumped up from the couch and ran to her.

"I'm okay. Just tired. I think everything is hitting me all at once," Angel grinned. "Why don't you take a shower so we can go to brunch?"

"I already took one." Steele pointed at himself.

"Did you or did you just change?" Angel glared at Steele.

Damn Angel had that mom look down pat.

"Okay, you got me." Steele sighed dramatically. "I'll go shower."

"Come on, Angel," Barrett held her hand and pulled her to the couch. "Let's just sit until he's done. If you feel bad again, we'll stay here. I can always text them you don't feel well, and I'll stay with you."

They cuddled and watched the cooking show Steele had been watching. Alex was going to love him if he showed an interest in cooking.

"Okay, I'm done." Steele came running into the living room with wet hair.

"Damn, that was fast." Barrett raised an eyebrow at him. Other than the wet hair, how had Angel known he hadn't taken a shower earlier? Usually Barrett could tell when someone wasn't telling the truth. He needed to step up his game to keep up with Steele.

"Did you wash the important places?" Angel asked.

"Yes, I did." Steele huffed. "Can we go now?"

"Angel?" Barrett hoped she would tell him the truth.

"I'm good," Angel smiled.

"Let's do it." Barrett stood and helped Angel up. She seemed to have a little more pep in her step, but he'd have to watch her. If this brunch turned out to be too much, he'd bring her back up to their room.

Upon entering Savor, they found everyone already seated at a long table for twelve. Osceola and Alex were at each end of the table. They left three seats between Sehoy and Tori, across from Holt, Bryce, and Maggie. Barrett pulled the chair out for Angel next to Tori. He told Steele to sit next to his mom, and he sat next to Sehoy. He tried to put as much distance as he could between Frey and Angel—just in case Frey got too sassy with Angel.

"Wow, this looks awesome!" Steele stared at all the food laid you.

"I'm Bryce. You're going to love Alex's cooking. It's the best."

"Thank you all for inviting us," Angel looked around the table.

Barrett saw Tori reach over and squeeze Angel's hand. Yeah, he missed sitting next to Angel, but Tori would catch her up on anything she didn't understand while giving her support. Not to mention Maggie sat across from her. The only girls away from her were Frey and his mom. He had better odds of a nice brunch with this seating arrangement.

After a quick prayer of thanks from Osceola, they all passed the food around and filled their plates. As usual, there were so many conversations going on at once that it was hard to focus on one until Frey said, "So, what are we doing for Barrett's and my birthday?"

"We're going to have a party for both of you and me on our floor, right mom?" Steele blurted between bites.

Barrett glanced at Angel, her spoon freezing in her mouth, eyes darting to Barrett.

Angel pulled the spoon out of her mouth, the corner of her lip lifted as she said, "Uhhh..."

"Yes!" Barrett interjected and placed a hand on Steele's shoulder. "We share a birthday with Steele, Frey. Isn't that awesome?" She needed to get with the program and get over her anger toward Angel. Barrett was not about to let Frey ruin Steele's excitement.

He glared at Frey and saw Holt's hand move under the table. Barrett didn't want to know what was going on under there but was glad for Holt's assist because Frey smiled at Steele.

"Sure is. So, big blowout party, Steele?" Frey raised her eyebrow at Steele. "Balloons, music, food, cake, and presents. And when we're done, we'll go downstairs and finish celebrating in the pool. What do you think?"

"Yay!" Bryce hollered. "I love going to the pool."

"Really?" Steele his eyes bugged out, and his fork slid out of his hands, making a clunk sound on the plate. "I've never had a big blowout party."

"We had small family parties at home, but not like what you're describing." Angel looked around the table. "I don't want to put you all out."

"It's not a problem." Sehoy smiled at Angel. "What Frey described is how we celebrate everyone's birthday. It's no trouble at all. I had already started the planning for their party. We'll just add Steele to the mix."

"I...I don't know what to say?" Angel stared at Barrett.

"Say yes," Barrett grinned. "I'm sure you can help my mom, since you know what Steele likes."

"I will take any help I can get," Sehoy piped up.

"Please, mom?" Steele turned to Angel with his hands in prayer mode. "It sounds like so much fun."

"O...Okay," Angel nodded, "yeah, sure."

Everyone hooted, hollered, or applauded. His family loved a good party.

"But only if I can help?" Angel looked around the table.

"Of course, dear," Sehoy took a sip of water. "We'll go over everything I've done so far later."

"Thank you, Frey." Angel looked directly at her. "It's really sweet of you to include Steele in your party celebration."

"Family sticks together, right Barrett?" Frey smiled.

Barrett took a sigh of relief. He knew his sister well enough to see that she was truly happy for him. "Yeah, we do."

Barrett stood, pushing his chair back, walked over to Angel, pulled her up and gave her a tight hug.

"I love you."

"I love you, too." She whispered in his ear.

Barrett jolted back and cupped her face. "Really, even after all this craziness?"

"Yes." Angel smiled and nodded.

Barrett wasted no time as he claimed her mouth and kissed the shit out of her in front of his family. They were all clapping, oohing and aahing except for Bryce, who covered his eyes and said they looked like his mom and dad.

Barrett knew Bryce meant Frey and Holt. They were his parents now, just like Barrett wanted to be Steele's stepdad someday. He could never replace Tools, but he had a lot to offer.

Barrett didn't care that everyone was watching his display of love for Angel. He wanted them to know how special she was to him. They broke the kiss when Steele tapped his back and said, "Can we finish eating now? Our party is in two weeks, and we have a lot of planning to do."

Barrett smiled against Angel's lips and gave her a quick peck. "Yeah, we sure can." He was floating on cloud nine. His girl just told him she loved him in front of his family. He would do anything right now. Instead of going back to his seat, he pulled his plate next to Angel's and sat in her chair, placing her on his lap.

"Barrett, what are you doing?" Angel laughed.

"Sitting with my girlfriend." Barrett answered and shoved a forkful of pancakes into his mouth. He'd waited all his life to feel this way about someone. Feelings of love, belonging, and family overwhelmed him. He wanted to remember this moment forever. Angel felt perfect sitting on his lap. He never wanted to let her go.

"I feel a little awkward eating brunch on your lap," Angel murmured in his ear.

"Give me this, just this once." Barrett gazed into her eyes. "I'm so happy right now. Besides, look around," –Barrett and Angel looked at everyone at the table– "no one's paying attention to us. They're all focused on the party and Steele."

"You've got a point," Angel chuckled.

"I love you." Barrett stroked her cheek.

"I love you, too."

*** Frey ***

Holt and Frey talked to Maggie and Mark last night and got the full rundown of the past two weeks' events. It had been a whirlwind, and she wished she'd been there for Barrett. During brunch, Frey watched her brother with Angel. Though the wedding events and her brother's shooting upset her, how could she not be happy for him, seeing how much he loved Angel?

Holt had come in this morning after his workout and repeated his conversation with Barrett. Angel and Steele had been through hell, and she wasn't about to wreak more havoc in their lives. Barrett looked at Angel the way Holt looked at her–eyes all soft and loving. She could tell her brother was all in with Angel.

When everyone had looked at Frey for her response about the party, she knew she had to let any animosity toward Angel go. She loved her brother, and his happiness came before any feelings of a ruined wedding. Because in the end, she still married Holt, and they got their honeymoon. They could have a reception with their family and friends another day or on their first-year anniversary. The important part was that she got to marry her best friend and share it with her brothers, mom, and dad.

So, as everyone stared at her, Frey let all the bad feelings go and got excited for the future. Everyone looked relieved. The icing on the cake was when they both declared their love for each other in front of everyone. It was beautiful. Frey couldn't be happier for them.

She watched Steele throughout lunch and was happy to see that he had a little hero worshipping going on with Barrett, similar to Bryce with Holt. They were all creating their happy families and Angel seemed to love Barrett, as much as he loved her. All she had ever wanted was for Barrett to stop his whoring ways and find a nice girl to settle down with and have babies. He'd found her.

Chapter 51

Surprise, Surprise

Angel

Two weeks had flown by, but not without a lot of hugging, crying, and understanding on everyone's part. There was lots of peace, love, and family on their floor. Frey and Angel had talked and were getting along as sisters should. Steele looked after Bryce like a little brother.

Angel, Maggie, and Tori put the finishing touches on the decorations for the big blowout party. Frey wanted to help, but they kept telling her that the party people should not have to decorate for their own party.

The night before the party, Angel convinced Frey to take Holt, Barrett, Bryce, and Steele to the local arcade. The video games would keep the little kids busy and Frey would keep the big kids in line and on time. Holt laughed when Angel asked Frey to come back on time. Apparently, Frey had a tendency to run late.

Angel went to stand on a chair to tape the streamer to the wall when she felt woozy and leaned on the wall.

"Are you okay?" Tori was holding the other end.

Maggie came down off her chair and ran over to Angel. "Get down from there and have a seat. You look ready to pass out. I'll finish that."

Angel stepped down and sat in a nearby chair while Tori rubbed her back.

After Maggie taped the end of the streamer to the wall, she tore the streamer and headed over to them.

"What's going on? Do you feel sick?" Maggie placed her hand on her shoulder.

"My stomach has been upset lately, and I keep throwing up. Sometimes, I get light-headed, and I'm tired all the time." Angel dropped her head into her hands.

"Have you gone to the doctor?" Tori asked.

"No, I was so focused on work last week, then Frey, Steele, and Barrett's party this week, that I haven't had time to schedule anything." Angel stood and tasted bile in her throat. "Oh no," she said before she covered her mouth and ran into Barrett's bathroom, emptying all the contents in her stomach in the toilet.

Maggie and Tori followed her in. "You need to go see the doctor." Maggie held her hair back.

"I'll call on Monday." Angel stood and walked to the sink to rinse and brush her teeth.

"Angel," Tori was watching her through the mirror, waiting for her to look at her. "I think you need to take a pregnancy test."

"What?" Angel gasped in shock. Barrett always wore a condom. Wait, no, he didn't. There was that one time he told her he was clean and several times after that when he slid into her bare. "Oh Shit. What if I am and Barrett doesn't want kids?" They'd never talked about it.

"I can assure you Barrett would love to have kids with you." Tori smiled. "Have you not seen all the attention he gives Steele? He already treats him like his son."

"He sure does." Maggie nodded.

"You're right." Angel relaxed and turned to them. "How am I going to get a pregnancy test if none of us are supposed to leave the resort unattended?"

"Leave it to me." Maggie held up her phone and sent a text.

"Who are you texting?" Angel watched in confusion.

"Isa...another one of our girls in our tribe," Maggie typed back and forth, focused on her phone.

"Isa is her best friend. Several of us get together and have girls' night. We'll have to do one soon so you can meet everyone." Tori smiled. "Although you'll meet everyone at the party."

"Okay, Isa will be here in about twenty minutes with a pregnancy test. She had an extra one at home that she never used." Maggie put her phone in her pocket.

"Is she pregnant?" Angel asked before brushing her teeth.

"Yup, six months. She's married to Thunder. He's our boss at the cultural center. You saw him at the wedding, but I don't believe you've been formally introduced. He's a nice person and an incredible boss."

"Let's get you to bed so you can lie down." Tori placed her hand on Angel's back after she spit out.

"I'll head downstairs and wait for Isa." Maggie said before she left.

Angel curled up under the covers.

"Are you going to be okay if you are pregnant?" Tori whispered.

Angel rolled over and faced Tori. "I always wanted more kids, and I would love to have them with Barrett. He's so caring and I love him."

"I'm glad." Tori smiled at her. "Scoot over."

Angel smiled and moved over. Tori arranged the pillows behind her and rested against the headboard. Crossing her ankles on the bed, she grabbed the remote, and channel surfed until she found a home improvement show. A few minutes into the show, they heard knocking on the door.

"I'll get it." Tori got up and went to answer the door.

Maggie came running into the room with another woman behind her.

"Isa, Angel," Maggie waved between them. "Angel, Isa. Now, go pee on this stick." Maggie tossed a paper bag on the bed.

"Hi Isa, it's nice to meet you." Angel got up and grabbed the bag. "Thank you for doing this for me. I'm sure its negative and Maggie made you run over here for nothing. Probably just a stomach bug."

"A stomach bug you've had for two weeks," Maggie challenged. "I don't think so."

"Nice to meet you too." Isa sat on the bed.

Angel walked into the bathroom and shut the door. Taking a deep breath, she read the instructions and peed on the stick. Angel was washing her hands when she heard knocking on the bathroom door. She opened the door to all three women staring at her.

"Come sit with us while you wait." Tori backed up to the bed and patted the comforter. "How long does it take?"

"It said about five minutes." Angel sat next to Tori. "Was this accurate when you tried it?" Angel asked Isa.

"It was." Isa smiled.

"When are you due, Isa?" Angel wanted to keep the conversation away from her because the wait was killing her. These were going to be the longest five minutes of her life.

Isa was rubbing her hands over her tummy. "I'm due on April 20th.

"Do you know what you're having?" Angel smiled.

"She's having a boy," Maggie blurted. "I can't wait to see who he looks like. I have dibs on him, looking like Thunder."

"A little Thunder running around would be so cute." Isa laid back on the bed with a dreamy look in her eyes. "Although, he says one day he would like a little Isa."

"I can't wait until he's old enough to come to the cultural center and learn all about his heritage–the Lakota side." Tori turned to Angel. "Thunder and I have known each other since we were kids. His sister Sarah and I are good friends. We both grew up on the Pine Ridge Reservation in South Dakota. Which, by the way, I meant to tell you guys, my sister is coming in April. She wants to stay for a while and see if she likes it here."

"You know she's going to love it here, right?" Maggie rolled her eyes.

"Yeah, I think so." Tori grinned. "She says she feels couped up on the reservation and is ready to live her life away from my parents. But I worry about her."

"I can't believe your dad is letting her come down here." Isa continued to rub her belly and closed her eyes. Since she also worked at a daycare, maybe she can help me with the baby?"

"I think she would love that." Tori pointed out. "I'll talk to her about it. She needs to have something to do or she will go crazy. My dad said since the LRs have disbanded and the majority are in jail, he feels more comfortable letting her come down to stay for a while."

"Are you excited she's coming?" Angel asked Tori. Angel had always wanted to have a sibling and envied anyone who had one.

"I am, but she can be a handful, especially when it comes to boys." Tori checked her watch. "The five minutes are up. Do you want one of us to get your stick, or do you want to do it?"

Angel stood and took a deep breath. "I'll do it." Angel strolled into the bathroom like she was going to the gallows. She picked up the instructions and re-read them. Two dark pink lines meant a positive result and the absence of lines showed a negative result. She closed her eyes, taking a moment to prepare for the outcome. If she was pregnant and Barrett didn't want a baby, she would be a single mom with two kids. She'd done it before. But this time she would do it without the LRs. She had a good job and a house.

However, if Barrett wanted children, would he want them so soon into their relationship? Now that she thought about, if she wasn't pregnant, she would be sad but could always have them later after they were married. Well, if they got married. So many ifs. But one thing was definite. She had to pick up the damn stick and see if there were two solid pink lines.

Angel grabbed the stick and nearly fainted. There was no confusion in the result because the two lines were solid and dark pink. Angel swung the door open.

"Well?" Maggie, Tori, and Isa said almost in unison.

Angel smiled and held the stick out in front of her.

"Oh, my God!" Tori was the first to jump up and hug her. "I'm so happy for you. I'm going to be an aunt for the second time."

"Second time?" Angel tilted her head and frowned.

"Bryce is my first nephew and now yours. This is so exciting!"

"Someone help me up!" Isa hollered.

"Come on, prego, you're not that big. Stop milking it." Maggie pulled Isa to her feet. "You've just gotten used to Thunder being at your beck and call."

"True." Isa smacked Maggie on her shoulder before turning to Angel. "Congratulations, Angel. I know Barrett will treat you just as good as Thunder treats me. Besides, us pregnant girls have to stick together. Let me know if you need anything."

"I am so happy for you," Maggie screamed and hugged Angel after Isa.

"Do you guys really think Barrett will be happy about this?" Angel bit her lip.

"No," Maggie answered first, and Angel's lip quivered.

"Stop teasing her, Maggie." Isa smacked Maggie again.

"Oh my God, Angel." Maggie winced. "I was just kidding. I think he will be over the moon."

"Angel," Tori glared at Maggie. "You'll get used to Maggie's sarcasm. It's an acquired taste. Don't worry about Barrett. He loves kids." Tori put her arm around her. "You should see him at the cultural center with the shelter boys. They love him."

"I hope so." Angel felt better knowing that all these people were close to Barrett, and they all agreed that he would be happy about her pregnancy. That calmed her nerves until she found the right time to tell him.

Maggie checked her watch. "Oh Shit, we gotta finish decorating. Everyone's going to be here in thirty minutes. Tori, you and I will do the standing on ladders and chairs. Isa you and Angel finish decorating the tables and organize the balloons."

"Yes, ma'am," Isa saluted Maggie.

Chapter 52

Best Present Ever!

Barrett

By the time Barrett, Frey, Holt, Steele, and Bryce came back from the arcade, Alex had already delivered the food and everyone else had arrived. They ate the food and caught up before opening presents. Barrett stood in the back with Alex, Holt, Mark, and George as they watched Steele tear through all his presents.

Barrett noticed Tori looking over several times at George. Had they been having trouble at the cultural center? Neither Alex nor Mark had mentioned anything. But maybe now that George was living there, they only discussed issues with him.

Finally, Tori walked over to them and stood in front of George. "George, can I ask you for a favor?"

George nodded and glanced at Alex. "Sure, Tori, what's up?"

"She's worried about her sister." Alex placed his arm over Tori's shoulder and kissed her temple.

"I'm not sure how I can help you?" George looked just as confused as Barrett.

"My sister is coming to visit in April, and I want you to keep her out of trouble." Tori pleaded. "I know you don't know her, and I will talk to her, but she's a little wild."

Barrett stood quietly. Damn, he was glad he was with Angel, because if Tori had asked him with her puppy dog eyes to watch over Lizzy, he damn well would, and judging by the crush she had on Barrett, it wouldn't have turned out well. Not that Barrett would have intentionally hurt her, but he wasn't interested in Lizzy.

"I will do my best. How wild are we talking?" George glanced at all of us. "Like Maggie wild?"

"Maybe," Tori winced.

"Oh, shit." Mark slapped George on the back. "You're gonna have your hands full."

"Nah, she's Tori's sister." George shook his head. "How wild can she be?"

Barrett heard Alex cough in his hand. Yeah, Alex knew just how wild Lizzy was.

"Thank you, George." Tori kissed his cheek. "I knew I could count on you."

Barrett watched Tori walk away, and he murmured to George. "Famous last words."

"Are you serious?" George faced him and crossed his arms. "She was fine the day of the shooting."

"She listened to you that day?" Barrett raised an eyebrow, questioning him.

"Mostly." George shrugged. "Everyone was panicking, so her behavior wasn't different from anyone else's. Well, except you, you fucking drama queen."

Barrett smirked at him. "Fucker. I hope she runs you ragged."

George burst out laughing. "I'll be fine. She won't be any trouble at all."

"Okey dokey."

Before Barrett could tell George about his encounter with Lizzy, Sehoy called Barrett to stand next to Frey and Steele at the front of the room. Most of the presents were for Steele except for two big gift bags. Holt placed one in front of Frey and gave her a quick kiss before he put the other bag in front of Barrett.

"Don't kiss me, fucker." Barrett whispered low enough that only Holt and Frey could hear him.

"I wouldn't dream of it. I only want my mouth on her." Holt pointed at Frey and blew him a kiss.

Barrett was about to get out of his chair and wipe that smirk off his face. But if he did that, his mom would kill him for ruining the party. So, he ignored Holt and grabbed his gift. It had been a long time since they'd received matching gifts.

"These are from Alex and I for our favorite twins." Holt grinned and stood back.

Barrett noticed Holt and Alex covering their mouths, glancing at each other. Those fuckers were up to something. Barrett pulled out a huge deluxe spa basket at the same time as Frey.

"Wow," Frey immediately pulled the cellophane off. "I love it."

"Funny," Barrett smirked at Holt as he took photos of Barrett holding his girly spa basket. "You guys suck."

"Language," Sehoy screamed at Barrett and pointed to the kids.

"Sorry, *chatski*," Barrett grunted.

"Mr. Barrett," Lucy came over with her hand out. "You owe me a dollar."

Barrett pulled out his wallet and gave her a one-dollar bill. "Sorry, Lucy." Lucy, Isa and Thunder's niece, loved to point out when anyone said a bad word. So last year, after Mark couldn't stop 'cussing', she asked Thunder if she could make a swear jar and collect a dollar every time one of them said a bad word. To date, Mark and Maggie paid her the most money. Their rate of cursing would pay off her college tuition in no time.

"Barrett, we just want to cater to your feminine side. After all, you're the one with the enormous tub." Alex winked at Angel.

Barrett turned to Angel and said, "I hope you like gardenias," before handing her the basket.

"No," Holt elbowed Alex, "we hope you like them."

"Why do they want you to like gardenias, Mr. Barrett?" Lucy stared at Barrett, confusion written all over her face.

"Uh..." Barrett couldn't think of what to say.

"Because when he puts all this in the bathroom, it'll smell like gardenias." Angel gets ten points for the save. He'd have to reward her later.

"Oh, cool." Lucy smiled and ran to her mom, Gaby, Isa's sister-in-law.

Barrett turned and kissed Angel. "Thanks."

"Don't mention it." She winked at him.

Barrett leaned down to her ear and whispered, "I can't wait for you to surprise me with the scent of gardenias all over your beautiful body."

Angel chuckled, "Oh, I'm gonna surprise you alright."

"Mom, can I put on my new bathing suit and head to the pool?" Steele had his arms filled with gifts.

"Sure, do you need any help?"

"No, I got it."

Barrett stood up quickly to swipe his key card since Steele's hands were full. He'd made him a key card for his birthday. It was in his pile of gifts, but with his hands full, there was no way he could reach it.

"Thanks," Steele smiled at him.

Steele came out a couple of minutes later, ready to go.

"We'll take the boys." Maggie walked toward Barrett. "Besides, Angel has another present for you." Maggie wiggled her eyebrows at him.

"Kids!" Maggie screamed, "let's roll out."

"What is she talking about?" Barrett turned to Angel, pulled her into his arms, and whispered in her ear, "Are we going to have some sexy time?"

"I need to talk to you," Angel answered.

"Okay everyone. We'll change and be down in a minute." Barrett pushed Angel into their room and shut the door.

Angel went to the couch and sat down.

"You sound serious. Is everything okay?" Barrett sat next to her and grabbed her hands.

Angel pulled her hands out of his and wiped them on her jeans. Her hands were clammy. Barrett didn't understand why she would be so nervous. She could tell him anything and he would understand.

"Whatever it is...," Barrett grabbed her hands again. "It's okay. We'll handle it together."

"I'm pregnant." Angel blurted.

"I'm sorry. What did you say?" Barrett wasn't sure if he heard her right.

"I said. I'm pregnant. But if you don't want a baby, it's okay. I can move back into my house and support Steele and the baby all by myself. You don't have to feel pressured to stay with us," Angel rambled.

"Are you sure it's mine?" Barrett spoke before realizing how what he said sounded.

"Oh, no," All the color drained from Angel's face. She stood and walked away from Barrett. "I didn't think about that. Do you think it could be Numbers' child? He wore a condom, but what if it tore?" Angel was now frantically pacing.

"I don't care." Barrett stood and grabbed Angel.

"Okay, I understand." With tears in her eyes, Angel pulled away from Barrett. "I'll pack our things and go."

"No!" Barrett yelled at her and grabbed her arm before she could leave him. He was fucking all this up. What he meant to say was that he didn't give a fuck if the child was Numbers. He would love that baby as if it were his. "Angel, I'm messing this all up."

Angel pulled away from him. "It's okay. I know I've flipped your world upside down. I'm sorry." Angel ran into the bedroom.

"Angel," Barrett followed her. "It's me who's sorry. Please, stop." Angel had grabbed her clothes and was throwing them on the bed. She wasn't listening to him, but he had to get through to her. On her next turn to go back into the closet, Barrett picked her up and threw her down on the bed. He quickly covered her with his body, leaning on his elbows so he wouldn't crush her. "I love you and I would love to have a baby with you. You just caught me by surprise, is all."

"What if the baby is Numbers?" Angel cried.

"I don't give a shit, but if you want, we can get a paternity test whenever it's safe for you and the baby." Barrett stroked her cheeks and wiped her tears. "Angel, I love you and I will love this baby no matter what. I never thought I would feel the way I do about any woman. But I can't breathe without you. I look forward to seeing your beautiful face every morning when I wake up and every night before I go to sleep. I love the way you love your son and I'm gonna love watching you with our child. Your laugh brightens my day. Your tears slay me, and I want to kill anyone who causes them. You are the best thing that's ever happened to me, and I'm selfish. I want to keep you forever." Barrett pulled Angel to the side of the bed and got down on one knee. "I'm excited about making a family with you and living out our days together." Barrett pulled a small black box out of his pocket, opened it, and offered it to Angel. A beautiful shiny, solitaire diamond, surrounded by smaller diamonds, sat on a simple silver band.

Angel gasped and covered her mouth.

"Will you marry me and be my best present ever?" Barrett held his breath, awaiting her response and hoping she wouldn't take too long, or he would pass out.

"Yes, yes, yes!" Angel threw herself at him, toppling them both onto the floor. "I love you, but I need to talk to Steele first."

"No need." Barrett settled her back on the bed. "I asked him for his permission earlier today and he helped me pick out this ring." Pulling it from the box, Barrett slipped the ring onto her finger. "Do you like it?"

"I love it." Angel held her hand out, admiring it before she cupped his face and gazed lovingly at him. "Thank you for including him. It makes it so much more special."

"Of course, I would include him. He's also my son."

Stay tuned for the last book in the Path Series:
Book 5: Blue Path
It is the story of Deputy George and Lizzy.
To be released later this year.

Chapter 53

Special Thanks

Neri

Thank you to my wonderful friend Michelle and for your help and support once again. My exceptional nephew-in-law, Dr. Dan, for always answering my medical questions even though I know you are super busy. As always, my helpful friend, K-9 Deputy Bryan Wright, for answering my law enforcement questions.

You are all so special to me and I can't thank you enough for everything you do for me. Your support helps me be a better writer.

I edited this book with the help of my friend Michelle. My usual editor, Deb wasn't available for this book. Please excuse any mess ups.

And to my readers, Thank You! For buying my books and enjoying this journey with me. You guys are the best!

Chapter 54

About the Author

Neri Lopez has worn many hats as a stay-at-home mom of triplets, graphic designer, and high school teacher (Spanish, Art, and Graphic Design). She lives in Florida with her husband, grown kids, and their fur babies, Mocha and Chewy. She is a crafter of all trades, including making jewelry, scrapbooking, knitting, crocheting, sewing, and painting.

Check out her website to sign up for her newsletter (emailed out every two weeks). You can also get the links to purchase her books, see all the translations, maps, and images of her characters and object in her stories.

website: sirenbookandcraft.com

(When you sign up for her newsletter, you will receive a FREE downloadable bookmark of Red Path.)

Neri loves to hear from her readers. You can email her at: sirenbookandcraft@gmail.com

Please write a review in Goodreads or Amazon, it truly helps authors to promote their books. Thank you in advance.

Or follow her on:

Facebook: Neri Lopez - Author

Instagram: Neri_Lopez_Author

The Path Series

Book 1: Red Path (Amazon Link - https://a.co/d/7NgFsGI)

Book 2: Unconquered Path (Amazon Link: https://a.co/d/dVu2Nmy)

Book 3: Wagering Path (Amazon Link: https://a.co/d/bVgZT8n)

Book 4: Unexpected Path (Amazon Link: https://www.amazon.com/dp/B0DR7GRP9Q)

Book 4.5 Novella: Double Trouble Path (Amazon Link: https://www.amazon.com/dp/B0DTGTN7D3)

Book 5: Twisted Path

Book 6: Blue Path (2025)